When Sunday Comes Again

When Sunday Comes Again

Terry E. Hill

www.urbanbooks.net

Urban Books, LLC
78 East Industry Court
Deer Park, NY 11729

When Sunday Comes Again Copyright © 2012
Terry E. Hill

ISBN 13: 978-1-60162-354-6
ISBN 10: 1-60162-354-2

First Trade Paperback Printing July 2012
Printed in the United States of America

10 9 8 7 6 5 4 3 2 1

Distributed by Kensington Publishing Corp.
Submit Wholesale Orders to:
Kensington Publishing Corp.
C/O Penguin Group (USA) Inc.
Attention: Order Processing
405 Murray Hill Parkway
East Rutherford, NJ 07073-2316
Phone: 1-800-526-0275
Fax: 1-800-227-9604

When Sunday Comes Again

Terry E. Hill

Chapter 1

The white lace curtains in Hattie Williams's open bedroom window rustled gently in the evening breeze, barely shielding the dark room from the glow of a full moon. The room smelled of talcum powder mixed with the sweet fragrance from a bouquet of roses picked from her garden that day. A cherry brown antique vanity served as the centerpiece of the room. It balanced an oval beveled mirror that towered above it. Crystal atomizer perfume bottles were symmetrically arranged on its surface, each containing the lilac, rose, and lavender scents that gently announced her arrival moments before she would enter a room. Three tubes of her favorite hand cream and a fabric-covered box filled with her Sunday gloves occupied the lowest shelf. A vase holding the red roses sat on the highest.

The sheets on the bed were the crispest of white, a true white achieved only from the addition of bluing poured by an experienced hand. Pillowcases printed with yellow and pink flowers and a patchwork quilt, sewn so many years ago by her mother, were tangled and strewn across the disheveled bed. Beads of perspiration gathered on Hattie's lip as she tossed restlessly in a fitful sleep. It was two o'clock in the morning.

"No. No, not the pastor. Not Pastor Cleaveland," Hattie sputtered as her gray hair thrashed from side to side.

The image of a man wearing a tailored black suit filled her dream. His eyes were wide open and staring straight at her. But there was no life, no sparkle, just an empty shell. He was lying in a pool of glistening blood. She could hear screams in the background, but no one was there except the lifeless body of her pastor, Hezekiah T. Cleaveland.

Her body convulsed as she tried in vain to revive the lifeless man in her dream. And then it happened. She felt the distinct presence of two people just beyond her dream's reach. One was familiar, but the other she did not know. Hattie could feel waves of hate and anger weighing down on her as she knelt over Hezekiah. Gradually, the source of the feelings moved closer and closer. The pain was almost unbearable. Hattie knew the source of this energy. It was one she had felt on so many Sunday mornings.

The second, unrecognizable force vied for her attention. There was warmth, but she couldn't see the source. The person hovered timidly in the background, afraid to move in closer, afraid to come into view. Hattie could clearly discern the emotions. There was an overwhelming sorrow, but permeating through it all, there was love.

She felt a cold hand on her shoulder. The touch sent a shudder through her sleeping body. She fought the urge to look over her shoulder, but she had no choice. The woman smiled down on her as Hattie looked up. The bright glow from her white teeth covered Hattie's and Hezekiah's bodies in light.

Hattie bolted upright in her bed and screamed out loud, "Oh, Lord! Why, Samantha? Why?" Her body was drenched in perspiration as her eyes fixed on her trembling reflection in the vanity mirror across the room. Her silver hair was tangled and tossed. Her hands shook as she cried out, "Hezekiah loved you so much, Samantha." Hattie prayed that it wasn't true. She hoped that this would be the one time her empathic gift had failed her.

Samantha Cleaveland stood in the floor-to-ceiling window of her office at the Cleaveland estate, wrapped in an aqua silk robe that caressed the curves of her long, graceful body. A carpet of green rolled over the grounds and palm trees lining the exterior of the property bristled in a gentle breeze rising from the Pacific Ocean below. Samantha stared at the vast blue void in the distance, which seemed to spill off the edge of the earth. A strand of velvety black hair tumbled over her chiseled cheek as she reached for a burning cigarette in an ashtray on the glass desk. With perfectly manicured fingers, she moved the stray lock from her view and took a long, deep puff from the cigarette. At thirty-nine years of age, she looked more the part of a glittering Hollywood starlet than the grieving widow of Pastor Hezekiah T. Cleaveland.

Her thoughts ebbed and flowed with each rhythmic wave of the ocean. Feelings of accomplishment over her recent appointment as interim pastor of New Testament Cathedral washed through her with every gentle beat of her heart. As the waters receded from the shore, memories of her late husband, Hezekiah, replaced her jubilation with loathing. She pondered the question of how she had come to hate the man she had once loved so deeply, and chastised herself for waiting so long to take fate into her own hands.

I should have killed him years ago, she thought as she took another puff from the cigarette. *He got exactly what he deserved for making a mockery of our marriage with a man and jeopardizing the entire ministry. He brought it on himself. God would have wanted it this way.*

Hezekiah and Samantha Cleaveland had been ecclesiastical royalty. The Cleaveland dynasty was known to millions of loyal viewers and contributors. Contributions ranged from the five dollars sent by the widow in Jackson, Mississippi, and the twenty dollars that came in like clockwork each month from the retired couple in Atlanta, Georgia, to the one-hundred-thousand-dollar anonymous "gift" that arrived each year from New York on Samantha's birthday. The money that poured in each week earned New Testament Cathedral the ranking of number six on the list of the top ten wealthiest churches in the country and allowed the Cleavelands to live in the cradled arms of luxury. A private jet was available at their beck and call. Drivers in black suits and a fleet of luxury automobiles stood at the ready twenty-four hours a day. Two Picassos hung in places of honor in their ten-bedroom mansion in Bel Air. The finest couture gowns, suits, shoes, and sparkling jewelry were available to them, often in exchange for only the honor of being worn by a Cleaveland.

Their glowing smiles were aired somewhere in the world twenty-four hours a day. She was the beautiful woman who stood lovingly behind the flawless man. "Can't you be more like Samantha Cleaveland?" was a common request made by lesser known pastors of their wives on every Sunday morning.

Together they had built the multimillion-dollar media empire and reigned over the world-famous headquarters of New Testament Cathedral in Los Angeles. They were the perfect couple. But in the quiet of their limousine or behind the wrought-iron gates of the estate, their life looked nothing like the one on the television screen.

Over the years and as the ministry grew, Samantha's resentment toward Hezekiah eclipsed the love she once had for him.

And then came the revelation that threatened to topple the entire ministry. She could have easily put the right spin on Hezekiah having an affair with another woman, as she had done many times before. But a man? Even her highly evolved public relations skills and heart-melting smile couldn't convince the ten-dollar-a-month donor from Tulsa to keep sending in her "love offering" if she learned that the great Pastor Hezekiah T. Cleaveland was in love with a man.

"He gave me no other choice," Samantha reasoned, looking out over the horizon. "It was either him or New Testament Cathedral. I know God would have wanted it this way."

A gentle tap on the office door drew Samantha back from the hypnotic spell of the sea.

"Come in," she said without turning from the window.

Etta Washington, the Cleavelands' housekeeper, entered the room, carrying a tray with coffee, a freshly baked scone, and the morning paper. She wore a simple black dress and sensible shoes. The lower half of her body was covered by a white apron. "Good morning, Mrs. Cleaveland," Etta said as she walked toward the desk. "I thought you might like a cup of coffee and a bite to eat."

Although there was other staff on the estate, Etta was the only one who lived in the house. She had seen the Cleavelands at their best and at their worst. Over the years the family had become the center of her world. Was the thermostat set at the right temperature? Were all the flower arrangements fresh and to their liking? Did the sheets on their beds have the proper thread count? Did the cook make enough of the fresh scones Mrs. Cleaveland liked so? These and all other concerns pertaining to the comfort of the Cleavelands were her domain, and she took pride in anticipating their needs long before they even knew them themselves.

Etta had learned early on that all she observed behind the double oak doors of the mansion was never to be discussed with anyone. Samantha's penchant for European cigarettes, their daughter Jasmine's frequent morning hangovers, or Hezekiah's occasional bouts with depression, which would leave him in a fetal position locked in his bedroom for days, were some of the secrets hidden from the world. They were all Cleaveland family secrets, and Samantha had repeatedly warned Etta, "If you ever tell anyone about this, you'll regret it."

"Put it on the desk," Samantha said to Etta as she extinguished the cigarette butt in the ashtray. "Is my driver out front yet?"

"No, Mrs. Cleaveland."

Samantha's body tensed when she heard the response. She looked up at the woman pouring the cup of coffee and asked, "Etta, how did you address my husband when he was alive?"

Etta's hand shook when she heard the question. The tremble was so slight, it was apparent only in a ripple in the cup of coffee. "I'm not sure what you mean, Mrs. Cleaveland," she replied softly.

"It's a very simple question, Etta. What did you call my husband when he was alive?"

"I believe I called him Pastor Cleaveland."

"That is correct. You always said, 'Good morning, Pastor Cleaveland,' or 'Can I get you anything else, Pastor Cleaveland?' Now that I am the pastor of New Testament Cathedral," Samantha said as she casually picked up the cup of freshly poured coffee, "I think it only appropriate that you address me as Pastor Cleaveland from now on. Is that understood?"

Etta looked stunned. She averted her eyes from Samantha's gaze. *You are not my pastor,* she fumed silently.

Etta's hand trembled again, but she gripped the tray firmly to hide any sign of fear from Samantha. She knew her life at the Cleaveland estate would never be the same now that the man she had admired and respected so deeply was gone. Hezekiah had, over the years, acted as a buffer between her and Samantha.

He had comforted Etta when Samantha's wrath, which always simmered just below the surface, was directed at her. "Don't take it personally, Etta," Hezekiah had said on many occasions. "Samantha is under a lot of pressure. You know she didn't really mean what she said."

Hezekiah would also remind the impatient Samantha, "Everyone makes mistakes," on the rare occasions that Etta had not served a meal in the exact way she had requested, or if the spotlight that pointed to the Picasso hanging in the foyer had not been turned on at exactly six o'clock each evening. Who would protect her now?

"Is that understood?" Samantha repeated in a sterner tone.

The wave of fear was followed quickly by revulsion. As Etta raised the tray, she straightened her back, looked Samantha directly in the eye and with a slight nod of her head replied, "Yes, I understand . . . Pastor Cleaveland."

Etta turned on her heel and walked to the door.

"Oh, and, Etta," Samantha called out to the retreating woman, "tell Dino to pull the car around now. I have a meeting at church this morning."

Etta stopped in her tracks without turning around and said, "Yes, Pastor Cleaveland," and then quickly exited the room.

The *Los Angeles Chronicle* lay where Etta had placed it on the desk. It had been three weeks since Hezekiah's murder, and every day the front page of the paper carried the latest update on the investigation and the state of affairs at New Testament Cathedral. PASTOR'S MURDER BAFFLES POLICE. GRIEVING WIDOW TAKES HELM OF THE SIXTH LARGEST CHURCH IN THE COUNTRY read the headline.

Samantha glanced down at the paper. A somber color photograph of the widow occupied a fourth of the page. Her grim expression gave curious readers no hint of what lay beneath the perfect skin, chocolate eyes, and sparkling white teeth. *Of all the pictures they have of me on file at that rag, they chose that one,* she thought. *I look like a goddamn nun.*

Samantha sat at the desk and unfolded the newspaper.

It has been three weeks since the brutal assassination of Reverend Hezekiah T. Cleaveland in his mega church, in front of fifteen thousand stunned parishioners and television cameras. The police still have no suspects or leads as to who was responsible for the murder, which sent shock waves through the American faith community. On Sunday, July 18, Pastor Cleaveland was shot in the head and chest by an unknown gunman, who fled on foot from the downtown Los Angeles mega church.

California State Bureau of Investigation spokeswoman Mandy Tidwell told CNN's Gideon Truman that Cleaveland had trauma to his head and body, but declined to elaborate. "We don't have any leads," she told the Chronicle *on Sunday.*

Officials have spoken with trustees and members of New Testament Cathedral, where Cleaveland had served as pastor for the past eleven years. "Pastor Cleaveland was loved by everyone who met him," said a longtime member who preferred not to give her name. "He was a loving father, husband, and pastor who . . ."

Samantha stopped reading and quickly scanned the rest of the article in search of her name.

Cleaveland is survived by his daughter, Jasmine Cleaveland, and wife, the Reverend Samantha Cleaveland. Shortly after his death, Reverend Samantha Cleaveland was installed as the interim pastor of the multimillion-dollar church and television ministry. Mrs. Cleaveland has yet to speak to the press about the circumstances surrounding her husband's death. It has been rumored, however, that she will give an exclusive interview to Gideon Truman in the coming weeks.

The article went on to tell of her courage, strength, and commitment to her husband's dream of completing the construction of the church's new twenty-five-thousand-seat, glittering crystal cathedral in downtown Los Angeles.

Samantha had been hounded by the press since her husband's death. Local, national, and international news networks, talk shows, and newspapers from around the world had been covering the investigation from day one, but she had skillfully avoided any contact with the media. Her silence had served only to increase her fame. This was just as she had planned.

Samantha closed the paper and walked back to the window. She looked out at a flock of salty white seagulls skimming the ocean surface in the distance, trees dancing in the wind and clouds drifting by.

Gideon Truman, she thought silently. *I wonder if it's true what they say about him. If it is, I'm sure Hezekiah would have liked him.*

Cynthia Pryce paced the living room floor in the twenty-third-floor penthouse. The blue sky dotted with clouds and the sun rising over rolling green hills in the distance were overshadowed in her presence. The glow of her morning skin rivaled the splendor of the panorama outside her window. Luxurious strands of burnt-caramel hair responded obediently to every tilt of her head. A creamy peach satin robe swirled around the calves of her long legs as she made a series of sharp turns in front of the windows. The face of Samantha Cleaveland on the front page of the *Los Angeles Chronicle* taunted her from the coffee table.

"Interim pastor," she muttered softly as she continued her march. "This isn't over, Samantha. Don't get too comfortable."

She felt a sharp snap of jealousy as she silently recalled the events of the last three weeks. *If only those idiots, Hezekiah and Lance Savage, hadn't gotten themselves killed, Percy would be the pastor of New Testament Cathedral today.*

She pushed the image of Samantha standing at the center of the pulpit before the entire congregation and all the cameras from her mind. A rage that she could hardly contain swelled in her stomach. *Pull yourself together, girl,* she thought. *This isn't over. You almost destroyed Hezekiah. You can do the same to Samantha.*

The slight glimmer of hope that her husband could still one day become pastor made the sight of Samantha's smug face on the front page of the newspaper hurt a little less. She reached down and, without looking at the paper, turned it over on the coffee table.

Just as she stood up, her husband, the Reverend Percy Pryce, entered the room. His tall frame was dressed in a smoky gray suit, a butter-yellow shirt, and a tie that picked up the hues in the suit, the shirt, and his rich almond skin.

"Is the paper here yet?" he asked coldly, without greeting her.

"It's on the coffee table. Of course, she's on the front page again."

"Why does that upset you so much?" he snapped.

Cynthia turned sharply toward him and said, "It upsets me because you should have been appointed pastor, not her."

"The trustee vote was unanimous. It's over, Cynthia. Samantha is the pastor. We just have to live with it."

"Wrong. They voted unanimously to appoint her as interim pastor. If everyone was so convinced that she was the best successor for Hezekiah, they would have made her permanent pastor. So it's not over. There's still a chance for us . . . for you to prove to them that you are the best person for the job. Hezekiah would have wanted it that way, and you know it."

"It doesn't matter what Hezekiah wanted at this point. If God wanted me to be pastor, he would have made me pastor. We have to live with the decision."

"Why are you so naive? It was Samantha's scheming that got her the position. God didn't have anything to do with it. The only thing we have to do is expose her for the conniving, greedy woman she is. If you would only do what I tell you and let me—"

Percy walked rapidly toward her at the window and cut her off. "You've done enough already. Lance Savage is dead because of you," he said.

"What are you talking about? I didn't have anything to do with his death."

The image of the *Los Angeles Chronicle* reporter Lance Savage lying dead on the floor of his home on the canals in Venice flashed in Percy's mind. "If you hadn't leaked the story about Hezekiah being gay to Lance, he would still be alive," he replied, barely containing his anger.

"The police don't know who killed Lance, and they haven't said anything about his death being linked to the story he was writing. Besides, who would kill him because of that?"

Percy looked away when he heard the question. No one, other than Associate Pastor Kenneth Davis, knew of his visit to Lance's home on the day he was murdered. Only they knew he had pushed the reporter to the floor when he refused to accept $175,000 in exchange for not running the explosive story detailing Hezekiah's homosexual affair. No one knew that they had fled the home, leaving the reporter's lifeless body on the floor, only to be discovered the next day by his housekeeper.

Cynthia continued, "Look at me, Percy. You have to be a man and fight for what is rightfully yours." Cynthia walked to him and put her soft hand on his cheek. "Darling," she whispered, "you were born to be pastor of New Testament Cathedral. We can make that happen. You just have to listen to me."

Percy bowed his head and tried to look away, but the soft touch of her hand caused him gradually, and unwillingly, to succumb to her breathless commands.

Cynthia was relentless. She raised his head and looked directly into his eyes. "I have it all figured out, baby. You have to trust me. Do as I tell you and everything will work out in our favor."

She drew him closer and placed his head on her shoulder. He could feel the warmth of her sweet breath on his ear. She expertly kissed his neck and lips. The intoxicating smell of her body replaced the fear and guilt with longing.

"I love you, Percy," she whispered. "Make love to me, baby. I need you inside me."

As she pulled him closer, she could feel the rigid evidence of his desire. His hands grudgingly tugged at the cord of her robe. He slowly removed it from her bare shoulders and let it drop to the floor, exposing her naked body for all to see in the floor to ceiling window. Percy caressed every inch of her creamy skin and felt her moistness as they panted in unison and pressed their lips together.

With nimble fingers she unzipped his pants and released his throbbing member. Cynthia raised her leg and rested it on the leather belt above his hip. With one hand she guided him into her and released a gasp when he thrust deep inside her.

"Just do as I say, baby," she repeated over and over as he made love to her in the window of the penthouse apartment. "Just do as I say."

Mondays were the hardest for Danny St. John. For him, the day marked the beginning of another week without Hezekiah. Another week he would not hear his voice whisper, "I love you, Danny." Another week he wouldn't feel his arms around his waist or taste the sweetness of his kiss.

Danny had rarely left his apartment in the three weeks since Hezekiah's murder. The air was stale and musty. All the shades were drawn, and the windows were closed tight. At times, he found himself stumbling through the house, wearing only baggy shorts, to the refrigerator for orange juice, or to the cupboard for saltine crackers and canned soup. He had no appetite for anything more substantial.

Parker never let Danny out of his sight. The scruffy gray cat followed his master from room to room. He sat on Danny's lap on the couch and curled next to him when he lay crying in bed.

The television in his bedroom had been on for three weeks. It was always either tuned to the local news, CNN, or the Home Shopping Network. Whenever he heard Hezekiah's name mentioned, he turned up the volume. The CNN reporter Gideon Truman offered the most comprehensive coverage of the killing. Although much of the information he reported was inaccurate, Danny found it difficult not to listen to the handsome journalist's account of the life and death of the man he had loved so deeply.

Newspapers were piled in heaps on the floor next to the couch in his small apartment. Each day the articles served to remind him that he would never see Hezekiah again. The headline on the Monday after the murder blazed PROMINENT LOS ANGELES PASTOR GUNNED DOWN IN FRONT OF HORRIFIED CONGREGATION. Wednesday's announced WORLD MOURNS THE DEATH OF PASTOR HEZEKIAH T. CLEAVELAND. The tragic headlines continued on Friday: SLAIN PASTOR TO BE LAID TO REST. MILLIONS EXPECTED TO VIEW TELEVISED SERVICE.

The stories never seemed to end, and they all landed with a thud on Danny's doorstep each day, courtesy of the *Los Angeles Chronicle*. The telephone on the nightstand next to his bed rang several times a day, but he never answered. The most frequent calls came from his friend Kay Braisden. "Danny, it's Kay again," her messages would say. "Honey, I know how you must be feeling right now. Please pick up the phone." When there was no response, she would continue. "Danny, I know I hurt you the last time we spoke. I'm sorry. I am so sorry. Please forgive me. I was just so surprised when you told me you were involved in a relationship with Hezekiah Cleaveland. I didn't know how to handle it. I was wrong."

On another day the message was, "You are my best friend, Danny. I should have been there for you, and for that I apologize. But I want to be there for you now. Please call me. I'm going to keep calling for as long as it takes for you to forgive me. I love you, Danny, and I'm praying for you."

Danny's eyes filled with tears each time he heard a message from Kay. He wanted to speak with her, but the right time had not yet come.

Chapter 2

Scarlett Shackelford's eyes were red and puffy from all the tears she had shed since Hezekiah's death. She now had the face of an angel touched by sorrow. Three weeks had gone by, but she had found only fleeting moments of relief from the agonizing grief she felt over the loss. This morning she sat at the dinette table in the kitchen window of the modest stucco tract home she shared with her second husband, David, and her daughter, Natalie.

The morning sun reflected off every surface in the bright and cheery kitchen. A tea kettle simmered on the stove. White-glazed tile countertops held stainless-steel appliances, a neatly lined row of cookbooks, and a ceramic rooster cookie jar that required beheading before it would yield its sugary treats.

The fact that Samantha Cleaveland was now the pastor of New Testament Cathedral only added to her misery. This was the same woman who had treated her so cruelly as a young girl; the woman who had fired her as Hezekiah's secretary after learning she was pregnant with his child; and the woman who she, in some remote corner of her heart, believed was involved in the death of the father of her daughter.

Only three people on earth knew Natalie was Hezekiah's daughter: Samantha Cleaveland, Hezekiah, and herself. Now only two were left to guard the secret. The responsibility of keeping such a secret was a heavy burden that she managed as best she could under the circumstances. She had told her husband, David, that Natalie was the product of her first failed marriage. Another tear escaped as she sat in the window. The kettle on the stove began to boil, but Scarlett's thoughts were on matters more important than the whistling water.

"Scarlett, turn off the kettle," came a booming voice from another room.

She did not respond.

"Scarlett, are you in the kitchen? Would you please turn that thing off?"

Still there was no reply.

Finally, David Shackelford huffed into the room, wearing only a robe and carrying the front section of the morning paper. The rich timbre of his voice matched perfectly his handsome face and muscular, six-foot-four frame. The robe he wore was stretched to the limit to conceal his well-contoured chest, and long runner's legs peeked through the front flap with every step he took.

"Honey, don't you hear the kettle? Why didn't you turn it off?"

Scarlett was startled when she heard his voice. "What?" she asked, looking blankly up at him.

"The kettle, it's been whistling for five minutes."

"I'm sorry. I didn't hear it," she said as she stood from the table. "My mind was somewhere else. Would you like a cup of tea?"

"Scarlett, what is wrong with you?"

She turned her back to him and mechanically began preparations for the tea. "Nothing is wrong. I just didn't hear it."

David walked behind her and sat the newspaper on the countertop. Samantha Cleaveland's face on the front page looked up at Scarlett. He took her by the shoulders and turned her around to face him.

"Scarlett, this has got to stop. This is unnatural. I know you cared for Pastor Cleaveland. It was tragic, but you have to be strong and accept the fact that he's gone. I know you're worried about the church, but Samantha will be fine as the new pastor. Everything will work out in time."

Scarlett jerked away from him and shouted, "Everything will not work out. You don't know what you're talking about. You don't know her. She'll ruin everything that is good about New Testament Cathedral. You don't know that woman like I do."

Scarlett began to cry and tried to walk around him, but he blocked her path. "Wait, honey, we have to talk about this. You can't go on like this. It's ruining our marriage. You're neglecting Natalie and—"

When she heard her daughter's name, she began to cry harder and fell into his arms. David stroked her head and tried unsuccessfully to calm her. "Honey, it's going to be all right. Hezekiah is in a better place, and there's nothing we can do about it. You've got to come back to us. Natalie and I need you."

"You don't understand, David," she said through her sobs. "Everything is so complicated."

"Then help me understand. I love you. We can work through whatever it is together."

"I can't . . . I can't tell you. You'll hate me if I do."

"I could never hate you, Scarlett. Now, tell me what is upsetting you this much."

Scarlett slowly pulled away from his chest, walked back to the dinette table, and sat down again in the window with her back to him. David did not move. She pulled a white paper napkin from a holder at the center of the table and dabbed her wet cheeks. The tears continued to flow, but the sobbing slowly subsided.

David waited to allow her to compose herself and then reiterated, "I love you, Scarlett, but you have to let me know what's upsetting you before I can help."

Scarlett looked out the window at a large blooming magnolia tree in her front yard. Their Japanese gardener raked leaves into a neat pile and waved to her, but she didn't wave back. His adolescent assistant revved a gas lawn mower in another corner of the yard. The loud roar of the engine suddenly filled the room.

David walked behind her and placed his hand on her shoulder. "Talk to me, Scarlett."

She clutched the soaked napkin in her fist and held it to her mouth. "I lied to you, David."

David planted his slipper-clad feet firmly on the yellow linoleum floor but did not speak. His hand remained on her trembling shoulder.

Scarlett placed her clasped fists on the table and took a deep breath. "My first husband is not Natalie's father."

David removed his hand from her shoulder and said, "Michael is not her father? Then who is?" He knew the answer before he said the last word.

There was a long silence before she spoke again.

"I was young, pregnant, afraid, and had no job. The only choice I saw at the time was to marry Michael and persuade him that Natalie was his. I didn't know what else to do. I didn't want to give her up. She's my baby. She is my world. I wouldn't give her up for anyone. I paid dearly for that mistake. Four years of hell. You know the story already. When Michael wasn't drinking, he was abusive."

David took a step backward but did not take his eyes off the back of her head. The wall around her well-kept secret crumbled with every word she spoke. There was no turning back now.

"Samantha tried to force me to give her up for adoption, but I refused. She didn't care about me or my baby. She only cared about her reputation. She only cared about how it would look for her husband to be the father of a child that was not hers. She only cared about how much money they would lose if anyone found out that Hezekiah was the father of my child."

David barely heard her last words over the lawn mower howling outside the window. His heart pounded in his chest. It took all of his strength to remain standing in the middle of the kitchen.

"I'm so sorry, David. Once the lies started, I couldn't stop them. But you have to believe I did it all to protect Natalie, not to hurt anyone, especially not you. I've tried a thousand times before to get up the nerve to tell you, but I couldn't." The sobbing began again. Scarlett placed her head on the table and cried into her arm.

David stood frozen in the middle of the room. He wanted to speak, but the words would not come. The churning lawn-mower engine drowned out the sound of her wrenching sobs and the pounding of his heart.

Dino Goodlaw, Samantha's driver and security guard, pulled the black Cadillac Escalade with tinted windows in front of the Cleaveland estate at exactly 10:00 A.M., just as he had been instructed.

Dino served as the loyal bodyguard, driver, and keeper of all things secret for Samantha and Hezekiah. His muscular frame and uncanny ability to disappear into the background made him perfectly suited to stand between the Cleavelands and dangers seen and unseen. But in the silence of his world, he also blamed himself for Hezekiah's murder.

"If only I had been closer to the pulpit, I would have been able to get Hezekiah to the floor before the second shot to his head," he had told the police hours after the murder. "Hezekiah would still be alive if I had just been a few feet closer."

From that moment on, he had vowed that he would die before any harm came to Samantha. "Any bullet aimed at Samantha will have to go through me first," he would say to his reflection in the mirror each morning while shaving.

A steel-gray handgun in his shoulder holster was visible for a brief moment as Dino exited the vehicle. He quickly buttoned his black suit coat to conceal the weapon before Samantha opened the front door.

The air was clear and smelled of ocean mist. Palm trees lining the winding driveway leading to the stately home stood like sentries guarding a king's palace. A cluster of butterflies fluttered around a bed of flowers at the foot of a double elliptical stone stairway leading up to the grand entrance of the home. The neo-Baroque covered porch with cream-colored wrought-stone columns and twelve-foot double doors served as the perfect stage for the statuesque woman.

Dino stood near the rear car door at the foot of the stairs. He checked his watch nervously and resisted the urge to pace the granite cobblestoned surface. When the front door finally opened, Samantha emerged, carrying a brown leather case. Strands of hair flowed like molten lava around her face as she walked down the stairs. She wore dark sunglasses and a mint-green pantsuit over a simple cream silk shell that only hinted of the perfect form that was beneath.

"Good morning, Pastor Cleaveland," Dino said as she descended. "Another beautiful day today."

"Good morning, Dino," she responded with a smile normally reserved for cameras, full arenas, and six-figure donors. However, Samantha and Dino shared a unique bond. They were the last people to touch Hezekiah when he was alive, and the first to touch his body when he lay dead on the pulpit floor. "How are you today, Dino? I hope you're sleeping better. I worry about you."

"That is very kind of you, Pastor Cleaveland, but it's my job to worry about you. Please don't give it another thought. I know you have enough on your mind these days."

Dino opened the rear door of the Escalade when Samantha reached the bottom step. She handed him the brown case and entered the plush automobile. When she settled in the rear, he passed the case back to her and firmly closed the door.

"I do have a lot on my mind, Dino," she said from the rear as the car drove down the rolling driveway, "but you were very brave on that day, and you've been kind to me through this entire ordeal. Just knowing that Hezekiah's killer is still out there somewhere makes it difficult some days for me to even leave the house. I'm still afraid, but knowing you're here makes me feel much safer."

Dino tensed when he heard the words. "With all due respect, Pastor, I may have been brave, but it wasn't enough. I failed you and Hezekiah," he said, approaching the wrought-iron gate at the end of the winding driveway.

"That is not true. You did everything possible to save him. No one would have guessed in a million years that someone would shoot him in front of the entire congregation. It took an astonishingly bold person to do something that brazen, and no one, not even you, could have stopped it." A faint smile crossed her lips as she spoke the words. "It was God's will, Dino. We have to learn to accept it and get on with the business of living."

Samantha soon grew weary of comforting the hulking Dino. He recognized the impatient look in her eye when he glanced at her in the rearview mirror, and simply replied, "Yes, Pastor Cleaveland. Thank you."

The estate's wrought-iron gate glided open at the sight of the car. Dino waved good morning to a uniformed security guard who was posted in the gatehouse. The man waived at Samantha as well. The tinted windows of the car shielded the guard from the look of disdain she gave in return to his greeting.

Dino merged cautiously into a trickle of Mercedes, red Ferraris, SUVs, and the stray Rolls Royce. Three cyclists in full yellow, red, and black riding gear kept pace with the flow, demanding their rightful place on the single-lane road. The tiled rooftops of other estates straddling the hillside could be seen through dense trees on the left; and a sheer cliff dropping to the bottomless canyon below, on the right.

As the two drove in silence, Samantha's cellular telephone rang. "This is Pastor Cleaveland," she answered in a tone befitting a recent widow.

"Good morning, Pastor Cleaveland," replied the apologetic voice on the telephone. It was Samantha's assistant, Veronica Cotton. "I'm sorry to disturb you."

"I'll be there in fifteen minutes. Is this something that can wait?" Samantha snapped.

"I have Gideon Truman on the line, Pastor Cleaveland. He insisted you would want to speak with him."

"Did I ever tell you I wanted to speak with him?" Samantha snapped again. "I don't want to speak with him, and tell him that I requested he stop spreading rumors that I've agreed to give him an exclusive interview."

With that, Samantha ended the call and rode in silence. The Monday morning Los Angeles rush hour traffic had subsided. Cars on the freeway moved at a decent clip. Dino was determined to get Samantha to New Testament Cathedral in the fifteen minutes she had anticipated.

The car turned onto Hezekiah T. Cleaveland Avenue. The street had been named in honor of her husband three years earlier. *I wish someone would knock down those street signs,* she thought silently. *I'm going to erase every memory of him from the face of the earth. In a year the world will forget he ever existed.*

To her left, Samantha saw the two-block-long and five-story-high New Testament Cathedral. In the midst of the dense urban setting, the church sat on ten acres of park-like grounds with cobblestone paths, rolling swaths of freshly cut grass, gurgling streams, and gushing stone fountains. A sweeping flight of stairs led to the glass entrance of the towering temple. From the street, a massive blown-glass chandelier could be seen hanging in the sun-drenched lobby. Writhing, spiraling cones of vibrant glass burst out in every direction from the light fixture's illuminated core.

Groundskeepers in green uniforms scurried about, mowing grass, pruning trees, and coddling roses, as the limousine drove by. On Samantha's right Hezekiah's legacy was slowly rising from the earth. Construction of the new twenty-five-thousand-seat crystal cathedral had continued at Samantha's insistence. Cement trucks churned along dirt roads. Scaffolding hung precariously along the side of the steel skeleton, and workers pounded, bolted, and soldered at all levels of the structure.

The car pulled into the reserved space near the administrative wing of the building. Dino scanned the parking lot before exiting the vehicle. He stood and did a 360-degree rotation to ensure no one was near the car before he opened the rear door.

Samantha extended her elegant Prada-clad foot from the vehicle. When she stood from the car, the morning light appeared like a pool at her feet and hovered around her head. The fiber of her mint pantsuit seemed to glow as she walked toward the building. Dino closed the car door and followed closely behind. He took a double step ahead of her and opened the door as she moved forward without altering her stride and stepped aside.

Samantha entered the office, which was filled with staff members. Young men in dress shirts and ties and women who looked like knockoff versions of Samantha studied glowing computer screens. Ringing telephones were greeted with "Thank you for calling New Testament Cathedral. God loves you, and so do we. How may I help you?" No one looked up as Samantha crossed the room, heading toward her office. They each had been instructed on the day they were hired, "Do not make eye contact with or address Samantha Cleaveland unless she speaks to you directly."

Samantha entered the outer office of the suite that had three weeks earlier been occupied by her husband. Her assistant, Veronica, sat upright at her desk when she entered. She wore a neatly tailored navy blue suit over a perfectly pressed white blouse and a floral scarf was draped over her shoulders.

"Good morning, Pastor Cleaveland," the attractive young woman said. "I'm sorry to have disturbed you earlier, but he was very insistent."

Samantha ignored the woman's contrition and instead said, "I want my entire staff in the conference room in ten minutes. Make it happen."

"Yes, ma'am."

Samantha looked coldly at the woman and said, "I've asked you not to call me ma'am. You're not in Mississippi anymore, and I'm not your mother. You will refer to me as Pastor Cleaveland. If *ma'am* slips from your lips again, consider yourself fired. Is that understood?"

Veronica looked down at the neat desk and responded, "I understand, Pastor Cleaveland."

"Good. Now, make sure everyone is in the conference room. Let them know that whoever is not present can pick up their last paycheck in accounting." The door to Hezekiah's office shut behind Samantha on the last syllable.

The large office, with antiques from around the world, overlooked the grounds of New Testament Cathedral from the fifth floor. The construction site across the street was partially visible in the corner of the window. Lush burgundy carpeting muffled the sounds of traffic below, and an oil painting of the Cleavelands hung over a fireplace encased in an ornately carved oak mantelpiece.

The message indicator on the telephone on the desk blinked as Samantha removed the dark sunglasses and sat in the high-back leather chair. She pressed a button and heard, "Hello, Reverend Cleaveland. This is Gideon Truman. May I offer my deepest sympathies for your loss. Pastor Cleaveland was a wonderful man. I never had the opportunity to meet him but heard good things about his work over the years, and everyone I've spoken to who knew Hezekiah speaks very highly of him. I understand this must be a very difficult time for you, but I would like to invite you to appear on my television program for an interview. You are a beloved American icon, and of course, the public is very interested in hearing from you and learning how you are handling the unfortunate death of—"

Samantha erased the message and prompted the next. "Hello, Reverend Cleaveland. This is Gideon Truman again. Your assistant just informed me that you believe I am spreading rumors about an exclusive interview. I can assure you that is not true. I have the highest respect for you and would never play such a manipulative game. I'm not sure how that got out there, but please believe that neither I nor anyone on my staff is involved. I would, however, be honored if you would allow me a few moments of your time to talk about a possible appearance on my program. Your assistant has my info. I hope to hear from you."

Samantha leaned back in the chair and spun toward the window. She could see a crane hoisting a steel beam up the side of the new cathedral. *You can wait a little longer, pretty boy,* she thought. *I'll let you talk to me when the time is right.*

The intercom buzzed, slicing through the silence. Samantha slapped the button and barked, "Yes? What is it?"

"I'm sorry, Pastor Cleaveland, but Catherine Birdsong is here. She would like a brief moment with you before the staff meeting."

"Tell her she can see me in three minutes, along with everyone else in the conference room."

"Yes, Pastor Cleaveland," was the timid reply.

Catherine Birdsong, the New Testament Cathedral Chief Operations Officer, stood at Veronica's desk in shock as she heard the line disconnect on the speaker.

The wool, steel-gray suit she wore stood stiff like a suit of armor. Only her hand shook as she spoke. "Who in the hell does she think she is?" she mumbled to the air as she turned and marched out of the room.

Chapter 3

It was ten thirty on Monday morning at New Testament Cathedral. The entire administrative staff had gathered rapidly in the building's main conference room, just as Samantha had ordered only ten minutes earlier. Everyone scrambled for the seats that were positioned farthest from the front and center of the room.

Men in suits, with neckties waving behind them, sprinted toward the conference room past panting, well-dressed middle-aged women, who, as they entered the room, searched frantically for any open seat. This was to be the first meeting Samantha had convened with the full staff since the untimely death of her husband.

Nervous chatter filled the room. "Do you know what this is about?" was heard from a table near the center of the room.

"Here we go. I don't think this is going to be pretty," said a man as he straightened his tie. "I just hope she doesn't fire me in front of the whole room."

Associate Pastor Kenneth Davis sat at a table in the front. The others at his table noticed the nervousness behind the thin veneer of composure. Reverend Percy Pryce shared a table with Catherine Birdsong and Naomi Preston, the director of public relations. Naomi sat with her eyes fixed on the front of the room. Her stiff, shoulder-length hair turned like a hat on the odd occasions she looked to see who entered through the rear door.

The room fell silent as a door in the front opened and Samantha appeared. She stood in the threshold for a moment and scanned the room. A smattering of applause began at the back of the room and slowly rolled to the front, until Samantha held up her hand, motioning them to stop immediately.

She walked to the front of the crowd and stood firmly. "Good morning, New Testament Cathedral family.

A jumbled chorus of "Good morning, Reverend Cleaveland," "Good morning, Mrs. Cleaveland," and "Good morning, Pastor Cleaveland" followed from the crowd.

Samantha threw the room a disappointed glare and said, "I see some of you are still not sure what to call me. Well, let me help you out. As of last week's board of trustees meeting, I am the pastor of New Testament Cathedral. Therefore, it is appropriate for you to address me as Pastor Cleaveland."

A collective look of bewilderment swept across the faces of everyone present.

Samantha continued, "Now that that is out of the way, let's get down to business. I want to first assure you that the death of my husband will in no way interfere with the operations of New Testament Cathedral. We will continue with all scheduled television broadcasts. Our elementary, middle schools, high schools, and college will continue to provide quality education to the future generations of doctors, lawyers, teachers, and missionaries. Our monthly magazine will continue to be published, and most importantly, construction of the new crystal cathedral will go on as scheduled."

Again, the room applauded, this time uninterrupted by Samantha. She flashed a short-lived smile and continued. "What that means for you is you will have to work harder and longer than you ever have before. I expect full and complete loyalty from everyone who works in this ministry. My husband and I have very different styles of management, and if you are given the opportunity to continue working here, you will soon understand what I mean by that."

Samantha took commanding and well-timed steps toward the center of the room as she spoke. "That brings me to my next point. No one in this room should feel secure in their job. Over the next few months you each will have to prove to me that you have what it takes to be a part of the New Testament Cathedral family."

She turned as she spoke until a full circle had been completed and eye contact had been made with virtually everyone in the room. "You will have to prove your loyalty to this ministry. You will have to demonstrate that you are willing to do whatever God asks you to do to spread his message to every living being on this earth. You will have to show me that you are able to raise more money than this church has ever raised in the past."

She paused to observe the looks of terror and fear on their faces and took mental note of those on which fear was not apparent. *You'll have to go, you and you,* she thought. "The last thing I want to discuss with you is a few structural changes. As of today I will be functioning not only as pastor but also as chief operations officer."

Subdued gasps were heard from every corner of the room, the loudest of which came from Catherine Birdsong. Samantha ignored them and continued. "Until further notice, all questions, payment requisitions, and personnel issues that were previously directed to Catherine will now come to me."

Catherine looked directly at Samantha with a questioning expression. She resisted the urge to stand and walk out of the room.

Samantha returned her gaze but spoke to everyone present. "Are there any questions?"

All eyes were focused on Catherine in anticipation of a heated exchange between the two most powerful people in the room. Catherine instead broke the eye contact with Samantha and cast her gaze down at the table.

"Good. I want every department head to contact my assistant to set up an appointment with me. Be prepared to give me a detailed report on the state of your division, the role of each of your employees, and to explain to me why I should allow you to keep your job."

Everyone in the room sat frozen in their seats. Some exchanged wounded glances, while others avoided eye contact with their tablemates.

"Now," she went on, looking menacingly across the crowd, "unless anyone else has something to add, I think we should all get back to work. Have a blessed day, everyone."

No one moved or exhaled until Samantha exited the room through the same door she had entered. When the door closed behind her, some slumped in their chairs, some stood dazed and bewildered, while others quickly exited the room.

Kenneth Davis's long legs quickly carried him across the room. He was the first to approach Catherine as she moved away toward the rear door. "Catherine, I'm so sorry. Did you know about this? Why didn't you tell me?"

Catherine did not turn around as she marched through the crowded room. Staff members stepped aside to clear her path. "I didn't tell you because this is the first I've heard of it," she said with her back to him.

The two were the first to exit the room. Kenneth struggled to keep up with her rapid pace as they walked side by side down the hall. "You mean she never talked to you in private?"

"That's exactly what I mean. The bitch fired me in front of seventy people."

"I didn't hear her say you were fired."

"Neither did I, but how else am I to interpret that performance? She now runs everything and everyone. She's always wanted me out of here, and now she has the power to make it happen." The two rounded the final corner in unison and stopped in front of Catherine's office.

"You need to talk to her and find out what her plans are. Don't assume she wants you out. If she did, I think she would have said it long before this morning."

"I'm so upset right now, I don't trust what I would do or say if I were alone with her. She had no right to humiliate me in front of everyone. She's evil, Kenneth. What possible motivation could she have to treat me like that? I've been loyal all these years to them both and to New Testament Cathedral. She's always been a power-hungry woman who doesn't care whom she hurts as long as she gets what she wants, and now that Hezekiah is gone, there's no one who can stop her."

"That might be true, but you still need this job. Where are you going to go? You love New Testament Cathedral," Kenneth said, escorting her into her office.

"I'm not so sure about that anymore. Hezekiah would have never treated anyone so cruelly. It's different now, and I'm not sure that I want to be a part of it."

"Just remember she is only the interim pastor. The trustees will see how wrong she is for the position and vote her out. You have to be patient and let her hang herself."

Catherine laughed out loud. "If the trustees were naive enough to put her in the position, they'll never vote her out. She'll manipulate them the same way she manipulated Hezekiah and everyone else she wants to control."

"All I'm saying, Catherine, is that you should speak with her first. Let her know that you aren't a threat. That you only want what's best for New Testament Cathedral."

Catherine sat at her desk and rested her head on the back of the cushioned leather chair, willing herself not to cry as Kenneth hovered above her. She took a deep breath and let out an exhausted sigh. "I'll think about it, Kenneth. But I'm not optimistic."

A fountain poured threads of water into a gently gurgling stream that wound through the center of the room. The only hint that it was a Japanese restaurant was the army of attractive and young Asian waiters moving silently from table to table, attending to the whims of diners. Gideon Truman checked his watch as the waiter poured more water into his glass. The trendy restaurant was dimly lit by modern lanterns hanging from the ceiling. The surfaces throughout the dining room were a mix of gleaming polished steel, cold gray cement, and highly glossed teak.

"Are you ready to order, sir?" inquired the waiter, who was wearing the regulation white shirt, black bowtie, and black pants.

"No," Gideon replied politely. "I'm waiting for someone. Looks like they're running late."

"I'll check back in a few minutes," the waiter said as he bowed his head.

Patrons of the restaurant discreetly craned their necks to sneak a glimpse at the handsome news reporter. Sushi chefs peeked at Gideon through the glass shield on the counter to ensure their illustrious lunch guest was comfortable and receiving the best service as they expertly sliced rich red strips of fresh tuna and molded fists of jasmine rice.

Gideon was used to the attention. At forty-five he was the host of a top-rated investigative news program on CNN. His talent for unearthing sensational facts that eluded his competition, coupled with a handsome yet boyish face, made him one of the most popular reporters in the country.

Every evening Gideon's face could be seen in the living rooms, bedrooms, and boardrooms of millions of American viewers. B-list celebrities clamored for the opportunity to appear on his program and be questioned to the point of tears as they confessed to being molested by their uncle when they were children, or to deny being the father of a silicon-injected stripper's love child. On the other hand, A-list celebrities, politicians, corporate CEOs, and heads of state did their best to avoid being caught under the glare of his bright light for fear of involuntarily revealing the one secret that would send their careers plummeting into the depths of public humiliation and obscurity.

His perfectly brown skin provided the ideal contrast for teeth that matched the luster of the finest Australian pearl. The warmth of his deep caramel eyes could seduce, comfort, and then, if he chose, dissect the powerful with surgical-like precision.

Gideon had not fully understood the impact of his striking looks until his first television job at a small station in Philadelphia. It was there he learned that most people were far more interested in what he looked like and with whom he slept than the stories he reported, a fact that never pleased him. There was always a subtle hint of embarrassment in his tone whenever he spoke to the cameras. It was as if he were saying, "I'm sorry if I am distracting you from this important story." This modesty provided viewers with yet another indescribable something that made him even more desirable.

Rumors of his questionable sexuality were frequently the topic of conversation at beauty salons, smart dinner parties, and on the cover of tabloids. No one knew definitively, but the gay community assumed he was "family," while ever-hopeful females defended his heterosexuality as if he were their husband-to-be or favorite son.

As Gideon reached for a full water glass, Cynthia Pryce approached the table. "Good afternoon, Mr. Truman," she said, extending her hand. Gideon bumped the table when he stood and gently took her hand. He appeared slightly rattled.

"I'm sorry. Did I startle you?" she said with a curious expression on her face.

"No. No, not at all. I must, however, confess that I wasn't expecting you to be so . . . Please sit down."

Cynthia smiled. "Thank you. To be so what?"

"Well, so attractive," he replied, uncharacteristically embarrassed.

Cynthia smiled and said, "Really? What exactly were you expecting?"

Gideon quickly regained his composure. "I'm not sure. Maybe a more matronly church-lady type, wearing lots of lace around her neck and a big hat with silk flowers."

They laughed gently. Both revealed pearly smiles that demanded the attention of diners from other tables.

After being directed by the chef, the waiter returned promptly to the table. "Good afternoon, ma'am. May I offer you something from the bar?" he asked Cynthia.

"I'll have a glass of dry white wine," she said without looking up.

"And you, sir?"

Gideon looked up with a smile and replied, "I'll have the same. Thank you."

When the waiter was out of earshot, Gideon spoke softly. "I must say, Mrs. Pryce, I was surprised when you contacted me. I've been trying to reach members of the board of trustees and senior ministers from New Testament Cathedral for three weeks now, but no one has been willing to speak with me. It seems a veil of silence has dropped over the entire church. It's almost as if you all have something to hide."

Cynthia smiled but did not speak. The waiter returned with the two glasses of wine and took their orders.

"Mr. Truman—"

Gideon interrupted, "Please, call me Gideon."

"All right then, Gideon, you mentioned secrets. How much do you know about Hezekiah Cleaveland's personal life?"

"At this point not very much," Gideon replied. "Only what's written about him on the church's Web site. As I said, no one has been willing to talk with me. That is, no one until now."

"Are you familiar with a *Los Angeles Chronicle* reporter by the name of Lance Savage?"

"Isn't he the reporter who was found dead in his home a few weeks ago?"

"That's correct," she said with a pleased expression. "Do you know anything about the story he was working on when he was murdered?"

"I don't. Did it have something to do with Pastor Cleaveland?"

Cynthia's response was interrupted by the waiter arriving with a small platter of intricately displayed sushi. When he bowed and left, she continued, "I'm not going to play games with you, Gideon. I happen to know the content of the story Lance Savage was working on."

"And how do you know that?"

"Because I was the source of his information," she said with a tinge of pride.

"Go on," he said, his words punctuated by a slight gesture of his hand.

"Before I say more, I'll need some assurances from you. What I tell you can never be attributed to me. I must remain anonymous. It will be up to you to prove or disprove what I say."

Gideon silently calculated the cunning of his prey and concluded that, if the information was as titillating as she seemed to believe, it was worth agreeing to her terms.

"That sounds reasonable. However, I must tell you that if what you say is in any way fabricated, I will be very displeased that you have wasted my time, and believe me, Mrs. Pryce, you don't want to lie to someone like me."

She smiled and said, "I can assure you that everything I'm about to tell you is absolutely true. And please, Gideon, call me Cynthia." Cynthia picked up her leather purse from the floor. From it she retrieved a folder containing a stack of papers and handed it to Gideon. "These are copies of e-mails I printed from Hezekiah's computer six months before he was killed. They are correspondences between him and his lover."

"When you say 'lover,' I assume you are referring to his wife, Samantha?" Gideon asked innocently.

"I'm afraid not. Hezekiah's lover was a man. A young man named Danny St. John."

Gideon took the folder, leaned forward, and asked suspiciously, "Are you saying Pastor Hezekiah Cleaveland was gay? Who else knows about this?"

"I'm not exactly sure. The only people I am aware of are Lance Savage, Phillip Thornton from the *Los Angeles Chronicle,* and my husband, Percy."

"How about his wife? Does she know about this?"

"That I don't know."

"Are you suggesting this has something to do with his murder?"

"I suspect it does. I don't know that for a fact, but think about it. In the week before the story was scheduled to run in the *Los Angeles Chronicle,* there were three deaths. All of them were people associated with Samantha Cleaveland. Lance Savage, the Reverend Willie Mitchell, and Hezekiah Cleaveland. It all strikes me as very suspicious."

"Who is Willie Mitchell?"

"Reverend Mitchell was a senior minister at New Testament Cathedral. He was also one of the largest individual donors to the new cathedral construction project and a man who would do anything Samantha told him to do. It was an open secret that he was in love with her, and she used that to control him."

"How did he die?"

"Poor man shot himself in the head on the night Hezekiah was killed," Cynthia answered with as much sympathy as she could muster. "It was such a tragedy."

"Do the police think there's a link between Hezekiah's murder and Mitchell's suicide?"

"No."

"So what makes you think there is?"

"Reverend Mitchell was madly in love with Samantha. So why would he kill himself after the man he believed stood between him and Samantha was now out of the way? It doesn't make sense."

Gideon still had not opened the folder that lay on the table. "Is Danny St. John a member of New Testament Cathedral?"

"No. He's a social worker who works with the homeless at an agency in downtown Los Angeles. I've never seen him before, but Lance told me he is quite beautiful. You should pay him a visit. You might like him."

Gideon ignored the poorly veiled reference to his orientation and opened the folder. The first e-mail was dated February twelfth two years earlier. It was sent from Hezekiah's New Testament Cathedral e-mail address to a Google address for Danny St. John.

> Hello, Danny,
> I'm between meetings and wanted to tell you how much I love you. I think about you so much sometimes, it's hard for me to concentrate. I was just counseling a couple whose marriage is falling apart, and all I could think about was holding you in my arms and kissing your body from head to toe. I love the way you taste, the way you smell, and the way you make me feel. I can't wait to see you tomorrow night.
> Love you,
> Hez

Gideon continued reading randomly through the stack of e-mails. They ranged in tone from completely innocuous to sexually graphic. Some were innocent communications, while others spoke to the undeniable emotional and physical bond between one of the nation's most powerful religious leaders and a young, naive social worker. After a while Gideon looked up from the papers at Cynthia, who had been studying him the entire time he read. There was silence at the table as they each planned their next move.

Gideon went first. "So, what do you want out of this? Our network has a firm policy that we don't pay for stories."

Cynthia had anticipated that these would be the salivating journalist's next words and reverted to her best minister's wife impression.

"I'm not seeking any type of financial remuneration," she responded indignantly. "I don't want anything but for God's will to be done. My heart goes out to Samantha. Who knows what diseases he may have given her? Also, what if this Danny St. John killed Hezekiah in a jealous rage? She needs to know for her own safety."

"Why didn't the *Los Angeles Chronicle* run the story?"

"It was scheduled to be their lead story on the Monday after the Sunday Hezekiah was killed. Obviously, Hezekiah being killed was a much bigger story than him liking to suck dick. And, afterward, I'm sure they realized there would be a significant backlash if they were thought to be maligning the dead." From the expression on Gideon's face, Cynthia realized her choice of words didn't fit with the preacher's wife image. "I'm sorry if I offended you."

"Not offended. Just a little surprised." Gideon took a mental note of the multifaceted woman and continued. "If this is true, it has the potential to be one of the most sensational stories of the year. Have you spoken to anyone else in the media?"

"No, I haven't. I wanted to speak with you first."

"Why me?"

"Because I believe you will handle the story in a way that will do the least amount of harm to New Testament Cathedral. You strike me as ethical, sophisticated, and talented enough to make the story about the man and not the ministry. Good people sometimes do stupid things. Hezekiah's behavior was certainly stupid, but the ministry he built is not. Millions of people around the world rely on New Testament Cathedral for hope, direction, and comfort. I think you can understand how important that is and will report the story in a way that will allow those of us who remain to continue to share the love of God throughout the world."

"That's a nice speech, Cynthia, but isn't your husband the next in line to become pastor if Samantha doesn't work out?"

Cynthia pulled her most offended expression from the depths of her gut and responded, "Yes, but that has nothing to do with this. I only want what's right for New Testament."

"Save the pious bullshit for your television audience. You seem to forget I'm a reporter. I knew everything about you and your husband ten minutes after you called me. I'm assuming your husband, Percy, isn't quite as ambitious as you are. What really happened, Cynthia? He didn't have the balls to throw Samantha under the bus and take over New Testament Cathedral after Hezekiah died? You had done all the dirty work by leaking the story." Then, to test her sensibilities even further, he added, "I wouldn't be surprised if you also had to fuck a few guys, or even girls, at the *Chronicle* to keep this story on track."

Cynthia leaned back in her chair unfazed as Gideon continued. "You would be the first lady of New Testament Cathedral today if Hezekiah hadn't gotten himself shot in the head the day before the story was scheduled to run. But you don't give up easily, because here you are, trying your damnedest to convince me to pin Hezekiah's death on his widow or his lover."

Cynthia looked him directly in the eyes as she reached for the folder between them. "I'll take those if you're not interested," she said with a wicked smile. "I'm sure I won't have a problem finding someone who is. Maybe Anderson Cooper, "she said wryly.

Gideon quickly placed his hand firmly on the folder. "Hold on. I didn't say I wasn't interested. I'm going to investigate the story, but on my terms. No one, including you and your husband, are off-limits. If I find out that your role in this was anything other than what you've said, it will be my decision whether or not to include it in my story."

Cynthia smiled slightly. "You don't frighten me, Gideon Truman," she said mockingly. "The role I played is exactly as I've described it. Just remember, if you call on me to corroborate any of this, you're out of luck. Based on your obviously brilliant skills of deduction, it shouldn't be too difficult for you to figure out why. I'll deny we ever met and sue you personally for libel if you ever try to drag me into this."

"It seems to me you've already dragged yourself into it, Cynthia. Can you get me an interview with Samantha? She won't take my calls."

"Don't worry about that. She knows you want to interview her, and she'll contact you when she feels the time is perfect for her to milk Hezekiah's death for her own benefit. By the way, when you do meet with her, don't forget to ask about his other extramarital affairs."

"What do you mean, other? Have there been more?"

"Of course there have been others, but none like this one. Who cares how many choir girls he's fucked over the years? That will all be eclipsed by the lovely Danny St. John."

Chapter 4

Reverend Percy Pryce's office was the third largest in the New Testament Cathedral administrative suite. The room's dominant colors were hues of grays and black, with a smattering of color in the form of autumn-toned pillows on a black couch, a green vase glimmering from the light pouring through the wall of glass, and a burst of fresh-cut flowers, which were delivered like clockwork each Monday morning to every office in the executive suite. They sat on the table near to Percy's desk.

Percy could smell the sweet fragrance of Cynthia's perfume still on his hands as he removed his coat and sat behind his large black lacquered desk. The fog that ecstasy brought slowly began to fade as the realization of his deeds came to the forefront of his mind. Once again the unsuccessful attempt he and Kenneth Davis had made to pay Lance Savage $175,000 in exchange for not running the incendiary story about Hezekiah played like a recording in his brain. The violent struggle with Lance Savage, which had left the living room of the little bungalow in shambles. The image of the reporter's crumpled body lying dead on the floor among the litter of one-hundred-dollar bills was ever looming.

His hands trembled slightly as he relived the scene. His palms felt moist and his mouth dry when the intercom buzzer sliced through the silence. "Excuse me, Reverend Pryce," exclaimed the disembodied voice.

"Reverend Davis is here to see you. Should I send him in? He said it will only take a moment."

Percy took a deep breath and rubbed his dewy hands together. "Thank you, Carol. Send him in."

Kenneth entered like a whirlwind, closing the door behind him. "She's out of control. We have to do something."

Percy looked up and calmly replied, "We only have ourselves to blame for this. We all knew who Samantha was long before Hezekiah was killed. We voted her in as pastor, and now we have to live with the decision."

"How can you be so calm about this? That woman is going to destroy this ministry with her ego." Kenneth walked anxiously toward the desk and continued. "This morning she announced that she is going to be functioning as the COO. She certainly knew how to run Hezekiah, but she doesn't know anything about running New Testament Cathedral."

Percy remained calm. "I think you're wrong. Samantha is a smart woman. The public loves her, and she raises more money than all of us put together. Some people think she's been running the church from day one and Hezekiah was only the front man."

"That may be true, but what about the spiritual needs of our members? You know as well as I do that if they can't write a check for ten thousand dollars or more, she won't want any part of them."

Percy paused and turned toward the window. He looked out over the grounds of New Testament Cathedral and replied mournfully, "I must admit that I worry about that too, Reverend Davis."

Kenneth sat down on the couch and, along with Percy, looked out the window. "And so you should. She's going to run this place like a coldhearted corporation. It will be all about money and her fame, not about saving souls."

The two men sat quietly, each searching the horizon for answers. Percy finally broke the silence. "Have you heard anything from the police about Lance Savage? Every time someone knocks on my door, I jump, thinking it's them coming to arrest me."

Kenneth moved anxiously to the edge of the couch. "I've told you to forget about that, Percy. There is no link between us and his death. As far as the police are concerned, Lance walked in on a burglar robbing his home and was killed."

"I just can't stop thinking about him lying there," Percy said nervously. "He's dead because of us, Kenneth. I don't know if God can forgive us for that. I don't know if I can forgive myself."

"It was an accident. You know it. I know it, and so does God. You didn't intend to kill him."

"Cynthia knows when something is bothering me."

Kenneth stood and walked behind Percy's desk. He spun the chair toward him, kneeled down in front of Percy, and placed his hand on his knee. "Have you said anything to her about this?"

Percy looked startled. "No," he replied emphatically. "I could never tell her I did something like this."

"Good. Let's keep it that way. As time passes, you'll learn to manage your feelings better, but for now don't say a word to anyone. Trust me, it will get easier. If you need to talk about it, call me. Understand?"

Percy nodded his head in affirmation, then turned away.

Kenneth continued, "The only thing we need to worry about now is Samantha and New Testament. We have to figure out a way to prevent her from being appointed as permanent pastor. Everyone knows you should be pastor, Percy."

"You sound like Cynthia. That's all she's been talking about since Hezekiah's death."

Kenneth stood up, sat on the desk and said, "You should listen to her. She's right."

"She might be, but there doesn't seem to be anything that can be done about it now. It's unlikely the trustees are going to reverse their decision. Once she starts bringing in money, they won't have any choice but to make it permanent. They're no match for her. No one is."

"You underestimate yourself, Percy. Cynthia believes in you. I believe in you, and so do thousands of other members of this congregation. You just have to have faith."

"I think I'll need more than faith to go up against Samantha. Right now I'm more concerned about Catherine. She's talking about leaving."

"Like I said earlier, Samantha is not stupid. She'll learn quickly that she can't run this place without Catherine. I'll try to talk some sense into her later this week."

"I don't think she'll listen, but it's worth a try."

"I think you, Catherine, Naomi, and I should meet. Let's put our heads together and see if there's anything we can do about this," Kenneth said.

Percy looked sharply at him and said, "You seem to have forgotten what happened the last time the four of us put our heads together to solve a problem." He stood up and walked away from the desk. "It was bribing Lance not to run the story. What were we thinking? It only made matters worse. Now the man's dead, for Christ sake."

"It was a good plan, Percy. He just got greedy and wanted more. It would have worked if you hadn't gotten so angry. We could have offered him more money."

"We should have never offered him any money at all," Percy said bitterly.

"You know we had no other choice," Kenneth rebuked. "A scandal like that would have brought this entire ministry down. At least that crisis was averted."

"Yes, it was averted, but at what cost? Two men are dead, Kenneth. Was it worth it?"

"How could you ask that? Of course it was worth it. You forget how many millions of people this ministry touches. You forget about all the people whom we've led to Christ. Was it worth it?" Kenneth repeated as his voice escalated. "Hell, yes, it was worth it, and deep down I believe you agree."

"Today my guest is the new pastor of the mega church New Testament Cathedral in Los Angeles and one of my dearest friends, the fabulous Reverend Dr. Samantha Cleaveland."

The audience of the nationally syndicated *Renee Adasen Show* was filled with well-dressed, smiling middle-class women who had collectively waited years for tickets to the talk show. The cantilevered seats held a sea of peach, blue, yellow, and spring pastels. Everyone stood to their feet and applauded when they heard Samantha's name.

Renee raised her voice over the applause and swung her arms in a sweeping motion. "Please help me welcome Pastor, Reverend Dr. Samantha Cleaveland."

The claps became louder and were accompanied by hoots of approval and gasps of admiration when Samantha walked onto the platform from behind a series of backlit blue panels and screens.

"So, you're so . . . gosh," the host said enthusiastically. "You're such an amazing woman. For those of

you who don't know—I can't imagine who that would
be—Samantha . . . I can call her Samantha because
we're friends." The comment was greeted with laughs
from the audience and a broad smile and a touch of
Renee's hand by Samantha.

Renee continued in a more somber tone. "Anyway,
there has been no modern-day tragedy since the King
and Kennedy assassinations, at least not one that I can
think of, that has moved the country like your story,
Samantha. For those in our audience who don't know
this, Samantha's husband, the Reverend Dr. Hezekiah
T. Cleaveland, was brutally assassinated. I don't know
any other way to put it, but he was assassinated in front
of you and the entire congregation of New Testament
Cathedral in Los Angeles. I mean you literally held him
in your arms as he was dying."

The cameras panned the audience. Women clutched
their chests and dabbed tears from their eyes. A close-
up of a woman shaking her head, with her hand covering her mouth, filled the screen for a brief moment. The
camera cut back to the two beautiful women sitting in
modern, comfortable chairs covered in butterscotch-
toned leather.

Samantha wore a simply cut black two-piece suit
and a white blouse with an oversize collar that revealed
only enough cleavage to remind everyone that she was
a voluptuous woman. Renee wore an apple red knit
dress with a round neckline that dipped slightly to the
left, similarly revealing enough flesh to remind viewers
that she, too, was a desirable woman.

The women faced each other at a slight angle. Their
perfect legs crossed at the knee, with one spiked heel
of their handmade Italian shoes planted in the carpet,
causing the tip to point graciously toward the audience.

"I know everyone would like to know. . . . I know I would. What was going through your mind at that moment?" the host asked unapologetically. "When you first heard the gunshots? I can only imagine how terrifying that must have been for you."

Samantha's expression, on cue, faded from that of a radiant television personality to grieving widow within seconds. "Renee, let me first tell you how much your support has meant to me through this very difficult time," she said sincerely.

Renee reached out, held her hand, and said, "That's what friends are for. I know you would have done the same for me."

The audience responded with loud yet respectful applause.

"So tell us, Samantha, what was going through you mind that day?"

"Renee, much of it is still a blur. It was a beautiful Sunday morning. Hezekiah and I were always our most happiest on Sundays. I was with him in his office before the service started, and like I always did, I straightened his tie, kissed him, and told him how much I loved him before he went out to the pulpit. I took my seat on the front row, and I remember thinking how lucky I was to be married to such a wonderful man—"

Renee interrupted, "Did you sense anything was wrong or that something bad was about to happen?"

"I had no idea. Everything seemed perfect. Hezekiah was about halfway through his sermon when I heard the first shot. I thought one of the overhead lights had burst." Samantha put the tip of her freshly manicured finger to her lips and paused before she continued. "Then I saw him lean forward and put his hand on his chest. That's when we all heard the second shot. There were screams coming from everywhere. It was horrible," she said with an air of introspection. "Just horrible. I honestly don't remember anything after that."

Renee dabbed a tear from her eye. She again reached across and took Samantha's hand and asked, "Do the police have any clue as to who may have done this?"

Samantha looked even more mournful and said, "So far they don't have any suspects. They think it might have been someone who had been stalking him for at least a year, but they're not sure. The Los Angeles Police Department has been wonderful. I have every faith that they will find the person or persons responsible for my husband's death."

Renee paused before continuing. "Yeah," she said, "I mean, for many people Hezekiah was an icon, but for you he was more than that. He was your husband, your partner, your lover. It must be surreal for you. . . . Is it disbelief? It's hard to believe still? It's still hard to believe he's gone?"

Samantha shifted uncomfortably in the chair and said, "It is, Renee. Some nights I turn over in bed and reach for him, only to find that he's not there. Anyone who's lost a loved one knows the grief is almost unbearable. It's as if you've lost a part of your own soul. I miss him more than you can imagine."

Renee pressed on. "Now, the entire thing was caught on tape?"

"Well, yes. It was Sunday morning service. There were cameras everywhere."

"Unfortunately, the tapes were leaked to the media and have been played . . . seems like nonstop since it happened. How does it feel when you see it now?"

"I haven't seen it. I haven't turned on a television or radio since it happened. I'm too afraid of hearing his name on the news or accidently seeing the footage."

"Well, unfortunately, I have seen it. I suspect most everyone in the country has seen it," Renee replied. "And like I said, it's surreal. I don't know how you've gotten through this with such grace."

"I can honestly say that I don't have any hate for the person who did this. My heart goes out to him, and every night I say a prayer for him. Its times like these that your faith is tested, Renee. This has, of course, tested my faith, but I know that God has a plan, and this has only increased my faith in him."

The last words triggered a round of applause from the audience.

Renee acknowledged the audience with an affirming smile and continued. "Now, this only happened a month ago, right?"

Samantha nodded yes. "It's been just over a month, and the amount of love I have received has been amazing. Thank you, America, for all the love and kindness you've shown me," Samantha said, smiling warmly past the camera to the audience. "Your love and the love of God are the only things that keep me going."

More applause erupted from the now entranced audience. Samantha was everything they had dreamt a friend of Renee's would be.

The host waited for the applause to die down and then continued. "Maybe you're not in this space yet—it's been a month since his death—but when you are able to go to the space where you're able to remember the warmest place and thoughts about your husband, what do you think those thoughts will be?"

Samantha contemplated for a moment and said, "I think what I will remember the most is his kindness. Not only to me, but to everyone he met. When people talked to Hezekiah, he had this uncanny ability to make them feel they were the center of his world. That whatever they were thinking or feeling at the time was important to him, and that he really cared. I loved him deeply, and I believe he also loved me just as much. I'll miss the feeling of security you get when someone cares so deeply for you and would do anything in the world to make you happy."

Renee followed another introspective pause with, "Do you remember the last thing you said to him or the last thing he said to you?"

"I love you."

Renee smiled and said, "I love you. . . . Isn't that a good thing? I understand that you've been selected to replace Hezekiah as the pastor of New Testament Cathedral."

Samantha feigned shock and quickly replied, "I could never replace Hezekiah. No one could replace him. He was a great man. He was my life. He was my soul mate, my rock, and most importantly, he was my friend. Sometimes I'm not sure if I can go on without him, but inevitably, at those lowest moments someone will say to me, 'Don't give up, Samantha. We need you,' or 'You can do it, Samantha. Do it for Hezekiah.' And, Renee, when I hear encouragement like that, I just . . . I get energized. They inspire me to work harder, to move a little faster, and to go on with the work my husband and I began together."

"You are amazing, girl. Isn't she amazing?" Renee asked over her shoulder of the audience.

Their unanimous response was given in thunderous applause.

"So what's next for you, Samantha?" Renee asked.

"I'm glad you asked," replied Samantha with a playful smile. "New Testament Cathedral is going to be bigger and better than ever."

The audience responded as if that was just what they wanted to hear.

"We are about to complete the construction of our new campus and twenty-five-thousand-seat cathedral. The television ministry is expanding now to South Africa, Thailand, and Australia. So we want the world to know New Testament Cathedral is very much alive and growing."

Renee stood up and said, "Wow." Samantha stood with her, and the two women embraced. The audience stood and clapped, as if to solidify the obvious bond between the two women.

Renee raised Samantha's hand as if she were a victorious prizefighter and said above the applause, "I said it once and I'll say it again. You're an amazing woman." She then faced the audience, still holding Samantha's hand in the air, and said, "Pastor Samantha Cleaveland, everyone. Thank you so much for being here with us today and sharing your courageous story. You are an inspiration and a role model to me and to women everywhere."

Samantha's and Renee's skin looked radiant, magnified on the sixty-two-inch flat-screen television that hung on the wall in Cynthia Pryce's den. Cynthia sat with her feet curled under her in one of two overstuffed black leather chairs that had been positioned at viewing distance in front of the television. A pair of Fendi black suede pumps lay strewn on the floor, and the black jacket of the Dolce & Gabbana pantsuit she wore that day had been tossed casually on the back of the chair.

The curtains were fully drawn and the room was dark except for the piercing glow from the two women on the screen. The room was filled with sleek Scandinavian chairs and a well-cushioned brown leather sofa. The dark stained teak floor offered no assistance in absorbing the crystal clear voices booming from the surround-sound speakers.

The clarity made it impossible for Cynthia to miss any syllable the two women spoke. Her silky hair shifted with every disapproving tilt of her head. As their words reverberated through the room, when they shared a knowing glance, and when the audience gushed, an invisible knife was driven deeper and deeper into Cynthia's heart.

Cynthia pointed the remote as if it were a gun and pressed the trigger when the credits mercifully began to scroll across the screen. The television went black, and Cynthia was left in silence to contemplate the spectacle she had just witnessed.

Is the American public so gullible that they can't tell when someone is acting? she questioned silently. *How could they not see her for the horrible, conniving bitch she is?* she thought, staring at her reflection in the screen.

It had been two days since Scarlett confessed to her husband that Hezekiah was the father of her daughter, Natalie. Two days of David avoiding eye contact when they passed each other in the hall. Two days of sleeping in separate bedrooms, and two days of wondering whether he would leave her life as quickly as he had come. Scarlett loved her husband, but her grief over Hezekiah's death made it difficult for her to worry about her domestic troubles.

Her sleep had been fitful, and there was no appetite. The little strength she had was used to comb Natalie's hair before school each morning and to greet her with a smile and a kiss every day after school. There were stretches of time during the two-day period that she didn't even know if David was in the house. Her thoughts rarely strayed from memories of the brief time she had loved and made love to Hezekiah, or the hurt she had endured at the hand of Samantha after she had learned that Scarlett was pregnant with his child.

David felt betrayed when he learned of the years of deception and lies. The pain was compounded by knowing Hezekiah Cleaveland had shared the secret with the woman he loved. His stomach churned when he thought of all the times he had shaken Hezekiah's hand after church with Scarlett standing by his side and Natalie in his arms.

"You outdid yourself with that sermon, Pastor," he had said to Hezekiah on several Sunday mornings. "You've made me want to be a better husband to my wife and a better father to our daughter."

The hurt festered in the silent home. Every time he saw Scarlett standing in the bathroom mirror or sitting and looking out the living room window, he would imagine Hezekiah groping her delicate body or making love to her in some cheap motel room. He could almost hear her gentle moans of ecstasy when he thought of Hezekiah pounding away at the woman he loved.

He wanted Hezekiah to feel the hurt he felt. *How do you hurt a dead man?* he had thought more than once. *If he wasn't already dead, I think I would kill him.*

Scarlett stepped from the marble and glass enclosure after a long hot shower. Beads of warm water rolled from her dripping hair, over the curves of her breasts, around her hips, and onto the carpeted floor. The water glimmered on her naked body as she wrapped herself in a plush pink towel. The room was filled with steam, leaving only a ghostly reflection in a wall of mirrors that stood before her.

The bathroom door opened, and David stood in the threshold as she dried her hair. "Does Samantha know about this?" he asked coldly.

Scarlett jerked her head in his direction. "You startled me. Why didn't you knock?"

"Now you want me to knock when I enter my own bathroom," he replied with a hint of irony.

"Yes, considering you haven't said a word to me in two days."

"Correction, Scarlett. We haven't spoken to each other in two days. You haven't answered my question. Does Samantha know about Natalie?"

Scarlett wrapped her damp hair in a towel as she spoke. "I told you she did. David, don't torture yourself over this. It doesn't concern you. This is my problem. I've handled it alone up until now, and I will continue to do so."

"What do you mean, it's your problem? You're my wife, and Natalie has been like a daughter to me."

"I appreciate that, David, but now that you know the truth, you don't have to worry about us anymore."

David looked confused. "How can you be so cold to me? I love you, and I love Natalie. Do you expect me just to turn off my feelings?"

"I don't expect you to do anything. I apologize if I've hurt you, but you need to understand that I did everything for Natalie, and for that I won't apologize. If you want to leave, that's up to you. I love you and I want you to stay, but I will understand if you choose not to."

"What does Samantha have to say about it?"

Scarlett did not respond. She turned her back to David and sat on the edge of the bathtub. The pain that had simmered just beneath her thin veil of confidence began to seep to the surface. She took a deep breath before she spoke. "I've already told you how she felt. She tried to force me to have an abortion. She threatened to publicly humiliate me and to say that I had seduced Hezekiah. At the time I was his assistant. She fired me and forbid Hezekiah to have anything to do with the baby."

"So why did you stay? Why didn't you leave the church?"

Scarlett stood abruptly and walked to him. She put her hand on his cheek and pleaded, "David, please don't dig this up again. Why are you torturing yourself? This happened years ago. Hezekiah is dead, and we have each other. Why does any of this matter anymore?"

Scarlett reached for his hand, but David grabbed her wrist roughly and pushed her hand away. "It matters because you lied to me. It matters because Natalie will eventually need to know who her real father is. It matters because the Cleavelands need to pay for how they walked away from her."

"Pay?" she asked. "I've never asked them for anything, and I never will. I've made it on my own for this long, and I will continue to do so with or without you."

"Why do you insist on making me the bad guy in this? I'm not the one who's been lying to you all these years. I'm not the one who's been lying to everyone that ever gave a dime to New Testament Cathedral, like Hezekiah and Samantha have been doing. Remember, I'm the guy who's been made a fool of while the three of you exchanged knowing glances behind my back. I'm the one whose wife has been in love with someone else for years. You've been acting like the grieving widow all this time, and now I understand why."

"You're not being fair, David. I love you."

"Don't give me that bullshit," he snapped. "You've hardly known I was in the house since he died. It was probably a relief that I didn't speak to you for the last two days."

"Is this about money? Because if it is, I told you I survived before I met you and I'll survive after you've gone."

"It's not about money!" he yelled with indignation.

She matched him tone for tone. "Then what is it? Is it about your ego? Are you afraid that he might have been a better lover than you? Are you concerned that his dick might have been bigger than yours? What is this all about?"

David froze in the middle of the bathroom floor. Her shocking words mingled with the thick shower steam and invaded his lungs. He didn't recognize the woman who stood before him. Although her face was distorted by the fog, he could still see her puffy eyes and sneering lips. The woman glaring at him through the mist was not the Scarlett he loved. She was not the woman whose gentle touch alone could make him forget all his troubles.

David had served as Scarlett's attorney when she divorced her first husband. The first day he saw her in his office, he knew professional boundaries were in jeopardy of being crossed. She had looked so fragile sitting across from him at the large mahogany conference table. From the moment the beautiful woman began to recount the physical and emotional abuse she had endured at the hand of her first husband, he was overwhelmed by a need to protect her and to destroy anyone that would do her harm.

And destroy he did. The eventual divorce settlement David won left Scarlett's first husband almost destitute. David was merciless and, by some standards, unscrupulous in winning her the million-dollar home in Brentwood, a vacation home on Lake Tahoe, full custody of the child he thought was his, alimony and child support so high that it forced her ex-husband to rent a studio in the less than affluent Leimert Park section of the city.

"It's about trust, Scarlett. It's about you not trusting me enough to tell me the truth about Natalie. It's about Hezekiah not taking responsibility for his daughter. If I had known, I would have made him pay."

"I know you would have. And that's another reason I never told you. I've never wanted anything from Hezekiah or Samantha. I saw how you destroyed my first husband, and I didn't want you to do that to Hezekiah."

"Why not? If Natalie is his child, he had a legal and moral responsibility to care for her," David said with a mix of lawyerly wisdom and wounded rage.

"I know what you're capable of, David. This would have consumed you. It would have been less about you looking out for Natalie's well-being and more about you wanting to destroy someone you felt had hurt me."

"Is that so wrong?" he asked, walking closer to her. His voice became calm as he cupped her bare shoulders with each hand. "I love you, and I love Natalie. I would do anything to protect you."

"That's just it, David. I didn't need you to protect me from . . ." Her voice trailed off as she held back tears.

There was no need for Scarlett to complete the sentence. The veil of sorrow that shrouded her face confirmed for David what he already believed.

"It's because you were . . ." David removed his hands from her moist shoulders and stepped back. "Because you *are* still in love with him."

Scarlett avoided his glare. "That's not true, David."

"Throughout our entire marriage you've been in love with Hezekiah."

"No, David," she pleaded.

"That's why you never left New Testament Cathe-dral."

"Don't do this, David."

"You wanted to be near Hezekiah Cleaveland."

Scarlett's knees went limp, causing her to wilt onto the edge of the bathtub. "David, please stop. It isn't true," she pleaded. "I love you."

"You don't love me. How could you?" David stood menacingly above her.

"Everything you've done since you met me has been to keep you close to Hezekiah. Pressuring me to join New Testament Cathedral, you accepting the appoint-ment to the board of trustees, insisting that Hezekiah officiate at our wedding. Were you still sleeping with him? How could I have been so stupid? It's always been about Hezekiah Cleaveland."

"It's not true, David," Scarlett cried. "I swear to you, none of that is true."

Chapter 5

The morning traffic had given way to cautious older drivers on their way to the local market or the post office, and the odd public bus making another round of the city. Danny stood alone in the window of his small apartment looking over Adams Boulevard.

In the distance he could see four homeless men sitting in a bus shelter. From their animated hand jesters, he assumed they had already drunk their morning's ration of alcohol and were making plans to get more. Danny recognized each of the men, as they had occupied various spots around his neighborhood for the last six months. He had never offered food or pocket change to the group of regulars for fear that if he did, they would discover where he lived and return for additional kindness. The apartment was his only refuge, and he refused to share it with the needy people he encountered on a daily basis in his job as a homeless outreach worker in downtown Los Angeles.

Danny's bohemian taste was reflected in the eclectic mix of flea market and garage sale finds that filled every room. His toes curled on the worn threads of an Asian rug he had found left on a curb in front of a home in Santa Monica. He took another sip from a steaming cup of tea pressed to his lips.

The endless parade of Joan Rivers jewelry, clothes for the plus-size woman, and revolutionary new cleaning products that promised to permanently rid his home of life's residue had kept his mind from lingering too long on the memory of Hezekiah. Danny hadn't slept the night before. His room glowed from the television, which was tuned to the Home Shopping Network.

Danny had spent his late teens and much of his twenties searching for the one person who would be willing to look into his eyes and, without reservation, tell him truly what he saw. Was there a hideous monster lurking behind his liquid brown eyes, waiting for just the right moment to pounce and devour his prey, or was an angel there only to serve and guard the weak and frail? Until Hezekiah there had been no one.

Hezekiah had shown him, through his gentle touch and tender kiss, that he was neither a monster nor an angel, neither good nor evil. He had shown Danny that he was more than a cliché, and too beautiful to label, that his love and his hate were one and the same, and that his fear and courage were of the same substance.

Among the jumble of his fears, the thought of forgetting all that Hezekiah had taught him about life, love, and about himself often emerged as the one whose weight seemed most unbearable. What if he forgot how to love?

The telephone in Danny's apartment rang intermittently the entire night. Each time the caller ID flashed the name Kay Braisden. Danny and Kay had been friends since college, before she had abruptly ended all communications when Danny revealed he was in a relationship with Rev. Hezekiah Cleaveland.

They were the same age and over the years had often celebrated their birthdays together. She was a devout Christian, the pretty, prim, and proper daughter of a pastor. Kay took great pride in the fact that she had graduated with honors with a master's degree in social work from one of the most prestigious Bible institutes in California and that she had read the Bible from cover to cover before she was twenty years old. Danny, on the other hand, was the soulful poet who preferred staying home to read or write on a Saturday night over sweating with the young, toned, and beautiful at the hottest new bar in town.

Danny stared at the glowing name on the telephone as it rang for the last time. The beep was followed by, "Danny, it's Kay again. If you're there, please pick up the phone." Then there was a moment of silence, but she did not disconnect. "Danny, I don't know what else I can say to—"

Danny's hand, of its own volition, reached for the telephone. "Hello, Kay."

"Danny, is that you?"

"Yes."

Kay began to cry. "Why haven't you returned my calls? No, don't answer that. I know why. I behaved like an idiot when you told me about Hezekiah."

"Yes, you did," Danny agreed flatly.

There was an awkward chuckle between her sobs. "I deserved that. Honey, I am so sorry. I've missed you so much the last few months. And then when I heard about . . ." Kay stopped mid-sentence. "How are you holding up through all this? When I saw it on the news, I almost fainted. All I could think about was the pain you must have been in."

"I wish I had died along with him," Danny said softly. "You weren't there for me. No one has been here for me. You were the only person I ever told about Hezekiah. You really disappointed me, Kay, and I don't know if I can forgive you."

"I deserve that, Danny. I feel horrible that I haven't been there for you. But I'm here now if you need me."

Danny was silent. He did need her now more than he had ever needed anyone. He needed someone to know the depth of his pain and loss. He needed someone who could remind him of the person he was before he met Hezekiah, because he had forgotten. He couldn't recall what his face looked like when he smiled. He didn't remember what his laugh sounded like or what his life was before the cloud of grief had descended and enveloped his entire world.

Kay interrupted the silence. "Are you still there, Danny?"

Danny began to cry. Kay was the first person to hear Danny's sorrow since Hezekiah's death. He had isolated himself and didn't allow anyone close enough to hear him cry. At work he behaved as if everyone else's problems were much greater than his own. No one knew of his loss. No one knew of his pain.

"It's okay, Danny. Let it out. I'm here for you, baby. I'm here," Kay said through her own tears.

Their combined sobs served as words for the next five minutes. Danny curled into a tight ball on his couch and cried with the phone clutched to his ear. His chest heaved as he gasped for air between deep wails. He needed someone to hear him cry, to acknowledge his pain, and to recognize his sorrow. Until that moment his loss didn't seem real. It was as if he were suspended in a dream.

"If a man cries alone, does he make a sound?" he had written in his journal one evening, while lamenting alone.

He does not, the scribe continued.
In the absence of sound, pain runs deeper.
When there is no shoulder to cry on,
the chill of sorrow is colder.

The weight of grief more unbearable.
If no one is there to share your loss.
The pain must live with you and you alone.

As their weeping gradually faded into sputtering breaths, Kay spoke. "Danny, I don't want you to be there alone. I'm coming home on the earliest flight I can get tomorrow."

"That's not necessary, Kay. I'll be all right."

"I know you'll be all right. That's not the point. We need our friends with us at times like this, and I am your friend."

Danny needed her desperately, but he continued, "You're busy, Kay. My mother is only ten minutes away. I can call her if I need to."

"Does your mother know about Hezekiah?"

Danny paused before answering. "No."

"Do you plan on telling her?" Kay asked in the tone of a woman who knew.

"No. She would never understand. I know my mother loves me, but I couldn't risk her abandoning me the way you—"

"I didn't abandon you, Danny."

"Bullshit, Kay," Danny said bitterly. "You didn't call me for months. You made me feel like our friendship all these years was a lie. That there were rules and limits you never bothered to tell me about. I don't want to take that chance with my mother."

"Your mother loves you so much, Danny. I don't think there's anything you could do or say that would change that."

"I'm not sure if that's true. She has her own preconceived idea of who I am. Anything that deviates from that and she's not interested." Danny sighed into the receiver. "Look at what happened when I thought you would never leave me. Our friendship was the one thing I thought I could count on, no matter what. But I was wrong."

"I deserve every horrible thing you have to say to me. There is no excuse for the way I reacted. All I can say is, I hope you can forgive me. You mean the world to me, and it hurts me to see you suffer alone like this."

Danny wanted to withhold his forgiveness, but it was impossible. He needed Kay in his life. "Our friendship is very important to me too."

"Does that mean you forgive me?"

Danny could hear a slight smile in her voice. He paused, not to decide if he could forgive Kay but rather to keep her in suspense for a moment longer. "Of course I forgive you," he finally responded. "Now, how soon can you get here?"

Kay laughed while wiping her tear-streaked cheek. "I'll be on the earliest flight I can get tomorrow."

White noise from sprays of water from a fountain in the middle of the cavernous glass room muffled the frenzied clamor of tourism. Gideon Truman sat in the lobby of the Bonaventure Hotel, intently studying his glowing BlackBerry. Faces from all corners of the world whizzed by, toting rolling suitcases, children, and cameras. Giddy bodies glided up and down the walls of the hotel in glass elevators along the perimeter of the lobby. Every surface glittered from natural and unnatural light. Concrete pillars dotted with pinpoint lights jutted from the marble floor up through the atrium's thirty-five stories to the rooftop revolving cocktail lounge and supported spiraling ramps that led guests upward through the lobby's core.

A hoard of plump Muslim women covered from head to foot in black burkas billowed behind an equally numbered group of their spouses in short cargo pants, overpriced tennis shoes, and brightly colored floral short-sleeve shirts. A gang of their collective offspring, in full summer gear, sounded like a gaggle of geese as their sandals slapped the marble floor while they darted playfully between the two groups of parents.

A steady stream of overly dressed couples paraded through the sliding glass doors of the main entrance. The men in gray and black suits with collars cinched at their Adam's apples and strangled by tightly knotted neckties escorted wives dressed in their cocktail party and Sunday-best outfits. One after another they made beelines to the main desk and inquired of the smiling attendants in blue blazers, "Where's the banquet room for the McDougal wedding reception?" Each time the attendants smiled as if it were the first time they had been asked that question all day, and pointed toward a row of double doors in the rear of the lobby. As the doors opened and the couples were pulled one by one into the wedding party vortex, the sound of Etta James's "At Last" could be heard, and it lingered until the doors closed again.

A tall, pale German man wearing white, yellow, and red plaid khaki shorts, leather sandals, white socks, and a Mickey Mouse cap complete with trademark stiff black ears, with his similarly dressed wife and three small blond children at his heels, stopped in his tracks when he saw Gideon, through an elaborate arrangement of tropical flowers, sitting alone in an overstuffed gray chair in the center of the room. His wife bumped into him, and the three little children collided into her.

Spoils of a day of foraging through the gift shops and concession stands at Disneyland hung from their bodies. Stuffed animals with price tags still connected were clutched under armpits. German-made shirts had been replaced by new white T-shirts with Minnie, Mickey, Donald Duck, and Tinker Bell emblazoned on each chest, and bulging gift bags filled with plastic trinkets that would remind them for years to come of their day at "The Happiest Place On Earth" dangled from the family's ten hands.

"That's Gideon Truman," the man said, pointing in Gideon's direction.

"Wo ist Gideon Truman?" the wife questioned in German with an irritated scowl. It had been a long day.

"Right there. See the black man der sitzt da drüben." he said in a mix of English and German and pointed again. As if responding to the wand of a conductor, the family looked in unison in Gideon's direction.

The wife squealed, "It is him," using her impeccable English for the first time that day. "He is so handsome. I want to take a picture with him. Quick. Get the camera from the backpack."

The portly woman quickly unloaded equal portions of her amusement park loot into the already full arms of each of the children, adjusted her bra under her Minnie Mouse T-shirt, and made an attempt at a dignified scoot toward the reporter.

"Excuse me. I am sorry to bother you, but are you not Gideon Truman, the reporter?"

Gideon looked up as if he had been expecting her to approach him. "Yes, I am not Gideon Truman," he said, flashing a dazzling smile.

The woman looked puzzled. "I do not understand. Are you or are you not Gideon Truman?"

Gideon's smile broadened. "I'm sorry. It was just a joke. Yes, I'm Gideon Truman."

The happy tourist clapped her hands loudly in delight and shouted to her husband, "It is him. Come. Come." Then she returned her admiring gaze to Gideon. "We are from Germany, but we have cable TV and watch you frequently. I am a big fan. May I please take a picture with you? Just one, please. It would make me very happy."

Gideon continued to smile as he turned off his Black-Berry and placed it in his pocket. "Of course. It would be my pleasure."

When Gideon stood, he towered over the woman. He placed his muscular arm around her as the husband approached with camera cocked and children and bags in tow. The little woman was enveloped under his arm and swooned into his heavily starched light blue button-down shirt. She could feel the finely woven raw silk of his dark blue trousers brush against her exposed calf. He smelled of sweet jasmine, or maybe it was sandalwood soap.

"Lächeln Sie," the husband said, pointing the camera in their direction.

"That means 'smile' in German," the woman said to Gideon through a beaming smile.

"*Ich weiß. Ich spreche Deutsch,*" Gideon responded.

The woman looked up in surprise as the camera flashed. "Are you German as well?" she asked.

"No. I worked in Berlin for two years. It's one of my favorite cities in the world."

The family retreated happily, carrying the prized souvenir, an image of Gideon Truman digitally etched in their camera.

Gideon returned to his comfortable seat and contemplated his next move. Cynthia Pryce had handed him the explosive twist of Danny St. John. He was now faced with the question of whether he should pursue the alleged homosexual affair, and inevitably sully the name and reputation of a much-cherished icon, or simply do what he had originally set out to do, report on the investigation into Hezekiah's murder.

He now held a piece of information that, if true, had the potential of toppling one of the most influential dynasties in the country and tarnishing the memory of one of the most renowned ministers of the twenty-first century.

Gideon was already famous, so the pursuit of acclaim would not factor heavily into his decision. He was potentially the only living reporter in the country that knew of Danny St. John. If he broke the story, it would serve to silence his many critics that claimed he was merely eye candy and not a serious journalist. Whenever he read the cutting critiques of his work, a chill would race up his spine. He had worked harder than his contemporaries but was never taken as seriously because his smile and dashing good looks always landed him on the cover and in the bowels of tabloid magazines. The question was, "Who is Gideon Truman dating now?" rather than "How did he find the nerve to ask the secretary of state that question?" The media coverage of his work usually read, "Gideon Truman looked devilishly handsome in a black Armani tuxedo at the inauguration ball," instead of "Gideon Truman asked the new president hard-hitting questions that were undoubtedly on the minds of every American."

A story this big would surely establish him as a serious journalist, worthy of the respect he so desperately desired. But at what cost would this be? New Testament Cathedral would likely be destroyed. Thousands, maybe millions, of people around the world would question their faith. One more high-profile black man would be subjected to a modern-day lynching and, in this case, would be unable to defend himself.

But the public has a right to know, Gideon thought. Hezekiah Cleaveland had set himself up as an icon. It was his decision to espouse a pious lifestyle that, if this is true, even he couldn't live up to. It was his choice to cheat on his wife and his choice to have an affair with a man.

It wouldn't hurt to talk to St. John, he thought, continuing along this line of reasoning. *I can't believe there's anything to this, anyway. I can decide whether or not to pursue it after I've spoken to him.*

Finding Danny's telephone number was an easy task. A visit to the Los Angeles mission where Danny worked, flashing a smile at the receptionist, and signing an autograph on the back of the mission's brochure yielded not only his cell phone number but also his home phone number, home address, and e-mail address, which he already had.

Danny St. John's name and telephone number appeared on the screen of the BlackBerry. After a brief hesitation he pressed TALK. The phone rang three times and then, "Hello. This is Danny. I can't take your call right now so . . . Well, you know the routine. *Ciao.*"

Gideon smiled when he heard the message. He also felt a warm flow rise from his belly as he listened to the deep, gentle timbre of the voice, which caused him to pause again.

"Hello, Mr. St. John. My name is Gideon Truman. I work for CNN. I'm covering the investigation into the death of Hezekiah Cleaveland. I was told that you may have known him. I was wondering if I might be able to speak with you briefly about this. I won't take much of your time, and I really would appreciate it. When you get this message, please give me a call on my cell at three-one-oh, five-five-five, four-four-five-five."

Hattie bent over in her garden to pluck another red tomato from a vine that slumped under the weight of a season's bounty. She stood on the rich soil between perfectly carved rows of greens, yellows, whites, and reds. The collard greens stood tall in the gentle breeze. They always reminded her of baby elephant ears when they flapped in the wind. Bushes of yellow zucchini shielded their precious fruits from the sun, and climbing green beans twisted and tangled themselves on elaborately constructed trellises made of wire and wood and set in a row.

The garden was her pride and refuge. It occupied the entire width of her backyard and one half of the length. A meticulous six-foot pink brick fence that her husband had built when the children were young served as the backdrop to the summer harvest. After each season, as soon as the last vegetable was plucked, Hattie would begin preparing the soil for the next round of crops. There was always something delicious growing in Hattie's backyard: carrots, onions, bell peppers, mustard greens and collard greens, broccoli, and cabbages. Always something to share with her neighbors, children, and friends.

The lower half of her body was covered by a faded yellow apron, tied securely around her waist, with oversize deep pockets that bulged from all the tomatoes she had picked. Moist dirt encased the soles of her sturdy black rubber shoes, and the wide-brimmed straw hat she wore caused a grid of light and shadows to form on her forehead.

Even with the warmth of the sun on her shoulders and the mud squishing under her feet, Hattie could not escape the memory of the dream she had had two nights earlier. Who was the other person, the one she could not see in the dream? Why didn't they show themselves to her? Why were they hiding from her? Was it a man or a woman? she pondered. Whoever it was, they clearly loved Pastor Cleaveland very deeply. Certainly more than Samantha had loved him.

Hattie shoed away a bee that buzzed near her ear, and another ripe tomato found its way into the apron's deep pocket. One of the many red and black dotted ladybugs in the yard landed on her shoulder. She did not brush it away. "Lord knows I can always use some good luck," she said, looking down at the ladybug.

Throughout her life, Hattie had always known what was going to happen to people around her long before it happened. She had cradled each of her four grandchildren in her dreams and had stroked their curly locks years before they were born. The vision of her mother's death at the hands of "sugar" had startled her from sleep many nights as early as seven years before the old woman succumbed to diabetes. The premonition of the man with the surprisingly dark skin sitting behind the desk in the Oval Office, just staring out the window, had come to her late one night two years before it actually became a reality.

She had learned to live with these foresights, whether they were good or bad. "Only you can change the course of a man's life," she often reaffirmed in her prayers to God and to herself. "And I ain't you, Lord, so let your will be done on earth just as it is in heaven." Hattie lived by these words. *Don't interfere with the paths men have chosen for themselves. It just ain't my*

*place. If they want to change it, that's between them
and their God.*

But today even her firm conviction left her wondering if she had done the right thing by keeping silent.
She had seen Hezekiah falling in the sanctuary days
before he was killed that horrible Sunday morning. She
had known well in advance that someone close to him
was trying to destroy him. Should she have warned
him?

"Pastor Cleaveland, you know I ain't one to meddle
in other people's business, but I feel I just got to tell
you. Something just ain't right around here," the conversation would have gone. "Now, I know you love your
wife, and so you should. But that woman is just pure
evil. She don't mean you no good, Pastor. One day that
woman's gonna do something terrible to somebody.
Maybe even you. I know she is. I can feel it in my spirit."

Of course, Pastor Cleaveland would have looked at
her as the kindly old lady that she in fact was, reached
for her weathered hand, and responded something
along the lines of, "Now, Mother Williams, I know your
premonitions have always been accurate in the past,
but this time I think you may have gotten your spiritual
wires crossed. Samantha loves me. You know that. She
would never do anything to hurt me."

It was not until the most recent dream that Hattie
learned who was behind the assassination of her pastor. The horror of the revelation had made sleep almost
impossible the last few nights. Every time she thought
about the coldness that passed from Samantha when
she touched her shoulder in the dream, the same chill
crept up her spine again. The light pouring from the
evil woman's smile that enveloped her caused her vision to blur momentarily. Hezekiah gazing up from the

pool of blood with that vacant look in his eyes made her stomach ache from pains of sorrow.

The figure she could not see still haunted her. "Who was it?" she questioned as she stood transfixed in the garden. "I hope that poor soul is not next."

Chapter 6

Gideon Truman drove the rented silver SUV to the entrance of the Cleaveland estate. He had finally been summoned by Samantha Cleaveland.

The call had come to his cell the day before. "Good afternoon. May I speak with Mr. Gideon Truman please?" the polite voice had asked with a slow, deliberate, and somewhat artificially sweet tone that hinted of Southern roots.

"This is Gideon Truman. How can I help you?"

"My name is Chantal Maxwell, Mr. Truman. I am Pastor Samantha Cleaveland's scheduling secretary. How are you today, sir?"

"Well, well. Finally, someone from New Testament Cathedral calls me back. I was beginning to take the snubs personally."

"Oh no, sir. Please don't take it personally, and thank you for your patience. I must deeply apologize for the delay in returning your calls, but as I'm sure you must understand, this has been a very difficult time for everyone at New Testament Cathedral, and especially for Pastor Cleaveland. You are not the only reporter we've had to put on hold over the last three weeks, but you should know you are one of the first we have contacted."

"I'm honored," Gideon said, barely concealing the excited tone in his voice.

"Mr. Truman, Pastor Cleaveland would like to invite you for lunch at the Cleaveland estate in Bel Air tomorrow at one o'clock. Would that be convenient for you, sir?"

"I'll be there," he replied quickly, forgetting to keep his excitement in check.

"Wonderful, sir. Would you like me to send a car for you?" The more she talked, the thicker her accent became and the slower the pace.

"That won't be necessary."

"Do you have any dietary constraints that you would like the chef to be made aware of?"

Gideon was surprised that no attempt was being made to conceal the conspicuous wealth of the Cleavelands: drivers, private chefs, Bel Air estate. *I guess the days of being embarrassed for getting rich in the name of the Lord ended with Jim Baker,* he thought.

"Thank you for asking, but I'll eat anything."

"Very well then, Mr. Truman. Also, Pastor Cleaveland has asked, will there be a film crew accompanying you? And if so, will they require any special accommodations? The estate is equipped with a state-of-the-art studio and media center."

Gideon paused, almost dumbfounded. "What was your name again, darling?"

"Chantal, Mr. Truman, Chantal Maxwell."

"Chantal, please tell Pastor Cleaveland that I'm hoping this will be the first of many conversations between her and myself. So, no, I won't be bringing a film crew with me this time."

"Yes Mr. Truman, I will pass that message on to Pastor Cleaveland. I look forward to meeting you tomorrow. I've taken the liberty of texting you a confirmation, the address and directions."

As she spoke the familiar beep on his BlackBerry sounded and the Cleaveland estate address and a Google Maps link appeared on the screen.

Chantal continued, "Now, if there is anything else I can do for you prior to your visit, please do not hesitate to contact me. May you have a blessed day, and remember, God loves you and so do we."

The telephone disconnected before his quick mind could form a snappy reply.

The next day Gideon found himself parked in front of the estate. "Good afternoon, Mr. Truman," a deep male voice said from the gatehouse. "Welcome to the Cleaveland estate. Pastor Cleaveland is expecting you. Please drive in and follow the road to the main house."

The grounds were surrounded by an eight-foot white stucco wall that extended so far up the street beyond the entrance that he was not able to see where it ended. The electronic iron gates, emblazoned with the initials *HC*, glided open. As he drove through, he saw a camera pointed directly at him. It followed him as he passed through the gates.

Within the confines of the stucco wall the temperature seemed to drop ten degrees. A thick canopy of trees and lush greenery gave the grounds an almost enchanted feel. The road was lined with palm trees standing at attention, as if they were guarding a castle. Movement to his left demanded his attention. Gideon did a double take. Three large peacocks on the shimmering green lawn flared their iridescent turquoise tail feathers as he drove by. In the background he could hear the muffled roar of the Pacific Ocean.

"If I start to hear harps playing, I'm leaving," he mumbled. The grounds were immaculate. He could see men in green uniforms riding in what appeared to be a golf cart filled with gardening equipment on a path to his right. A tennis court with striking white lines was followed by a gazebo that looked out over the ocean. Then he saw what he assumed was a guesthouse tucked behind a grove of even more trees.

Finally, he could see the main house looming ahead. As he drove closer, the dense cover of trees unfurled like curtains on a stage. The house was drenched in sunlight, which seemed to appear just as he approached.

It was a magnificent glowing white Mediterranean villa flanked on each side by spectacular views of Los Angeles and the Pacific Ocean, and above by a strikingly blue sky dotted with fluffy white clouds. Gideon never remembered seeing the sky such an amazing shade of azure before. Two massive stone double stairways curved around a fifteen-foot stone fountain pouring water into a pond filled with night-blooming water lilies and black, gold, and white koi fish, led up to a covered porch. The landing held four twenty-foot-high carved pillars, two to the left and two to the right of what were the largest and most intricately carved wooden doors he had ever seen.

Before he could completely stop the car, a gentle tap on the side window startled him. A tall, well-built man who appeared to be of Italian decent, wearing a black suit and dark sunglasses, opened Gideon's car door.

"Good afternoon, Mr. Truman. Welcome to the Cleaveland estate. Please leave your keys in the car. I assure you it will be well taken care of."

Gideon noticed a brown leather strap under his coat as the man gestured for him to exit the car. *Armed security?* Gideon thought. *She must be terrified with the killer still on the loose.*

"Security's pretty tight around here," Gideon said, exiting the car.

"Yes, sir. We do take every necessary precaution. You will be very safe during your time with Pastor Cleaveland. Enjoy your lunch, Mr. Truman."

With that, the armed man climbed into the SUV and drove around the side of the house.

Gideon stood for a moment alone at the foot of the stairway. In every direction he looked, he could not see the perimeter of the property. The only sounds he could hear were the occasional high-pitched calls of the peacocks and the splash of the fountain.

In his career Gideon had interviewed two presidents, a host of A-list celebrities, war heroes, and the Pope, but he had never been as nervous as he felt at that moment. *Must be the peacocks,* he thought as he began the ascent up the stairs. He checked his breast pocket to make sure he had his recorder, a pen, a pad, and his BlackBerry. As soon as he set a foot on the porch, the double doors swung open.

A woman appeared in the center of the doorway. The first thing he noticed was that her skin was as smooth as alabaster. Her features were fine and worthy of her pale complexion. Shoulder-length hair, the most perfect shade of deep dark red, flowed in slow motion, as if blown by an unseen wind, as she walked toward him with an extended hand.

I see Samantha Cleaveland likes to surround herself with lovely things, both animate and inanimate, he thought as he walked to the beautiful young woman.

"Welcome to the Cleaveland estate, Mr. Truman," the woman said, exposing a smile too perfect for even her flawless face. "I'm Chantal Maxwell. We spoke on the telephone yesterday."

"Thank you, Chantal. I've been looking forward to my visit."

"Please come in. Pastor Cleaveland will be down shortly," Chantal said, directing Gideon over the threshold and closing the doors behind him.

The foyer surpassed the splendor of the exterior of the home. The oval-shaped room was bathed in warm golden light. Gideon couldn't tell if it was natural or artificial. Double doors on the left and on the right led to the living and dining rooms. A round marble table stood in the center of the room, balancing the most elaborate floral arrangement he had ever seen.

Two stairways on the left and right, with black wrought-iron banisters contoured to the shape of the curved walls, led up to a second-floor landing that overlooked the foyer.

Gideon's eye went directly to the painting that hung on the wall opposite the main entrance. He pointed at the picture and stammered, "Is that . . ."

"Yes, it is, Mr. Truman. Pastor Hezekiah Cleaveland gave it to Mrs. Cleaveland on their thirteenth wedding anniversary."

It was the first of two Picassos in the Cleaveland home. The deconstructed portrait of a woman whose dreamy expression had mesmerized the world for decades, ignored the two standing in front of her. Painted hands formed the triangle in her lap through which all life must pass. Her slanted head and blissfully closed eyes hinted of the erotic dreams that caused her pouting red lips to smile.

Gideon resisted the urge to blurt out, "Holy shit!" and instead said to Chantal, "He must have really loved her."

"Yes, he did, Mr. Truman. This way please."

Gideon followed the young woman and her smoldering red hair into the living room. Antique furniture and classic French, Italian, and Flemish masterpieces were arranged throughout the cavernous room. The placement of each object was so precise that Gideon correctly surmised that the blueprint was the work of one of the world's renowned interior designers. Finely woven Persian rugs served as the canvas upon which the well-thought-out ensemble of wingback chairs, marble-topped tea tables, and satin couches were displayed. A massive crystal chandelier hung in the center of the room, and Lalique vases glittered throughout. A cold black Steinway baby grand piano rested in front of a wall of glass that overlooked the grounds.

Gideon's eyes soon found their way to the second Picasso, which hung over a gaping fireplace. The five women of *Les Demoiselles d'Avignon* looked unimpressed as they surveyed the room. Their faces were primitive, and the jagged edges of their pink flesh formed sharp angles that jutted out in every direction.

An eight-by-six-foot oil painting of Hezekiah and Samantha hung on the wall opposite the Picasso. Their two smiling faces served as the perfect aesthetic counterbalance to the seductive five women across the room. But as lovely and masterfully executed as the two paintings were, their beauty was eclipsed when Samantha Cleaveland entered the room.

"Good afternoon, Mr. Truman."

Gideon tore his gaze away from the paintings and turned to see Samantha standing in the threshold, enveloped in a pool of light from the foyer. She wore a powdery pink pantsuit that had obviously been sewn in strict obedience to every curve of her statuesque form. A pair of flat Ferragamo shoes, the exact color of her suit, barely touched the carpet as she glided toward him.

Gideon could not move. His feet felt like they each weighed a hundred pounds. She was, he thought, one of the most beautiful women he had ever laid eyes on.

Gideon had forgotten that Chantal was in the room until he heard her voice. "Mr. Truman, this is Pastor Samantha Cleaveland," she said, as if introducing a guest on a late-night talk show. As she spoke, she took a step back to clear the path between Samantha and Gideon.

"It is so nice of you to come on such short notice. I hope you didn't have any trouble finding the house," Samantha said.

As she spoke, she extended her hand. Gideon was distracted once again, this time by the glitter from a diamond bracelet on her wrist, which seemed to catch every particle of light in the room.

"Thank y—you for inviting me," he stuttered. "Finding the home was a challenge."

"It's a bit hidden, but when my late husband first saw it, he insisted on having it."

"It's a beautiful home."

"Thank you. It was built by a steel magnate. He lived here for less than a year. I originally was not very fond of it, because it's so large, but now it's filled with so many of our memories, I could never dream of moving."

As the two spoke, Chantal exited the room, unnoticed. The only evidence that she was ever in the room came in the form of a click as she closed the double doors behind her.

"I hope you're hungry, Mr. Truman. My chef has prepared a special meal for us. He apparently is a fan of yours."

Gideon's years of experience as an investigative reporter slowly began to emerge through the fog of awe. He silently chastised himself for the momentary paralysis caused by the extravagance of the estate and the stunning beauty of the woman now standing before him.

Pull yourself together, man. You've interviewed royalty, for God's sake.

"I'm afraid I won't be able to stay for lunch, Pastor Cleaveland. I simply wanted to meet you to get a feel for who you are as a person and to discuss your appearance on my television program."

Samantha looked slightly disappointed. "I'm sorry to hear that. My chef will be disappointed. Can I at least offer you something to drink?"

"Water would be fine. Thank you."

"Chantal, please have Etta bring water for Mr. Truman and coffee for me," Samantha said into an intercom sitting on a tea table next to the sofa.

"Yes, Pastor Clea—" came Chantal's disembodied reply as Samantha disconnected the line.

"Please sit down, Mr. Truman."

For the first time since she had entered the room, Gideon was able to move his feet. Samantha sat on the sofa in front of the fireplace topped by Les Demoiselles d' Avignon, and Gideon sat in a plush chair opposite.

Samantha spoke first. "Let me say, first of all, that I have not agreed to appear on your television program. I, too, first wanted to meet you and get a feeling for who you are. As you can imagine, I am cautious about speaking to the media. They have not always been kind to my husband and I."

"I completely understand." Gideon removed the recorder from his pocket. "Would it be okay with you if I record our conversation?"

Samantha did not blink and simply replied, "Of course."

Gideon placed the recorder on the coffee table between them and began. "Pastor Cleaveland, let me start by extending my deepest sympathies on the loss

of your husband. I never met him, but by all accounts
he was a great man."

Samantha's face turned somber. "Thank you. It was
a tragic loss, not only for me and my daughter, but for
all the members of our congregation."

"How are you doing now?"

"Right now I'm living my life one day at a time, and
every day is a challenge. The only thing that keeps
me going is my knowing that it was God's will that he
be taken from me. I don't know why, and may never
know, but I do find comfort in knowing that all things
work together for good for those that love the Lord. Are
you a religious man, Mr. Truman?"

"Somewhat. I imagine that you must miss him terribly. Can you talk a little about your relationship? What
he meant to you and how his death affected you?"

There was a gentle tap at the door before it opened.
Etta appeared, carrying a silver tray holding a crystal
decanter filled with water, a goblet, and a cup of steaming coffee, and moved toward Samantha. She placed
the tray on the coffee table and poured the water. "Will
there be anything else, Pastor Cleaveland?" she inquired coldly. Her tone didn't go unnoticed by Gideon.

Samantha looked lovingly up at Etta and replied,
"Thank you, Etta dear. That will be all for now."

As Etta moved toward the door, she could hear Samantha say, "That is my housekeeper, Etta. She's been
with us for years. She's like a family member. I don't
know what I would have done without her. Now, where
were we?"

"You were about to tell me about your relationship."

"Hezekiah meant the world to me. Not only were we
partners in building the ministry, but he was—please
excuse the cliché—he was my soul mate. When I was

growing up, I never imagined I could love someone as much as I loved him, or be loved by someone as much as he loved me. Over the years, we went through so many trials and tribulations and fought so many battles together, but each one only served to strengthen our union. We were a team, partners, lovers, and he was my best friend."

"How has his death affected you personally?"

"I'll be honest with you, Mr. Truman. There are some days that I think I can't go on without him. But then I remember how much he loved me. I also think about how much he loved the ministry we built together, and I know that he would want me to continue building the vision that we shared."

"And what is that vision?"

"It is a simple one, to share the message of God's love with every living being on earth."

"And you are well on your way to achieving that, a global ministry, the sixth wealthiest congregation in the United States, a multimillion-dollar cathedral, university, and multimedia complex currently under construction. Some have speculated that without Hezekiah, the ministry might not be able to continue growing at the incredible rate that it has over the last ten years."

Samantha's face tensed for a fraction of a second, then returned to that of the lovely grieving widow. The brief and almost undetectable change would have easily gone unnoticed by a television camera or a sanctuary filled with adoring worshippers, but to Gideon's experienced eye the faint facial contortion hinted that he had touched on a sensitive topic.

"What some people fail to realize, Mr. Truman, is that Hezekiah and I were equal partners. We built the ministry together. So it's not as if I'm trying to fill shoes that I haven't been wearing up until now."

Gideon decided not to pursue the line of questioning, but rather to save it for when the cameras were rolling. Instead he replied, "Pastor Cleaveland, you strike me as a woman who is capable of doing just about anything."

Samantha smiled. "I'll assume you meant that as a compliment. But I have no doubt that the ministry will continue to grow. Not because of who I am, but because of God. This is his ministry and I am his servant and I truly believe this is God's will."

"If I may change the subject, do you have any idea who might have done this to your husband? Was it an enemy from the past, a deranged viewer, an ex-lover possibly?"

Again, her brief facial tic registered. "I have no idea who killed my husband, Mr. Truman, and I assure you that Hezekiah was completely faithful to me, if that is what you're implying."

"I'm sorry. I didn't mean to offend you."

"I'm not offended, but I do want to be assured that if I were to appear on your television program, infidelity will not be one of the topics you broach. There would be no point, because Hezekiah was completely and utterly devoted to me and would never have broken the vows of our marriage. I know because he was that kind of man."

"I assure you, Pastor Cleaveland, that I will not touch on any topic that is not substantiated by fact. Have the police given you any indication that they are any closer to finding out who killed your husband?"

"The Los Angeles Police Department has been absolutely amazing throughout this entire ordeal, but I'm afraid they are at a loss as to who assassinated my husband."

"How does it make you feel knowing that this person is still out there? Are you at all concerned about your own safety and that of your daughter?"

"I, of course, am concerned, but more so for my daughter. As I'm sure you experienced when entering the property today, security on the estate is very tight. I never travel alone and am always surrounded by a number of highly trained security guards, seen and unseen. I must admit that sometimes it terrifies me that his killer has not been caught. I am afraid for my life, but I will not allow fear to control me. There is work to be done, souls to be saved, and a message to be preached. I've made the promise to God, to the members of my congregation, to Hezekiah, and to myself that I would go forward, and I will not allow anything or anyone to stop me."

A chill traveled up Gideon's spine as the woman spoke. Beneath the beautiful veneer, he detected the soul of a woman who would stop at nothing in her quest for power, wealth, and fame.

"Do you have any questions for me, Mrs., excuse me, Pastor Cleaveland?" he asked and once again noticed her stiffening cheek muscle. "I do hope that you will agree to appear on my show. I know my viewers would love to hear from you."

"Only one. Why?"

"Why what?"

"Why do you want me to appear on your show? And, please, be truthful. I detest dishonesty."

Gideon calculated at lightning speed his response. He knew her consent hinged on his answer. "Because millions of viewers would tune in if they knew a woman as beautiful and powerful as you was sitting across from me."

"If you had said anything other than exactly that, I would have known you were lying. Have your people call my office to make the arrangements."

"Wonderful," Gideon said, barely containing his pleasure.

"The head of my security team will need access to your studio at least one day prior," Samantha said, standing to her feet to indicate the meeting was to end.

"My studio?"

"Yes. Isn't that where you plan on conducting the interview?"

Gideon stood obediently, following her cue. "I appreciate your willingness to come to me for the interview, but I was hoping we would be able to conduct it here in your home, in this room, as a matter of fact."

Samantha looked at him intently. "Here?" she questioned. "I don't think I'm comfortable with that idea."

"Oh . . . I had assumed you would be more comfortable if we did it in your home. I also wanted to show my viewers a different, more intimate side of you, Pastor Samantha Cleaveland at home. Something I believe the American public has never seen before."

The opulence that even took me by surprise when I arrived at the estate, Gideon thought as Samantha pondered the possibility. *The peacocks, the burly security guards, the lush rolling grounds, the fountains, and Picassos. If it weren't done so tastefully, it would be considered vulgar. No surprise she doesn't want the public to see this.* He refused to let the opportunity pass to interview Samantha Cleaveland in her home.

"You are correct, Gideon. We have never had cameras in our home. You see, my late husband and I always viewed this as our sanctuary. The one place we could go for peace and privacy."

"I assure you, Pastor Cleaveland, no hint of this location will be given, and we'll only show areas of the home that you preapprove and are comfortable with."

There was a silence that seemed like an eternity to Gideon. Samantha scanned the room and made a mental note of the more expensive pieces that would have to be removed before filming. The pricier pieces of art were at the top of the list.

"All right, Mr. Truman," she finally said. "You can do the interview here. However, I don't want any exterior shots of the house."

"Agreed," he quickly replied. A small concession for the opportunity to film the bounty contained within the walls of the Cleaveland estate.

After exchanging pleasantries and gracious goodbyes, Gideon was met in the foyer by Chantal.

"Hello again, Mr. Truman," she said, matching his stride as he walked to the door. "I trust your visit with Pastor Cleaveland was a pleasant one."

"Yes, it was. Thank you. She is a remarkable woman."

Chantal did not respond.

"What's it like working for someone as powerful as Pastor Cleaveland? I would imagine she can be very demanding."

"I feel very blessed that I am able to serve such an anointed messenger of God."

"I'm sure you do, but what is she really like?"

As the two reached the threshold, Chantal opened one of the double doors. "Thank you for coming, Mr. Truman. Your car is waiting at the bottom of the stairs. Have a blessed day."

Before Gideon could respond, Chantal gently closed the massive oak door. Once again, he stood looking out over the grounds. Again, he could hear the call of the peacocks in the distance and the gentle whoosh of the fountain. The sun seemed brighter than it had been when he entered the house. Every flower petal seemed to have a ray of light dedicated to its beauty. Drops of water in the fountain shimmered like crystals falling into a lake of diamonds. This was an enchanted place, and now it was even more so after being in the presence of Samantha Cleaveland.

As promised, his car was waiting at the bottom of the stairs, accompanied by yet another security guard wearing the regulation black suit and dark sunglasses. Again, Gideon noticed the revolver-shaped bulge in his coat. As Gideon descended the stairs, the man opened the driver's side door. "Thank you for visiting the Cleaveland estate, Mr. Truman," he said in a rich baritone. "Will you be able to find your way back down to the city all right?"

"Yes, thank you," Gideon said as he entered the car.

"Very well then, sir. Have a nice day," the man said as he gently closed the car door.

Gideon drove the car to the main road. To his left he could see a mother deer and her fawn nibbling in a dense patch of brush. A flock of Canadian geese flew overhead in a V formation, honking as they landed on an open stretch of lawn to his right. He instantly regretted agreeing to not show the exterior of the estate. "America would never believe this," he said out loud. "How many old ladies' pensions does it take to pay for all this?"

The wrought-iron gates glided silently open as he approached. He could see the poorly camouflaged lens of a camera on the gatehouse follow him as he exited onto the road. At the bottom of the long, winding hill the smog of the real world slowly became visible again. In the rarefied heights of the Cleaveland estate, smog was apparently not permitted. The preening peacocks were replaced by dusty gray pigeons, and instead of the soothing purr of the flowing fountain, he heard blaring horns and sirens from ambulances whizzing by.

Gideon felt disoriented. Samantha Cleaveland had left a distinct impression on him, but he could not figure out what it was. Yes, he was repulsed by the lavish exhibit of wealth: the shameless disregard for the sacrifices made by members of her church to maintain a lifestyle that would make most Hollywood celebrities jealous.

Yet Samantha Cleaveland was undeniably one of the most beautiful women he had ever been in the presence of. The way she carried her body through space, the sensuous, almost breathy tone of her voice, which seemed to echo in his head, when she spoke. Only a woman like that could eclipse the timeless splendor of Picasso. Only Samantha Cleaveland could make you look away from the breathtaking city and ocean views when she walked into the room.

Every piece of exquisitely designed furniture in her home was in exactly the right place. Every jardiniere and statue was positioned perfectly to display its beauty and craftsmanship. Every exotic flower was pointed in the precise direction to capture the light and reveal its humble magnificence to the fullest. But still it all paled in Samantha Cleaveland's presence. It all seemed to fade into the background when the woman entered the room.

An intoxicating vapor seeped from her pores. Her seductive brown eyes invited those under her gaze to let down their defenses and trust the pearls that dripped from her red lips. However, Gideon couldn't help but sense that there was something sinister lurking just beneath the well-polished veneer, something simmering behind the sparkle in her eyes. A thing that was capable of destroying anything, and anyone, in her path to protect and maintain what she had made.

That was the Samantha Cleaveland that he now knew he must expose. He wanted his viewers to see the real Pastor Samantha Cleaveland. More importantly, he wanted to see her for himself.

I wonder if she knew about her husband's alleged affair with a man, Gideon thought. *She doesn't strike me as the type that would look the other way. She's got too much to lose. I think it's time for me to meet this Mr. Danny St. John.*

Chapter 7

Danny had managed to shave, shower, and dress himself that morning. His boss had called the day before and told him he had missed too many days in the last month and he either had to get a doctor's note or come in to work the next day.

"I can't keep covering for you, Danny," he'd said in a sympathetic yet firm tone. "I'm worried about you. Are you doing any better? You haven't told me what's wrong with you, and you don't have to tell me if you don't want to but . . ."

"I understand Gregg, and I appreciate you not pressuring me. I'm sorry I've missed so many days, but I'm doing much better now. I'll be in tomorrow."

The large room in the homeless drop-in center in the skid row section of downtown was filled with haggard and weather-beaten men and women who had survived another night on the streets of Los Angeles. Some were watching television on a big screen, while others sat quietly, sipping tepid coffee from paper cups. Old women surrounded by plastic shopping bags and bundled in tattered coats huddled against walls, trying to be invisible. Young children clutched their mother's thighs as they spoke to attentive social workers in cubicles piled with boxes of clothing donations.

A group of six men sat on folding chairs in a corner and exchanged stories they had accumulated from the night before. "The cops showed up at three o'clock in the fucking morning and made us pack up all our shit and move out of the park," a little man with sunburnt skin and a missing front tooth said to the captivated group. "Bastards took my shopping cart and everything I couldn't carry away in my arms."

"Some strung-out crackhead tried to rob me last night over on Sixth Street," another began. "Son of a bitch pulled a knife on me." The man then lifted his shirt and showed the group a gash that ran from his left nipple to his belly button. "Cut me here, took my last fucking beer and all the money I panhandled yesterday."

Some attempted to wash away the city's dirt in the facility's shower area, while others slept in heaps on the floor, trying to recover from a night of aimless wandering.

Danny sat in his cubicle. There were eighty-seven e-mails waiting for his attention, and the red blinking light on his telephone indicated there were twenty-eight messages waiting to be heard.

The cubicle was only large enough to fit two chairs in front of his desk. The five-foot-high gray carpet–covered partitions offered little privacy for the exchange of often personal details between client and social worker. A picture of Parker, Danny's cat, was pinned to one of the cubical walls and surrounded by flyers announcing the latest shelter opening, food basket giveaway programs, free clinics, and dozens of other services available to his clients.

A weathered old man sat across his desk. Danny could smell the stale remnants of Night Train and cigarettes on his breath. His grizzled hair and mustache were stained yellow, and his face and hands were covered in dried blood and scabs. The heavy jacket he wore was covered in dirt from every corner of the city, and his left big toe stuck out from the tip of his worn over shoes.

"I haven't eaten in two days," the old man sputtered. "Somebody stole my County debit card last week. I need that card, man. I ain't been able to get my medical marijuana in over a week now."

Even though Danny had heard the sad story a thousand times before, his eyes were filled with a compassion that comforted the weary homeless man more than any words he could have spoken. Danny would listen intently to every tragic story he was told as if it were the first time he had ever heard it. He made a point of looking directly into the eyes of each person who sat at his desk and, as often as possible, shook their hand regardless of how grimy they looked. When appropriate, he would gently touch the shoulder of those beaten down by life. No person he encountered was unworthy of his time, compassion, and expertise.

The noise in the drop-in center made it difficult for Danny to speak to the man. Wobbly shopping cart wheels clanked against the cement floor, multiple conversations meshed into an indecipherable hum, and children cried in their mother's arms.

"I'm sorry to hear about your card being stolen," Danny said to the man. "I'll contact your eligibility worker and request that another be sent to you here as soon as possible. When we're done here, you should go to the dining area and get something to eat."

The man did not respond, but Danny could see the sense of relief in his face. As the two men continued their conversation, Danny noticed the noise level in the center had dropped to a whisper. The only sounds he heard were the occasional sniffle, cough of a small child, and Judge Judy on the big-screen television.

What's going on out there now? he thought to himself. Then, suddenly, the center's receptionist appeared at the opening of his cubicle. "Danny," said the young Asian woman wearing faded denim jeans and a baggy white sweatshirt, with a sense of excitement in her voice, "there's someone here to see you. He said it's very important."

Danny looked annoyed by the interruption. "Have they signed up on my list? I've already got nine people in the lobby waiting to see me."

The receptionist's excitement level increased slightly. "No, he's not on your list, Danny," she replied discreetly. "He's not a client, Danny, and I think you should see him as soon as possible."

Danny could see the disappointment on the old man's face. "He's going to have to wait. This is not a good time," he said to the anxious receptionist.

To his surprise a broad smile appeared on her face. She walked closer to the desk. With her back to the old man, she looked Danny directly in the eye and said through her smile, "Trust me, Danny, you don't want to make this guy wait."

Danny looked puzzled but agreed. "Okay," he said grudgingly. "As soon as I'm done with Mr. Wycliffe, you can send him in."

The oddly delighted receptionist hurriedly exited the cubicle. Danny returned his attention to the man. "I'm sorry about that interruption, Mr. Wycliffe. Where were we?"

Danny spent another fifteen minutes with the man, filling out documents, making telephone calls on his behalf, and loading him up with clean socks, vitamins, and a bar of soap. The old man slowly stuffed the items into his coat pocket and staggered from the cubicle. Before Danny could place the document he had completed into a file, the receptionist appeared again at the entrance to his cubicle.

"Danny," she said in a now professional tone, "Mr. Gideon Truman is here to see you."

Danny froze in place. The documents he held were suspended above the manila file folder. A look of surprise and curiosity came across his face as Gideon Truman appeared in the entrance to his cubicle.

When Gideon saw Danny sitting behind the wooden desk in the cluttered cubicle, he saw a world of sharply conflicting contrasts. Danny's rich brown skin seemed to flicker in the dingy cubicle like a firefly trapped in a jar. His eyes were so clear, they seemed almost transparent. The purity in his eyes forced Gideon to avert his gaze for the briefest of seconds. His perfectly carved shoulders and chiseled swimmer's frame were surrounded by rickety metal bookshelves stacked with worn binders and tattered books containing the once latest treatments for alcoholism, borderline personality disorders, and chronic substance abuse.

Gideon was paralyzed at the sight of the beautiful young man. For a brief moment he was oblivious to the smell and sound of the human misery within the walls of the homeless drop-in center. The man that sat before him had overwhelmed his senses. His thoughts went immediately to Hezekiah Cleaveland. *He must have been a hell-of-a-man to attract two such uncommonly beautiful people.*

Danny looked suspiciously up at Gideon and waited for him to speak.

Gideon willed himself back to the task at hand. "Hello, Mr. St. John," he sputtered, regaining control. "I'm sorry to disturb you at work, but I was very anxious to speak with you."

Danny placed the papers in the file, stood up, and cautiously shook Gideon's warm hand.

"My name is Gideon Truman."

"I know who you are," Danny replied.

"Is there somewhere we can speak privately? I promise I won't take up too much of your time."

"You can use the conference room, Danny," the receptionist interjected. "There's no one in there now."

Danny again looked irritated at the eager receptionist. "Thank you," he said, motioning for her to leave. He turned to Gideon. "I'm not authorized to speak to the media on behalf of this agency. You'll have to speak with my boss. I believe he's in his office. You can wait here and I'll get . . ."

Gideon looked intently at Danny as he spoke. He couldn't help but notice the long eyelashes that seemed to flutter in slow motion as his lids opened and closed. To Gideon's eye, Danny was enveloped in a warm and inviting mist that seemed to emanate from his core. The air around him was somehow immune to the stench that filled the rest of the drop-in center.

Gideon hadn't expected to meet such a beautiful man in the bowels of skid row. Danny's voice echoed in Gideon's head in the same way Samantha's had. His voice was hypnotic. In this encounter it became plausible that this man was Hezekiah Cleaveland's lover. He understood clearly how a powerful man could fall in love with Danny St. John. It would be harder to believe that he could resist.

"Danny, may I call you Danny? This isn't about the homeless. I'd like to speak with you about Pastor Hezekiah Cleaveland."

Again Danny froze in place. Struggling to regain his composure, he said slowly, "Hezekiah Cleaveland? Isn't he the pastor who was killed recently?"

"Yes, he is, Danny. Did you know him?"

Danny feigned surprise and forced a laugh. "Why would I have known Hezekiah Cleaveland?"

The two men locked eyes for what seemed forever. Then Gideon looked over the five-foot-high cubicle partition and saw that every eye in the cavernous waiting area was looking in his direction. The eager receptionist had returned to her counter but watched his every move. The group of men who had been exchanging war stories in the corner was silent. Pairs of beady eyes peered from beneath piles of sooty clothes on the floor. All activity in the room had stopped. Gideon was comfortable with the attention, but he felt the need to protect Danny, for reasons he could not understand at the moment.

"Danny I would really prefer it if we had this conversation in private."

Danny also saw the effect Gideon's presence had on the facility. He walked from behind his desk and simply said, "Follow me."

Gideon followed Danny through a maze of cubicles; eyes were peeping out at every turn. Gideon smiled as someone greeted him. "Hey, aren't you Gideon Truman?"

"Yes, I am," he replied politely.

"Danny, you in some kind of trouble?" came from another cubicle.

The two entered a dark room together. Danny turned on a light, which flickered and sputtered before it fully lit the room, revealing dingy white walls. Four small folding tables were arranged in the center of the room to form one larger conference table, which dominated the stark space. It was surrounded by a hodgepodge of twelve tattered plastic, worn fabric, and faded leather chairs. Posters of wide-eyed children pleading for compassion and homeless men looking longingly into the camera hung on the walls. A large, round white-faced clock with bold black numbers ticked loudly as the second hand propelled the two men forward in time.

Gideon closed the door. "Would you like to sit down?"

"I'd rather stand," Danny responded curtly. "I don't have much time. There are nine clients waiting for me . . ."

"I understand. I'll get straight to the point. I'm doing a story on the life and death of Pastor Hezekiah Cleaveland. Your name came up during an interview with someone who worked very closely with him. So I'll ask you again. Did you know Pastor Cleaveland?"

"I've already told you I didn't know him."

Gideon reached into the breast pocket of his coat, removed a sheet of neatly folded white paper, and handed it to Danny.

"Do you recognize this e-mail, Danny?"

Danny unfolded the paper and read silently.

From: Danny St. John
Sent: Wednesday, December 16, 2010 9:37 A.M.
To: Hezekiah Cleaveland
Subject: Re: Lunch

Okay. See you then. I love you too.
D.

Danny St. John
Social Worker
Los Angeles Homeless Drop-In Center

From: Hezekiah Cleaveland
Sent: Wednesday, December 16, 2010 9:36 A.M.
To: Danny St. John
Subject: Lunch

I miss you, Danny. Are you free for lunch today
at two o'clock? I'll pick you up at work.
Love you,
Hez

Pastor Hezekiah Cleaveland
New Testament Cathedral
Los Angeles, California
Remember, God loves you and so do we.

Danny remembered the e-mail as if he had just received it that morning. His hand began to tremble
slightly as he reached for a chair at the table and sat
down. "Where did you get this?" he asked without looking at Gideon.

"I can't tell you that, Danny. But I can tell you I've
seen dozens of other e-mails between you and Hezekiah."

Danny sat motionless, staring at the white paper.

Without thinking, Gideon walked next to him, placed
his hand on his shoulder, and gently said, "I'm very
sorry for your loss. I can tell from the e-mails that he
loved you very much."

The gentle touch of Gideon's hand and his kind
words released a single tear from Danny's welling
eyes. He could almost smell Hezekiah in the room. The
weight of Gideon's hand on his shoulder made him remember Hezekiah's touch; and the salty tear, the taste
of his lips.

Gideon sat down in the chair next to him and covered the hand that held the white paper with his own.
"How long were you together?"

Danny had no wall to hide behind. There was no
hedge to duck under. His emotions had again bubbled
to the surface for all to see. "Two years," he replied
softly.

"You must feel very alone now that he is gone," Gideon said instinctively. There was no hint of guile, no clue of an ulterior motive or tone of deception in his voice. He could feel Danny's pain as if it were his own. Although his eyes were dry, he still felt the moisture of Danny's tears on his own cheeks, as if they each had fallen from his own eyes. Gideon had never felt the pain that accompanied the loss of someone so loved, but today he felt the pain that was the companion of sorrow.

Gideon released Danny's hand and put his arm around his shoulders. Danny rested his head on the nape of his neck and wilted into his comforting embrace. Gideon was helpless as the pain melded them into one. He couldn't tell if the gentle sobbing was coming from his lips or from the man in his arms. Loneliness enveloped the two like a damp blanket and made their bodies quiver from the cold.

"It's okay, Danny," he whispered. "I know Hezekiah loved you."

When Danny heard the words, his cries deepened.

"I know that you loved him too," Gideon continued.

"I did," Danny said through his tears. "I loved him, and he loved me."

The raw confession of love released the first tear from Gideon's closed eyes. He didn't question the source of the tear, because it seemed natural and right. In that moment he wasn't the hard-hitting investigative reporter. He wasn't the award-winning newscaster or the host of a syndicated television show viewed by millions. He was simply a man who held in his arms someone he felt he had loved forever.

Chapter 8

Samantha sat behind the desk back in her old office. The room and all its contents were completely white except for an arrangement of thirty-six long-stemmed, blood red roses. The flowers sprayed from a large etched-crystal vase sitting in the center of a liquid glass, round conference table that was surrounded by ten white high-back leather chairs. The plush snowy white carpet showed no hint of footprints or remnants from treading shoes. There was not a speck, twig, or fleck on any inch of the entire room. There were eight massive mirrors, each framed in carved white lacquered wood. No light fixtures were visible anywhere in the room, yet each surface was illuminated from sources unknown. The room was a stark, yet elegant canvas that served only to display Pastor Samantha Cleaveland.

From the window she could see construction cranes scaling the skeletal walls of her New Testament Cathedral, which was being built across the street. Cement trucks churned, drills whizzed, and hammers pounded, but there was no sound in the snow-white cocoon. Samantha's glass desk held only a white telephone and a white computer screen. There were no papers or mementos, family pictures or holders of things normally associated with a workstation. The glass was so clear that the telephone and computer screen seemed to float in the air.

The sound of the intercom pierced the stark white silence. "Excuse me, Pastor Cleaveland," interrupted the voice. "Catherine Birdsong would like to see you. Shall I send her in?"

Samantha did not hesitate. "Yes, send her in."

Samantha spun her white leather chair to face the office door and waited, steely-eyed, for the door to open.

Catherine entered, fueled by anger and hate. She didn't pause at the threshold but instead walked purposefully toward the desk at the opposite end of the long room.

"What can I do for you, Catherine?" Samantha asked matter-of-factly.

Catherine found no need for decorum. "You can start by telling me what I've done to deserve being treated with such disregard."

"I'm not sure I know what you're talking about."

"You know exactly what I mean. You humiliated me in front of my entire staff. You demoted me without having the common decency of first explaining to me why."

Samantha remained seated and said, "First, let me remind you who you're speaking to, Ms. Birdsong. I'm not Hezekiah, and I don't have an overwhelming need to be nice or polite to the hired help. Secondly, I feel no need to show you the respect that you have never shown me, and I don't have to explain my actions to anyone."

Samantha rose from the chair, walked around the desk, stood squarely in front of Catharine, and continued. "I haven't fired you yet, Catherine. I'm giving you the opportunity to prove that you can be loyal to me and meet my expectations. I'm not Hezekiah. My standards are higher."

"Everyone here knows you're not Hezekiah, Samantha."

"Do not call me Samantha," she snapped. "If you are to remain in my employ, you will address me as Pastor Cleaveland."

Samantha took a step closer and continued. "God in his wisdom saw fit to take my husband from me. I don't know why, but I have learned to accept it as his will. God has also seen fit to place me at the helm of this ministry, and I will do everything in my power to make sure it grows even larger than Hezekiah could have ever imagined. In order for this to happen, I need to surround myself with people who share my vision. And to be honest with you, Catherine, I've never felt you ever really understood what I'm capable of."

"I think I understand perfectly what you are capable of."

"No, I don't think you do. You see, Hezekiah underestimated me, too, and you see what happened to him."

Catherine looked at her curiously. Samantha's words slowly registered. Catherine felt a chill envelop her body as Samantha stared coldly into her eyes. There was fear like none she had ever experienced, a fear that could be caused only by the presence of pure evil. Catherine took a step backward and looked away from Samantha's frozen glare.

"I . . . I understand, Pastor Cleaveland," Catherine stammered and physically demurred. "I don't ever want to be perceived as an impediment to achieving your vision for the ministry."

"No, you don't," Samantha chimed firmly.

"I hope you know that was never my intent."

Samantha did not respond but held her gaze.

"I apologize if I ever made you feel unsupported. I think you are an amazing woman . . . Pastor Cleaveland."

Samantha gestured with her head for her to say more.

"I think it would be best for all parties involved if I submitted my resignation, effective immediately."

Samantha broke her gaze and slightly relaxed her posture. She turned away from the wilting woman and returned to her seat. "I think that would be best, Catherine."

Catherine looked bewildered and dazed. She attempted to speak, but Samantha interrupted.

"I will have security meet you in your office while you clear your things."

Catherine looked at her one last time and said, "Thank you, Pastor."

She began the long walk to the door over the harsh white terrain. Her pointed shoes left no indentations in the woolen snow. As she reached for the door handle, she heard Samantha call out and turned abruptly.

"Catherine," Samantha said.

"Yes, Pastor?" she asked hopefully.

"Please don't speak to anyone on your way out," Samantha said with a smile usually reserved for television cameras. "I'll inform your staff you decided to leave us for unexpected personal reasons."

Samantha's personal security guard, Dino, opened the rear door of the black Escalade at the construction site of the new sanctuary. Samantha extended the tip of her brown alligator pump from the rear of the car. Her four-inch spiked heels landed firmly in the soft dirt.

"Shall I wait at the car, Pastor Cleaveland?"

"No, come with me," she instructed Dino as she walked toward the shell of the building. "This may be a difficult conversation."

Dino unsnapped the leather holster under his left arm, then buttoned his jacket. Construction of the new sanctuary had not stopped after Hezekiah's death. Samantha had received a call on the Monday after the assassination from the site foreman, asking if they should stop working for a day of mourning.

"No," Samantha had answered abruptly. Then she'd remembered she was in mourning. "No. Please have your crew report for work as planned," she'd said with an added dose of grief. "I know Hezekiah would want the work to continue."

"Hello, Pastor Cleaveland," said a round, ruddy-cheeked man wearing a plaid shirt and faded denim overalls.

Benny Winters was the general contractor for the cathedral construction project, which would soon be the new twenty-five-thousand-seat home of New Testament Cathedral and its media complex.

Samantha did not extend her hand but instead continued her stroll into the building. "This is the first time I've been on-site since my husband's death, and I want to make sure you and I are on the same page."

Dino followed a short distance behind the two.

"First, let me say how sorry I am about what happened to Pastor Cleaveland," Benny said, removing his fluorescent yellow hard hat in respect. "He was an amazing man."

"Thank you, Benny. We all miss him very much. My first question is, are we on schedule?"

Benny looked surprised. "Yes, ma'am, we are on schedule. Building inspectors from the city were out just last week and gave a green light to the HVAC system. The satellite tower is en route on a barge from Beijing as we speak and will be in place by the end of next month. The subcontractors handling the stained-glass windows have been here every day this week, preparing for installation next month."

Samantha, Benny, and Dino continued the tour through the interior of the building. Workers balanced on ladders connecting webs of electrical wiring. Sturdy men and women in hard hats drilled, hammered, sawed, and screwed as the three walked past. The smell of cut lumber and burning solder filled the building

The three entered through the main doors of the new sanctuary. The cavernous room spilled down in cantilevers in front of them. The pulpit seemed like it was a mile away. The ten-story-high, slanted, and jutting cathedral walls were constructed of five hundred thousand rectangular panes of glass. They were woven together by threads of glistening steel, forming a patchwork quilt of light and blue sky.

"We've got three new JumboTron screens waiting to be installed. There's going to be one there, there, and there," Benny said, pointing to the front and both sides of the sanctuary.

Samantha looked out at the massive effort laid at her feet with mild amusement. "Where will the waterfalls be placed?"

Benny looked bewildered. "Waterfalls?" he asked cautiously. "There are no waterfalls in the plans."

Samantha looked perturbed. "I told Hezekiah I wanted waterfalls."

"I'm sorry, ma'am, but he never discussed that with me. I'm afraid we're too far along in construction to make major changes like that."

"Nonsense," she snapped. "I want one on either side of the pulpit. Each constructed with boulders that lead to pools of water on the pulpit. Don't worry. I'll oversee the design personally."

"But, ma'am, that's just not possible. Something like that could add at least a million onto the cost and . . ."

Samantha looked Benny in the eye, and Dino stepped closer. "You seem to misunderstand me, Mr. Winters. I'm not asking your permission. I'm telling you what I want. This is not a debate."

Benny's bulbous head became flushed. He noticed the imposing Dino staring coldly at him over Samantha's shoulder.

"Is that understood?" she asked after a brief silence.

"I suppose we can move the two side JumboTrons a little farther from the front and place the fountains there, but . . ."

"Please, no buts, Mr. Winters. If you are unable to make this happen, please let me know now so that I can have you replaced."

"Replaced?" he barked loudly. "What do you mean? We're in the final stages of . . ." He saw Dino move in closer. "I haven't made a move on this project without Pastor Cleaveland's approval. You can't—"

"You are not in a position to tell me what I can or can't do, Mr. Winters. My husband is dead, and I am now the pastor of this church. I am paying for this cathedral. I am signing your check, and I am going to be the one standing on that pulpit every Sunday. So what I say goes. Is that clear?" she asked, with her tone escalating at each syllable.

Dino slowly unbuttoned his jacket without taking his eye off Benny. Benny could see the leather strap leading to the bulge under his armpit.

He looked over his shoulder into the structure that had been his life for the last two years. Sweat began to form in crevices all over his little round body. He then looked again at Samantha, took a deep breath, swallowed, and replied, "Yes. I understand, Pastor Cleaveland."

"Good," she answered in a slightly softer tone.

Dino rebuttoned his jacket.

"Now, tell me more about the pipe organ. I'm not sure it's going to be big enough. Where is the baptismal pool going to be placed? I want to see swatches of all the carpets Hezekiah selected and samples of the tiles. Our tastes were very different. I want the pastor's suite of offices to be in a different location than the one Hezekiah selected. Follow me. I'll show you where I want them."

The conversation continued for the next three hours, with Samantha changing much of what Hezekiah had approved and Benny repeatedly responding, "Yes, Pastor Cleaveland," as Dino closely monitored the exchange.

After the lengthy talk with Benny at the construction site, Samantha went back to her office. She had made a point of changing as much of the building design as possible, especially elements that she knew her husband had been the most excited about: the color of the carpet, the marble in the baptismal pool, the custom light fixtures that Hezekiah had designed himself, the tile in the hallways and, especially, the design of the podium. She changed the solid mahogany podium to a glass one so the cameras would always have a full and complete view of every curve of her figure. Give the men a reason to send in checks and the women a reason for envy.

"Excuse me, Pastor Cleaveland. You have a call from Brother David Shackelford. He would like to speak with you for a moment. He said it's important."

"What does he want?"

"He wouldn't say what it was regarding. Only that it was very important that he speak with you."

"Why do you put these people through to me without screening the call? Tell him I'm busy and to make . . ." Samantha paused mid-rebuke. She remembered that she was only the interim pastor and would possibly require Scarlett's vote to make her position permanent.

Samantha despised Scarlett for the affair she had had with Hezekiah when she was his secretary, and hated her even more when she learned she was carrying his child. When Hezekiah appointed her to the board of trustees, Samantha knew it was only to keep her from leaving the church. Samantha had forbidden him to have any contact with the child. But she could see the way he looked so lovingly at her some Sunday mornings from the pulpit. She could see that he loved the little girl that Scarlett held in her arms as much as he loved Jasmine.

"Never mind. Put him through." She paused a moment, then said, "Brother Shackelford, so nice of you to call. How is Scarlett? I know she took Hezekiah's death very hard."

"I would imagine that you more that anyone knows just how hard she took his death," he replied ominously.

David sat in his car, looking out over the Pacific Ocean from a parking lot at the Santa Monica Pier. The iconic blue and white arch over the pier that read SANTA MONICA *YACHT HARBOR * SPORT FISHING * BOATING CAFES was to his left. The sky was dotted with clouds. Seagulls perched on the edges of rusted trash cans, waiting for the stray french fry or hot-buttered popcorn kernel to drop from a passing tourist's sticky fingers. White foam from waves danced at the battered wooden feet of the

pier, which strained under the weight of a whirling
Ferris wheel, concession booths, a roller coaster, and
the sandaled feet of tourists from every corner of the
world.

He had been parked in the same spot for two hours.
The car smelled of cigarettes and alcohol. He had
driven around the city until he ended up at the end of
the earth in Santa Monica after the shocking revelation
from his wife. He hadn't realized that he was in the
parking lot until the pimply-faced parking attendant
said, "Sir, sir, that'll be ten dollars."

Samantha sat upright in her chair. She deliberately
placed the solid gold pen she had been using to sign
thank-you letters on the desk. "Yes, I know how much
she cared for Hezekiah," she said, proceeding cautiously.

"I would imagine they were very close when Scarlett
was his secretary. What do you think, Pastor Cleaveland?"

Samantha did not respond.

"Samantha? May I call you Samantha? Are you still
there?" he asked coldly.

"Yes, I'm still here. Brother Shackelford, I appreciate
you calling with condolences, but I was just about to—"

"Oh, this isn't a condolence call, Samantha. By the
way, why don't you call me David? After all, we're almost related."

"I'm not sure what this is about, but I really must be
going."

"I think you'll want to hear what I have to say, Samantha."

"Then, please, say it. I'm very busy."

"I'm afraid you are not in a position to rush me, Samantha." David's tone turned aggressive. "Wouldn't
you like to know how Natalie is holding up, or are you
that cold of a bitch?"

Samantha did not speak.

"You can imagine how difficult it must be for a child to lose a parent."

"I don't know what you're talking about," were the only words Samantha could think of to stall for time to plan her next move. "Have you been drinking?"

"As a matter of fact, I have. I've got a half-empty bottle of Jack Daniel's sitting between my legs like a hard dick. Oops, I hope I didn't offend you, Pastor. I get like that after a few drinks."

Samantha knew there was no need to pretend. "What do you want?"

David laughed loud and hard, so hard that it quickly turned into a bone-rattling cough. He tossed a smoldering cigarette butt out the car window and onto the pavement. "I don't know what I want," he finally replied.

"Is this about money?"

"Don't insult me," he shouted.

Samantha removed the telephone from her ear. "Calm down, David," she said softly. "I didn't mean to insult you."

David dropped the cell phone into his lap and took a deep breath. He could feel the familiar racing of his heart. His eyes blurred, and the sound of the rhythmic beating of ocean waves seemed to throb in his head. He knew from experience that a panic attack was sure to follow. He began gasping for air. Beads of perspiration formed on his forehead.

The attacks had, years earlier, forced David to abandon a full partnership in one of the city's most prestigious law firms. While standing before judges and packed courtrooms, he would suddenly experience an overwhelming and all-consuming fear. White-collar clients who he knew were guilty of fraud, embezzle-

ment, and other gentlemanly crimes sat on the edge of
their seat. Jurors would stare blankly at the frozen lawyer. Bailiffs would stand at attention, fearing the statue
that he had become mid-sentence would reanimate in
a violent rage. After the third incident, the other partners in the firm decided his work should include only
cases that didn't require court proceedings. His cases
now consisted of advising rich old ladies of the best
way to disperse their worldly possessions after their
deaths.

"Hello . . . David. Are you there?" came Samantha's
voice from his lap.

The pier and the sun-drenched tourists began to spin
in time with the Ferris wheel. David shut his eyes tight
and took three deep breaths, as his therapist had rec-
ommended. As the panic slowly subsided, he retrieved
the telephone from his lap.

"Samantha, are you still there?" he finally asked breathlessly.

"Yes, I'm here. Are you all right?" Samantha asked.

"I'm fine."

"Are you sure?"

"I said I'm all right!" he shouted. "I don't need your
sympathy. I don't need anything from you but the truth.
Was Hezekiah Natalie's father?"

"I'm not comfortable having this conversation over
the telephone. Why don't you go home and sober up?
Come to my home later this evening, and we can talk
about this there."

After the telephone conversation with Samantha,
David went home. Scarlet was in the kitchen when he
arrived.

"David, where have you been? I've been calling your
cell. Are you all right?"

David didn't look at her or respond. He walked past her, placed his keys calmly on the white tiled counter-top, and exited the room.

Scarlett followed him through the narrow hallway. "David, I know you're hurt," she called out to his back. "Honey, we have to talk about this." She matched his stride and touched his broad shoulder. "David," she cried. "Please, stop and look at me." The tears began to fall again.

David stopped abruptly but did not turn around. He could hear the gentle sobs in her voice.

There was silence as she caressed his shoulders with both her hands.

Then he spoke. "Are those tears for me or for your pastor?" he asked coldly.

Scarlett dropped her hands from his shoulders. They each stood frozen in front of their bedroom door, in silence.

David waited for a reply, but there was none.

"That's what I thought," he said, reaching for the door. He paused again while gripping the handle, hoping for a response. His gesture was greeted by a chilling silence, which answered even more questions than the one he had asked.

David entered the bedroom and gently closed the door behind him. She felt the guilt and shame associated with breaking a man's heart. She did not shun the embarrassment that came with lying to the world for so long. But intermingled with these painful feelings was a faint hint of relief. *At least now he finally knows the truth,* she thought as she walked through the long hall back to the safety of her sunny kitchen.

Chapter 9

The Cleaveland's mansion felt like a crypt to David as he squirmed from side to side in the stiff chair. David sat alone in the living room of the Cleaveland estate. Everything was in its proper and precise place. Oil paintings looked down on him with judgmental eyes. Crystal vases stood aloof, as if warning him to not come too close. Elegant wingback chairs and tufted couches, though plush and beautiful, seemed uninviting and foreboding. There was a dead, still quiet. He could faintly hear the waves outside the French doors surrounding a baby grand piano, which he dared not approach.

David had been in the home only once before. Hezekiah had requested his legal advice on a generous bequest by a wealthy church member. The deceased family had contested a will that left two million dollars to New Testament Cathedral and nothing to three children and four grandchildren. David was successful in proving the validity of the will. He charged New Testament Cathedral nothing for his services. "This is the least I can do for you. Scarlett has told me how kind you were to her when she worked for you," he had told Hezekiah as they exchanged a bonding handshake.

What an idiot, he thought. *If I'd known, I would have kicked the fucking bastard in the nuts.*

He didn't hear the door open as Samantha walked into the room. David was startled when she spoke.

"Hello, David," she said as she approached. "Thank you for coming. I hope you're feeling better."

Samantha wore a sleeveless, chocolate, silk-crepe halter-neck dress that draped in the front over her full breasts. The sensuous and meticulously crafted garment cascaded from a single point on a gunmetal chain around her neck, which was closed with an oversize gold lobster clasp. Her feet were strapped in a pair of black sandals, which David guessed must have cost at least one thousand dollars.

When he heard her voice, David jumped to his feet and stumbled slightly. His awkward move did not go unnoticed by Samantha.

"Please sit down. You still seem a bit tense. Would you like a drink? I usually have a sherry in the evening. My housekeeper, Etta, is out, but I'd be happy to get it for you."

Like most men, David was mesmerized by the woman that stood before him. Her casual demeanor was countered by a beauty that caught most off guard. He couldn't take his eyes off her silky black hair. It looked like every strand had been attended to separately, then combined to form ribbons of shimmering black water pouring from a fountain. The room seemed to come to life now that she was present. Was there music playing softly in the background now? Did the chairs seem more inviting? Was that the call of a peacock he heard in the distance?

"Yes, I'll join you. I wouldn't want to interfere with your evening routine," he said in an attempt to appear at ease.

Samantha poured them each a glass of sherry from a decanter on a console behind one of the couches. "Let's sit down," she said, handing him the cut glass.

Samantha sat down in an equally stiff chair directly in front of David. They were separated by a cream-colored, six-foot distressed wood coffee table with claw feet. The table held an alabaster bust of a Greek goddess, a spray of exotic flowers, and three crystal bowls. There was a large black Bible with gold embossing in the middle of the table.

David stared blankly at the ancient leather-bound book.

"It's beautiful, isn't it?" Samantha said, sipping from her glass. "It's a sixteen-eleven King James, first edition pulpit Bible, very rare. There are less than two hundred of them in the world. It was a gift to us from Pope John Paul the Second."

David looked up in amazement.

Samantha immediately stared directly in his eyes. "Now, what was that nonsense you were talking about this afternoon? You sounded a bit disoriented. I was concerned about you."

David took a sip of sherry. "I wasn't disoriented, and you know exactly what I was talking about, don't you?"

"Unfortunately I do. I take it Scarlett has told you our little secret."

"The *secret* is not so little anymore. Natalie is five years old."

"I'm aware of that. I see her occasionally at church. She's a lovely little girl," Samantha said with a warm smile.

The patronizing tone of the woman sent a chill up David's spine. His head quickly became clear and lawyerly. "Don't patronize me, Samantha. You and Hezekiah abandoned her. Scarlett made a mistake, but it wasn't only her fault. Hezekiah was just as guilty. But you kicked her to the curb without any regard for the child. What kind of heartless, hypocritical monsters are you?"

Samantha listened quietly until he finished. "That's not entirely true, David. Did Scarlett also tell you that I offered her a substantial amount of money?"

David looked surprised. He tried to read her face for a trace of deception, but there was none apparent.

"I also offered to relocate her to another state," Samantha continued, "but she turned it all down."

"I don't believe you. She said you tried to convince her to have an abortion."

"I don't deny that. At the time it seemed like the right thing to do."

"The right thing for you!"

"Yes, for me, but also for New Testament Cathedral and for Scarlett. She was young, alone, and stupid enough to get pregnant by my husband. Hezekiah wasn't going to leave me for her, so what other options did she have? I presented her with good choices, and she foolishly turned them all down."

David was repulsed by the casual way she spoke of the life-altering events.

"Ask her, David. Ask her how much money I offered her to leave the state." Samantha's tone grew harder. "You're a big boy, David. You know how much was at stake. There was no way I was going to let some young, silly girl destroy all that I had built because she couldn't keep Hezekiah from getting into her pants."

David flinched at the harshness of her words.

"I'm curious, David. Why did she tell you this now? Hezekiah has been dead less than a month. Does she want to cash in on this death?" Samantha stood from the chair and walked around the dazed man to a writing desk behind him. She removed a checkbook and pen from a drawer. "Now that Hezekiah is dead, she realizes she'll never have him," she said with a slight laugh. "So how much does she want? One million, two? I hope she's going to be reasonable about this."

David leapt to his feet. He could take no more of the callous woman. He rushed to the desk and snatched the checkbook from under Samantha's moving pen. David threw the checkbook across the room. He grabbed Samantha's wrists, forcing her to stand directly in front of him. Her hair glided across her face with the abrupt turn.

"You disgust me," David said in her face. She could smell the sweet sherry on his breath. "Scarlett doesn't even know I'm talking to you. She has no interest in your fucking money, and neither do I."

Samantha tried to twist from his powerful grip, but he held her tight.

"Then what do you want?"

"I want you to pay for what you did to Scarlett. I want you to know how it feels to lose everything. I want you to suffer, and I wish your husband was alive so that he could suffer with you. I'm going to the press. I want everyone in the world to know what hypocrites you are."

Samantha stopped struggling to free herself from his grip. "Haven't we all suffered enough, David? If you go public with this, you'll ruin Natalie's life and everyone will know your wife for the whore that she is."

David quickly released Samantha's hand and slapped her hard on the cheek. Her head jerked from the blow. He grabbed her wrist again and pulled her back to his face. "I'm willing to take that risk as long as you are brought down in the process. You'll be preaching to bums on skid row after I get through with you."

A wicked smile crept across Samantha's face as a drop of blood fell from her lips. She tossed her hair from her eyes. The strands brushed against his cheeks, and she said, "There must be something I can do to make this right for you, David. You're a reasonable man, and I'm a reasonable woman. We can work out some arrangement that we both can benefit from."

Samantha moved closer, until their bodies were pressed together. David could smell a hint of lilac in her hair. He could feel the warmth of her breath. Her breast pressed against his heaving chest.

"I'm so lonely, David. Please don't do this to me," she pleaded breathlessly. "I need someone like you in my life right now." Samantha leaned forward and kissed him on the lips. "I don't want to be alone," she whispered, pressing her lips to his. "I need you near me."

He could taste the sweetness of her blood on her lips as she gently kissed him. A momentary confusion and fear overtook him. The image of Scarlett crying at the kitchen table flashed in his mind. *What is happening?* he thought. *What am I doing? This is Pastor Samantha Cleaveland.* Then he saw Hezekiah shaking his hand while he held Natalie in his arms. *Nice sermon this morning, Pastor,* David heard himself say as Hezekiah touched the little girl's head. *She is such a beautiful little angel. You are a lucky man, David.*

Yes, I am, Pastor.

Fear and confusion were replaced with betrayal and rage after seeing the image. David held Samantha at arm's length and looked in her eyes.

"Don't push me away, David," she pleaded.

David saw Hezekiah's face again, but this time it was pressed against Scarlett's lips. With that thought he slapped Samantha again hard on the cheek. Her hair twirled from the impact of the blow.

"I don't care if you hurt me," Samantha whimpered. "Do whatever you want to me. Beat me, hurt me, but don't leave me."

David grabbed her shoulders and yanked her head to his and kissed her deeply. The flow of blood increased from the roughness of his kiss. His large hands groped the fullness of her body through the silk dress.

"Make love to me, David," she panted.

Samantha could feel David's erection pressing against her stomach. She knew now he was hers to possess. In a frenzied motion Samantha ripped open his shirt. Little white buttons popped free from his fresh white shirt and scattered to the carpet. His chest heaved as she caressed him and undid his belt buckle.

"Do whatever you want to me, David. Hurt me, slap me, but please make love. I'm yours."

David unfastened the lobster clasp from her neck. The weight of the gunmetal yoke dragged the dress over her breasts, around her hips, to form a pool of silk at her feet.

David could feel her hand guide his erect member as he caressed her exposed breast and kissed her moist lips.

In unison they fell to the carpet. Samantha pulled his full weight to her, and he landed on her with a thud, with his shirt draped from his shoulders and his pants around his ankles. As they writhed on the floor, he entered her with one violent thrust.

Her hair formed a velvet fan on the carpet as she threw her head back and cried out in ecstasy. "Hurt me, David," she panted. "Harder. That's it. As hard as you want to."

With her commands his thrusts intensified. Each one delivered harder than the one before. "You bitch," he moaned in time with each blow. "You fucking bitch."

As he pounded into her flesh, she moaned in agony and pleasure. With each plunge her cries became louder and his breath more shallow.

"I'm going to cum you, bitch," he moaned. "You fucking whore, you're going to make me . . ."

Before he could finish his last assault, his entire body stiffened, and he let out a gut-wrenching cry.

Samantha matched his tone. "That's it, David. I want all of you inside me," she demanded.

For moments afterward they lay tangled and twisted in each other's arms, until the room slowly stopped spinning.

Samantha stroked his temples and nuzzled under his cheek. He belonged to her now to do with as she pleased.

Hattie Williams hummed along with the hymn on her crackling radio.

"Walk in the light.
Beautiful light.
Come where the dewdrops of mercy shine bright.
Oh, shine all around us by day and by night.
Jesus is the light of the world."

A large mixing bowl filled with snapped green beans rested in her lap. A straw basket filled with the vegetables from her garden was at her feet. She reached into the basket for another handful of fresh beans. One at a time she nimbly snapped off the tips of each bean and peeled away the stringy strip along the side. She then snapped each bean into three equal parts and dropped the pieces into the bowl.

"I am on the battlefield for my Lord."

The next hymn on the radio began, and this time Hattie sang along. "I am on the battlefield for my Lord. And I promised him that I would serve him till I die. I am on the battlefield for my Lord."

Hattie sat in her favorite chair in the kitchen window, looking out over the garden. The mint-green and white vinyl chairs had never been reupholstered, yet they were as bright and fresh as the day her late husband had brought them home. The glossy green cracked-ice Formica table with polished chrome legs and apron had dutifully served her family breakfast, lunch, and dinner for over sixty years.

As she reached for another handful of beans, she heard the doorbell ring. Hattie looked at the rooster clock that hung above the window over her sink. It was 3:27.

"Lord, now who could that be?" she said, placing the bowl on the table. Hattie opened the front door without hesitation to reveal a solid metal screen and security-bar door. She could see only the silhouette of a man standing on her porch.

"Good afternoon, ma'am," came the greeting from the shadow. "My name is Gideon Truman. I'm looking for Mrs. Hattie Williams."

"I'm Hattie Williams," she replied cautiously. "How can I help you?"

"It's very nice to finally meet you, Mrs. Williams. I've been trying to find you for a week now. I'm a reporter with CNN, and I'm doing a story on the life of your pastor, Hezekiah Cleaveland. May I trouble you for a few minutes of your time?"

Hattie hesitated for a moment, but her Texas roots prevented her from not inviting the man into her home.

She unlatched the security-bar door and said, "I don't know how I can help you, but come on in." Hattie directed Gideon to the living room. "It's hot out today. Can I offer you some lemonade or ice water?"

Gideon accepted graciously. "Yes, ma'am. That is very kind of you. Lemonade would be very nice, but only if it's not too much trouble."

While she was in the kitchen, Gideon looked around the small but comfortable room. *I'll bet she hasn't moved any of this furniture in fifty years,* he thought. Gideon felt oddly at ease in the home. *Amazing how everyone's home from her generation always feels and looks the same.*

A wool, braided, oval rug lay in front of the couch. A carved wooden coffee table held sundry bric-a-bracs, each with its own sentimental significance. Photographs of the children, grandchildren, and great-grandchildren had been placed on the walls, tables, and shelves. Gideon felt like he was in his grandmother's living room in Texarkana, Arkansas.

After a brief moment Hattie returned to the living room with a tall, clear glass with embossed flowers, which she placed on a coaster on the coffee table. She sat down and with a huff said, "Arthur is really acting up today."

"I'm sorry, ma'am. Who's Arthur?"

Hattie laughed. "You're too young to know anything about Arthur. But keep living. You'll meet him soon enough." She could see the look of confusion on his face and said, "Arthritis, boy. I'm talking 'bout arthritis. My knee is aching badly today."

"I'm very sorry to hear that. Is there anything I can do?"

"Nothing nobody can do. Just got to keep moving, or else you lay down and die, and I ain't ready to die just yet." Hattie rubbed her swollen knee and continued, "So you said you were writing a story about Pastor Cleaveland. What kind of story, exactly?"

Gideon proceeded with caution. He knew it was common for someone of Hattie's age to hold her secrets close to her chest. "First, let me extend my condolences on the loss of your pastor. I know that must have been difficult for you."

"It's so sad. So, so sad. But you got to believe everything happens for a reason. God don't make mistakes."

Despite the expensive clothes and the transparent smile, Hattie felt a warmth surrounding the handsome man. *He's got an old soul,* she thought. *I bet his people are from Texas.*

"I agree with you, ma'am. God does not make mistakes. I'm investigating his death, and I'd like to talk to the people who were the closest to him. I know you are one of the founding members of New Testament Cathedral and a trustee, so I just wanted to ask you a few questions."

I wonder, does his mama know about the homosexual thing? Shame. He's such a good-looking boy. Sho'll would make some pretty babies, she thought.

"New Testament Cathedral is one of the largest churches in the country, and Pastor Cleaveland touched so many people, I wanted to do a kind of tribute to him on my show."

Gideon's words said one thing, but Hattie heard another. *So you trying to find out who killed him,* she thought. "I think that would be very nice. He was a great man and deserves some kind of tribute," she said.

Hattie felt a power around Gideon that she usually only felt around politicians or corporate executives. *Sure is a powerful man to be so young and not be a politician,* she thought.

"What newspaper did you say you write for?"

"I'm sorry, Mrs. Williams. You misunderstood me. I don't write for a newspaper. I'm a television reporter. I have a program on CNN."

That explains it, she said to herself and nodded.

Hattie trusted Gideon. The slick, well-mannered, smiling reporter didn't impress her. What lay beneath the surface was what mattered to her. *His heart is in the right place,* she thought. He'd been hurt as a child. He looked to God for healing and found it. *I hope he finds a good man soon,* she thought. *Too nice of a young man to be alone in this world.*

"You're not drinking your lemonade. Is it too sweet for you?" she asked.

"No, ma'am. It's perfect."

Gideon saw a familiar glimmer in Hattie's kind eyes. It was the same twinkle he would see every time he looked in his grandmother's eyes. At that moment he missed her very much. *I really should go and see her soon,* he thought.

"God's given you a gift, boy," his grandmother would say every time Gideon went to visit her in the little shotgun house in Texarkana. "Don't waste it."

"How's your grandmother doing? Is she still with us?"

Gideon froze as he lifted the glass of lemonade to his lips. He didn't remember saying anything about his grandmother out loud.

"Don't look so surprised, boy," Hattie said casually. "You got a good spirit, and somebody's praying hard for you. I assumed it must be your grandmother."

Gideon sat the glass on the coaster and blotted his moist hands on his trousers. He was quiet for a moment. He did not question the old woman's wisdom. He knew from a lifetime of experience with his grandmother that there were some people in the world who saw and knew things that most others did not.

He smiled at Hattie and said, "You are correct, Mrs. Williams. I was raised by my grandmother, and yes, she is still alive. Her name is Virginia."

"That's good, 'cause she still has a lot more she can teach you. You need to get home and see her soon. She misses you."

"Yes, ma'am, I was just thinking the same thing."

"Now, young man, I can't sit here, talkin' all afternoon. I got a basket full of green beans that need snappin'. What did you want to ask me?"

Gideon had interviewed some of the most powerful, notorious, and famous people in the world, but he found himself unprepared for Hattie.

He reached into the breast pocket of his coat and took out a small recorder. "Do you mind if I record our conversation? It's easier than taking notes."

Hattie did not reply but simply nodded her head in approval. Gideon pressed a red button on the little box and placed it on the coffee table between them.

"How long had you known Hezekiah Cleaveland?"

"I've known both Hezekiah and Samantha since they first started New Testament Cathedral fifteen years ago. Their first church was just a block from here. My husband and I, rest his soul, and my grandkids used to walk there every Sunday morning. Couldn't been more than ten members back then. But I knew he was somethin' special."

"How do you mean special?"

"Are you a religious man?"

"Yes, ma'am. I was raised in the church."

"Then you'll understand what I'm about to tell you. God loves everybody, but He put some people on this earth to do great things. I knew Hezekiah was one of those people the moment I laid my eyes on him. Deep calling unto deep. He was covered in light the first time I saw him, and it stayed around him until the day he died. The Bible says sometimes those gifts are a vexation. It's a heavy burden to carry. That's why I stayed with him all these years."

"To intercede on his behalf?" Gideon said as if a light had just turned on in his head.

A pleased smile came across Hattie's face. "You are a religious man. Not a day went by that I didn't pray for Hezekiah."

"Did he know that?"

"He would sometimes call me at three or four in the morning and simply say in the phone, 'Mother, would you pray for me?' and hang up."

Gideon saw a single tear fall from Hattie's brown eyes. She reached for a crumpled handkerchief from the pocket of the floral-print apron tied at her waist and dabbed her cheek.

"When I saw him lying on the floor, covered in his own blood, that Sunday morning," Hattie continued, unprompted by Gideon, "I couldn't help but feel I had let him down."

"It certainly wasn't your fault. There was nothing anyone could have done to prevent it from happening."

"I knew. I knew something terrible was gonna happen," she said, looking out the window.

Gideon leaned forward in the chair. "How did you know?" Gideon asked gently.

Hattie looked him in the eye, smiled, and said, "Old people just know some things, boy."

Gideon knew Hattie would say nothing more on the subject and decided to move on. "Can you tell me about your new pastor, Samantha Cleaveland?" he asked.

Hattie looked back to the window, sighed, and dabbed her cheek again. "What would you like to know?" she asked while clearing the thoughts of Hezekiah from her mind.

"Just give your general impressions of her. How do you think his death has affected her? Do you think she will make a good pastor? Things like that."

"Whether or not she'll make a good pastor is in the hands of the Lord."

"Then I assume you don't see the same light around Samantha Cleaveland as you saw around Hezekiah." Gideon sensed Hattie was holding back. "This can be off the record if you'd prefer. Would you like me to turn off the recorder?"

"No need," Hattie scoffed. "There's no light around Samantha Cleaveland."

"But it's my understanding that you and the other members of the board of trustees voted unanimously to make her interim pastor. If you didn't see any light around her, why did you vote for her?"

Hattie didn't hesitate in her response. "Because I love New Testament Cathedral. I believed that she's the only person right now that can keep the ministry together. She will keep people coming in the doors and turning on the TV every Sunday morning. You've seen her. She's beautiful, and people around the world love her, but there ain't no anointing there. New Testament needs her until God sends us the right shepherd. People need that church, and I didn't want to see it fail. That's why I voted the way I did."

Gideon was honored by her candor. "Thank you for being so open with me, Mrs. Williams. I assure you I will not use any of this in my story."

"I know you won't," she said calmly. "Because that's not why you came here."

"Then, why do you think I'm here, ma'am?" he asked, somehow knowing that she actually knew the answer.

"Because you want to know who killed Hezekiah."

Gideon tried to conceal his discomfort. He felt vulnerable and exposed sitting in the chair, facing the old woman. It was as if she could see parts of him that he himself didn't know existed.

Gideon felt weak. There was no point in denying the truth. "So who do you think killed Hezekiah Cleaveland?" he asked, not as the acclaimed reporter, but as the vulnerable little boy sitting on his grandmother's couch.

Hattie gave a wry smile. "I know a lot of things, son. For example, I know you're about to meet somebody you've been looking for your whole life. And they've been looking for you too. I know you're scared to death that one day people will find out about that secret you've been hiding for so long. But don't worry 'bout that, boy. People are gon'na love you no matter what."

Hattie paused to allow the handsome young man to digest all that she had said. Gideon struggled to maintain his composure. Then she continued, "I know there's a dark cloud near you, and you seem to be walking right into it. Do you know what that means?"

Gideon could hardly speak. He managed to choke out, "No, ma'am."

"It means you might be gettin' in over your head with this one. Be careful, boy. You're heading toward someone who's more dangerous than you could ever imagine."

Kay Braisden exited the green and white cab in front of Danny's apartment. She tipped the driver five dollars.

"Thank you," said the scruffy, woolen-capped driver. "Hope you enjoy you stay in L.A."

Kay rolled her single black canvas suitcase to the door. The wheels made a clanking sound on the pavement, which Danny could hear from his apartment. Kay and Danny were the same age, but she looked older and wiser. She wore comfortable traveling clothes that hid the fact that she had gained weight since the last time they saw each other, three years earlier. Her hair was in a tight bun knotted on the back. Kay never wore makeup, and today was no exception. By Los Angeles standards, she was a plain girl who most people would forget a few minutes after they met her. Their friendship had survived the distance. They would talk two and three times a week before Danny told her about Hezekiah. In between telephone calls were text messages and e-mails.

Have you seen bouncy Beyoncé's latest video? one such benign text message from Kay had read. Wish had legs like those.

Danny's responses were typically. LOL . . . last time i saw u did have legs like hers just shorter ;).

LOL . . . , came Kay's rapidly texted reply.

But after Danny told her about Hezekiah, all communication had stopped for months.

Before she could lift her hand, the door opened. Danny stood in the threshold, and they looked in each other's eyes. She could see he had been crying. Kay extended her arms, and Danny gladly stepped into her embrace.

"I told you I would pick you up at the airport," he said, still in her arms. "Why didn't you call?"

"It was just as easy for me to take a cab," she said, squeezing him tighter. "I've missed you so much, Danny St. John."

"I've missed you, too, Kay Braisden. I'm so glad you're here."

Danny placed her suitcase in the little entry hall and made them each a cup of tea. The two sat on the couch, Danny's legs curled under him and Kay sitting sideways, looking Danny in the eye.

"How are you holding up?" she asked, already knowing the answer.

"It's been weeks, but every day it feels like it just happened. When is it ever going to stop hurting?" Before Kay could respond Danny answered his own question. "I don't think it ever will."

Kay took his hand and said, "I can't tell you how sorry I am for not being there for you when you needed me."

Danny did not respond.

"It all just took me by surprise. You never mentioned anything about him to me in the entire two years you were seeing him. Why didn't you tell me?"

"Because I was afraid you would react the way you did. I knew you wouldn't approve, and I was already feeling guilty enough without you adding to it."

Kay looked embarrassed. "And of course, I, like an idiot, acted true to form."

Danny paused and then said with a smile, "Yes, you did."

Kay smiled with him. "I don't know why I reacted the way I did. I'm not as old- fashioned as you may think."

"Then what happened? Why did this have such a negative impact on you personally?"

Kay had decided before she boarded the plane in Washington, D.C., that she would—no matter how painful it would be—tell Danny the truth about how she felt about him. From the first day they met in college, she had been in love with him. She'd followed him everywhere he went for their entire undergraduate years. She would join the same clubs on campus. She arranged her class schedule so she could take as many classes with him as possible. He never touched her in a way that was sexual. She had longed to kiss him on so many occasions but never got the nerve. To her painful dismay, he would always introduce her as "my best buddy, Kay," to his friends and family. But she'd wanted so much more.

"Danny, I reacted the way I did because I wanted so much more for you. It's not because you're gay," her self betrayal began. "It hurt me so deeply that you didn't tell me about Hezekiah sooner. We've always shared our secrets with each other, and I was angry that you didn't trust me enough to tell me the biggest secret of your life." Kay sat her now tepid cup of tea on the coffee table. "It's selfish, I know, but that's the embarrassing truth. I felt left out of your life."

A tear dropped to her cheek as she spoke. It fell from the pain of not being able to summon the courage to tell the truth to the man she had loved for so many years.

Danny lifted his hand and gently brushed the tear from her cheek. She grabbed it before he could remove it. Her heart fluttered as she held his soft hand. "I'm so sorry, Danny," she said through mounting tears. "Can you ever forgive me?"

"I forgive you, Kay," Danny said gently. "Now, come here and hug me. I need a hug."

Kay could feel the warmth of his breath on her shoulder as they embraced. She could smell the familiar scent of his favorite sandalwood soap on his skin. His strong arms held her tight as she cried more tears of unrequited love.

"Do you want to talk about it?" Danny asked, still holding her close.

Kay froze, and the tears abruptly stopped. *Had he seen through that clumsy attempt at hiding my real feelings?* she thought. *Could he possibly feel the same way about me?* For a brief moment she felt a glint of hope. "Talk about what?" she asked without breathing.

"About my relationship with Hezekiah," Danny said curiously.

The hope that had made her heart miss a beat at the thought he could possibly love her in the same way left as quickly as it had come. "Of course, of course," she said, embarrassed, wiping tears from her cheek with the back of her hand. "I want to hear all about it. But only if you feel up to it."

Danny was eager to tell someone he knew about Hezekiah. In the two years of their relationship he had never spoken his name to anyone.

Danny leaned back on the couch. He cradled the cup of tea in his lap as he spoke.

"I met him purely by accident on the street. I was helping a homeless person downtown, and he pulled up next to me. He said there was a homeless woman near his church and asked if I would speak to her. After I helped her, he asked if he could do outreach to the homeless with me one afternoon. Kay, I swear it all was so innocent at first. I had no idea he was gay, and it never crossed my mind that he was attracted to me. But when we were alone in my apartment—"

"Alone in your apartment?" Kay interrupted. "How did that happen?"

"He came with me one afternoon to do outreach. You know, handing out socks, vitamins, condoms to people on skid row. When we finished, his driver was late picking him up, so he asked if he could hang out with me until he came." Danny paused and looked at Kay. "Are you sure you're all right hearing this? You seem tense."

Kay suddenly became conscious of the fact that her fist was clenched in her lap and her jaw was tight. She took a deep breath and replied, "I'm fine, Danny. It's important that you talk about it. It's part of the healing process. Go ahead. I'm listening."

"Well, anyway," Danny continued, "we went back to my apartment, and everything seemed perfectly innocent. We sat right here on the couch, just like you and I are right now, and just talked. He was nothing like the man I'd seen on television. He was funny, vulnerable, and relaxed and, I guess, just a normal guy. He wasn't that bigger-than-life, one-dimensional cutout."

"A normal guy who just happened to be one of the most famous people in the country and married," Kay said.

"Are you judging me? Because if you are, I don't need it," Danny said defensively." Believe me, I've already judged myself. If you are, we can stop this conversation right now."

"I didn't mean it that way. I'm sorry. Go ahead."

Danny proceeded with caution. "I was walking him to the door, and we stopped right over there," he said, pointing to the arched threshold leading from the living room to the entry hall. "We stood directly in front of each other, looking into each other's eyes and not saying a word. Then it was like a magnet pulled us together. We made love the first time that afternoon right here on the living room floor."

Kay felt her stomach tighten. She tried to push the image of their two male bodies writhing on the floor out of her mind.

"Kay, he was an amazing person. Not because he was so special or unique, but because he loved me like no one has ever loved me before. He once told me he knew every inch of my body and remembered everything I'd ever said to him. I can't tell you how much that meant to me. That someone knew everything about me. I was so lonely at the time I met him. You had moved away. I rarely went out. I was working seven days a week just not to be at home alone. And, more than that, I was also afraid."

"Afraid of what?" Kay asked with a level of compassion that even surprised her.

Danny thought for a moment. "Afraid that I would never find someone to love me."

A tear fell from Danny's eye as he spoke.

"I had been alone up until that point. I was afraid I would never find someone that wanted to know who I really was. Not just a body or a paycheck, but a person who loves, who has fears, who makes mistakes. Someone who was interested and cared enough to know that I like my coffee with two sugars and a drop of cream. That I love to watch Woody Allen movies on Sunday afternoons, curled up on the couch. Someone who cared that I have panic attacks. That Picasso is my favorite artist or that I've never been to Las Vegas. And after learning all the insignificant and silly and even the horrible things about me, he loved me even more in spite of what he'd learned. Hezekiah was that person. He took the time to discover things about me that I didn't even know myself. And with all he knew, he still loved me."

Danny tried to stop talking, but he couldn't. He needed someone to understand. More importantly, he needed Kay to understand.

"He was the head of a multimillion-dollar ministry, and I never set foot in his church until the day of his funeral. I wasn't a part of that part of his world, and when he was with me, neither was he. He wasn't Pastor Hezekiah T. Cleaveland with me. He was simply Hez. That's what I used to call him."

"Did you ever meet his wife?"

Danny shifted slightly on the couch. "No, and I never wanted to meet her. I, of course, knew about her, and toward the end he told her about me, but I begged him to never tell her who I was."

"Why?"

Danny looked mournfully out the window at the traffic below. "To be honest with you, Kay, I was afraid of what she might do."

Kay looked surprised and said, "Afraid she might hurt you?"

There was silence. Danny shifted again. His body tensed, and the hand holding the cup of tea trembled slightly.

"Danny," Kay said into the silence. "What do you mean? Did she threaten you in any way?"

Danny looked her in the eye and said, "I wasn't afraid for myself. I was afraid of what she might do to him, and I think I was . . ."

Kay sat upright on the couch. She placed the now cool cup of tea on the table. "Danny, you're not saying you think she had something to do with his death?" she asked in disbelief.

Danny did not respond.

"Danny, that's crazy. You're talking about Samantha Cleaveland. She's . . . she's Samantha Cleaveland, for Christ's sake. How could you think that? The woman is a saint, a beautiful and strong God-fearing woman. Look how well she's managed with such grace and dignity after his death. People love her."

Danny shook his head gently. "You don't know what she's capable of. Hezekiah would tell me things about her that even frightened him."

"Danny, this can't be true. I watch her every Sunday morning. She's like a role model to me. I love Samantha Cleaveland. Everybody loves Samantha Cleaveland."

"I know, Kay. But beneath that exterior there's an evil woman who would do anything to maintain and further her position in life. She built New Testament into what it is today, not Hezekiah. He admitted that

to me. She pushed him into television. She persuaded
him to build the new cathedral. He didn't want it. She
forced him to buy that mansion in Bel Air and hire the
drivers and security guards. He didn't want any of that
stuff. He told me he hated that house."

"I don't believe any of this. You must be mistaken,"
Kay said defensively. She looked at Danny and saw the
disappointment on his face. She could see the hurt her
last statement had caused.

"I didn't mean it that way, honey," she said, reaching for his hand. "I simply meant maybe Hezekiah
stretched the truth to ease his own conscience. This
whole affair—I mean relationship—must have been
very difficult for him."

"It was," Danny said. "On the day he was killed, he
had planned to announce that he was stepping down
as pastor."

Kay gasped and clutched her hand to her gaping
mouth. "No," she said in disbelief.

"Yes, and Samantha was the only person, other than
me, who knew. I never believed she would ever let that
happen. If he'd stepped down because of a homosexual
affair, she would have lost everything. The credibility
of the Cleaveland dynasty would have been in sham-
bles, and everything she'd built would have crumbled
around her two-thousand-dollar Gucci shoes. Even the
great Samantha Cleaveland wouldn't have been able to
salvage it."

Kay sat in disbelief. She couldn't stop her left leg
from shaking. Her foot bounced nervously on the faded
throw rug in front of the couch. "This is incredible," she
said, her voice trembling. "I can't believe what you're
telling me. You actually believe she killed him."

"Of course she didn't pull the trigger, but I believe
she was behind his murder. Have you seen the footage
of the service that Sunday morning?"

"Everyone in the country has seen it. Gideon Truman played it almost nonstop on CNN for two weeks."

"Didn't anything about it look strange to you?" Danny asked.

"The whole scene looked strange. Who would have ever imagined that he would have been killed on live television on a Sunday morning in front of his entire church?"

"More than that, what about the obvious outrageousness of the entire melee? I mean her performance after he was shot. When she rushed to the pulpit and cradled his head to her chest. It all looked rehearsed to me. Every move she made appeared choreographed. I could swear she was trying not to get his blood on her white suit."

"Danny, you're being cruel. She doesn't deserve that. The woman had to witness the man she loved being shot in the head."

"All I'm saying is she knew she was about to be humiliated in front of the entire world and, more importantly, she was about to lose everything. That is the perfect motive for murder. The police haven't been able to find any suspects. They can't find anyone with a motive. They're not looking at her, because she's too smart for them. She's fooled the police, just like she's fooled everyone else in the world. She doesn't fool me. Even though I have never met her, I feel like I know her better than anyone. Hezekiah told me everything."

"Have you talked to anyone else about this?"

"No. You're the first person I've spoken to." Danny paused for a moment. He suddenly remembered the conversation he had had with Gideon Truman. "I take that back," he said, as if a light had been turned on in his head. "I forgot that I've spoken to Gideon Truman."

Another gasp escaped from Kay's lips. "*The* Gideon
Truman? From CNN? You talked to Gideon Truman?"

"He came to my job and asked a bunch of questions.
Someone gave him copies of e-mails between Hezekiah
and me." Danny shuddered as the words escaped.

"That means someone out there knows you exist,"
Kay said.

"I never thought of that."

"Maybe you should talk to the police."

"And tell them what? That I was Hezekiah's lover
and I believe his wife had him assassinated? They
would believe I killed him before they believed she did
it."

"Oh my God, Danny, this is horrible. I'm afraid for
you. Your life may be in danger. You suspect someone
killed Hezekiah because he was about to come out of
the closet. Who's to say the killer doesn't know about
you too? You've got to talk to someone. Maybe you
should speak to Gideon Truman."

Danny remembered how kind Gideon had been to
him in the grungy little conference room at his job. He
remembered how gentle Gideon was when he wept on
his shoulder and the comforting words he'd whispered.
I know Hezekiah loved you.

"What good would that do? He can't protect me."

"He can help the police find the killer. He's been
investigating Hezekiah's murder from the beginning,"
Kay said urgently. "He's dedicated more time to the
story than any other network. You have information
that might help him find the killer. If you are in danger,
then that clearly helps you."

Danny considered her words. He hadn't feared for
his life before, and he still didn't. The thought of the
killer, possibly Samantha, knowing his identity did not
frighten him. His world had been so empty without He-

zekiah in the past few weeks, he couldn't think of many reasons to cling to life, anyway.

Kay could sense his hesitation and said, "If your safety is not motivation enough to talk to Gideon, then think about Hezekiah. Don't you want the killer to be caught? And if it is as you suspect, then the world needs to know the real Samantha Cleaveland."

Chapter 10

The grounds of New Testament Cathedral glistened in the afternoon sun. Plush grass flowed like a tranquil river over the ten-acre compound. Gurgling fountains and the coo of pigeons provided a soothing soundtrack for a tense conversation between the four coconspirators.

Cynthia Pryce walked between Reverend Kenneth Davis and Catherine Birdsong; her husband, Percy, kept pace in the rear. The four walked along the cobblestone paths, pausing intermittently to say "Hello" or "Welcome to New Testament Cathedral" to groups of passing tourists.

They had assembled at the request of Kenneth. Meeting out in the open seemed like the safest way to talk without being overheard. An innocent scene: four leaders of the church taking a leisurely afternoon stroll along the sloping knolls. All the pathways led to a fifty-foot cross carved from white marble. The cross served as the centerpiece of the garden. It rose up from a circular mound of exotic orchids, perennials, and shrubbery. The flower bed was encircled by iron benches, for contemplation, that Samantha had commissioned from an artist in Paris.

"We've got to do something," Kenneth said as he waved to a couple in the distance. "She's not suited to be pastor. Her heart isn't in the right place. Samantha is going to destroy this ministry if we don't replace her."

"I agree," Cynthia said, looking straight ahead.

"First, she humiliated Catherine in front of the entire staff, and then forced her to resign," Kenneth continued. "Benny Winters called me in a panic this morning, saying she's demanding changes to the new cathedral design that could run into the millions. I'm afraid to think of what she'll do next. Replace me? Force you and Percy out of the church?"

"There's nothing that can be done, Kenneth," Catherine said. "Everyone loves her. Our television ratings have almost doubled since she took over. Contributions have been pouring in like never before. Did you see how much we took in last week? It was more than we usually get in a month."

"This isn't about money, Catherine," Cynthia interjected. "It's about God's will, and I agree with Kenneth. Her heart is not in the right place. I don't believe for a minute that she's interested in bringing souls to Christ. She's about the almighty dollar, and I'm not afraid to say it."

"Cynthia, please," Percy said from behind.

"Well, someone had to say it, Percy, and you all know it's true. The only thing that's important to her is maintaining her embarrassingly lavish lifestyle. I can't believe that any of you think that it's God's will or that you would sit idly by and allow her to fleece all the saints that support this ministry. The thought of all those lovely people sending in their hard-earned money to buy her another piece of art just breaks my heart. Every night since she's been pastor, I've prayed that God will forgive us for being negligent stewards over the blessings he has given this ministry."

Percy walked behind with his head held down. He'd never seen Cynthia pray in the fifteen years they had been married.

"But what can be done?" Kenneth asked.

Cynthia spoke before anyone could respond. "There are five votes on the board of trustees. Yours, Kenneth, and Percy's, Scarlett's, Hattie Williams's, and Samantha's. I know Scarlett can be persuaded to vote her out. I'm not sure about Hattie. But even without her, that's three to two."

"It's not a question of votes, Cynthia," Percy finally said. "It's a matter of how a move like that would be received by the congregation. If she's replaced, we run the risk of a mass exodus of members and supporters. We could be left with half the congregation."

Cynthia stopped dead in her tracks and turned swiftly to face her husband. Percy froze in his steps, and everyone stopped with her. The four formed a circle in the middle of the pathway.

"I don't think that is true, darling," she said icily, looking her husband directly in the eye. "You are mistakenly assuming this is a personality-driven ministry. I don't believe it is. I have faith in God and in our members that they will be loyal to the message and not the messenger, and so should you," she said pointedly.

Percy did not respond but instead met her gaze with equal contempt.

"You're all forgetting one important piece of this," Catherine said, breaking the petrifying silence. "Who could replace her?"

Again there was quiet, until Kenneth said, "Well, I think that is obvious. Percy, you were always the heir apparent."

Percy looked down at the pavement and faintly said, "I don't think . . ."

"Slow down, Kenneth," Cynthia interjected before Percy could finish his response. "I think it's premature to have that conversation. Percy and I have never thought in those terms. It would mean a significant adjustment in our lives. We would need to pray about it before he could even consider becoming pastor. What's important at this stage is that we all agree that Samantha cannot be made permanent pastor of New Testament Cathedral."

"I think we've established that we agree she should be removed," Kenneth said. "But it seems like a moot point since we don't know where Scarlett and Hattie stand on this. Someone should speak with them. It's obviously a very sensitive subject, so it has to be handled with the utmost tact."

"I agree," Cynthia said. "It obviously can't be Percy. Catherine, you are technically an employee of the board of trustees, so I think it would be inappropriate for you to have that conversation with them."

"That's fine with me," Catherine said, relieved.

"So, Kenneth, that leaves either you or me," Cynthia said, dismissing the others in the little circle. "What do you think?"

Kenneth looked off into the distance. "Because Samantha is a woman, it might be interpreted as chauvinistic if I was the one suggesting to them that she be replaced."

"I never thought of it in those terms," Cynthia said believably. "Then I'll speak with them."

From the window of her fifth-floor office, Samantha looked down on the assembled group. *So they finally got up the courage to meet,* she thought. *How dare they do it on my property and out in the open?* She could see that Cynthia was at the center of the conversation. *I suppose she thinks that spineless husband of hers is man enough to replace me.*

Samantha walked back to her desk and calmly sat down. *Poor, silly woman,* she thought. *She really doesn't know what I'm capable of.*

***

Hattie Williams pulled the damp white sheet from the bulging wicker laundry basket at her feet. She wore her favorite short-sleeve sundress covered with yellow sunflowers and a white apron with a red trim border that she had stitched on by hand. She stood in her backyard, under the clothesline that was suspended between two metal poles. It was the same clothesline that her husband had installed at her insistence fifty years ago.

"We don't need a clothesline," her husband, Howard, had said. "I just bought you that brand new Maytag washer and dryer."

"Don't argue with me, Howard. Ever since I've been using that dryer, my sheets and pillowcases ain't been nearly as white as I like them. The washing machine is fine, but I ain't got no use for that dryer. The sun makes clothes white, and it kills germs. The sun was good enough for my grandmama and my mama, and it's good enough for me. So go downtown to Mr. Kroger's hardware store and get the rope and some poles. I want my clothesline."

Howard knew even back then that once Hattie had made her mind up about something, there was nothing he could do to change it.

"And don't get no cheap rope," she said as Howard gathered his keys and headed to the door. "I want that line to last, so get some good sturdy rope."

Last it had. The ropes that extended from the now rusting poles had not been changed in the fifty years since Howard strung them up on that Saturday morning in 1961. Hattie found the edges of the sheet and extended it above her head. She fastened the first corner to the cord with a wooden clothespin. Arms still raised above her head, she applied the next pin to the center of the sheet and finally the third at the end. The sheet billowed gently in the breeze. Hattie took a step back and looked at the white fabric with pride. *Good enough for my mama,* she thought.

It was a perfect day for drying laundry. The sun had reached its high point. The air was still, except for the occasional breeze that danced between the pillowcases and towels. As Hattie reached down into the basket for the next sheet, she felt a familiar twinge in her stomach. The twinge that heralded the coming of understanding. The feeling foretold of images to come. Hattie stood upright and waited patiently for the vision to begin. She stared blankly into the white sheet that she had just hung as the images slowly began to appear.

The sun had descended from the heavens and rested in the upper right corner of the sheet. The golden rays flowed down onto what she immediately recognized as the sanctuary of New Testament Cathedral. The room was full of saints. She could see rows and rows of colorful felt, straw, and satin Sunday hats. The crowd seemed to be energized by the rays of the sun.

She could hear chords of heavenly music coming from the pipe organ. Everyone was singing in unison, "Walk in the light. Beautiful light. Come where the dewdrops of mercy shine bright. Oh, shine all around us by day and by night. Jesus is, Jesus is the light of the world."

Hattie found comfort in the beautiful refrain. She had sung it herself on many Sunday mornings. There was joy in the hearts of all those present. She could feel the love and contentment emanating from every row, aisle, and corner of the sanctuary. Then, suddenly, legions of people began to pour down the center aisle toward the pulpit. She could see tears of joy in their eyes.

Thank you, Jesus, Hattie thought as she saw the new converts make their way to the pulpit. *So many souls coming to you, Lord.* It was by far more people than Hattie had ever seen accept the invitation to the church. Their arms were waving in the air as they walked briskly to the pulpit. She could hear them shouting and crying out, "I've been gone for so long. I've made so many mistakes," and "I'm so tired of running. I'm ready to come home." The chorus of pleas from the repentant filled the room.

Hattie was overwhelmed with joy at the sight of so many souls turning their lives over to God. She felt her own eyes fill with tears as she witnessed the scene that unfolded on the white canvas of her freshly washed sheet.

With her eyes wide open, she followed the crowd as they made their way to the front of the church. Hattie suddenly began to feel the temperature around her drop as the throngs of people formed a crowd at the foot of the pulpit. Even though she could still see the sun in the corner of the sheet, the rays were no longer sufficient to warm her exposed arms or sooth her arthritic knee. The room slowly dimmed, but to her surprise, the praises from the crowd continued to grow louder and more insistent.

As quickly as it had come, the joy she felt suddenly turned to dread. She feared how the scene would finally play out. Hattie braced her spirit and said a silent prayer. *Lord, give me strength.*

And then she saw her. Samantha stood at the edge of the pulpit. Her arms outstretched, welcoming the euphoric masses. She was radiant. Like a queen. The elaborate gold-jewel-festooned robe she wore glowed so brightly that it eclipsed the now waning sun. Samantha did not speak. She looked lovingly over the masses as a shepherd would over a flock of sheep.

Hattie resisted the sight of so many people being persuaded by Samantha to come to the pulpit. Her heart was both joyous and crestfallen. Although she tried, Hattie wasn't able to blot from her mind the images of the thousands of transformed people standing at Samantha's feet. She stood as the helpless witness to the future of New Testament Cathedral.

The emotional scene ran its course and forced Hattie to view every tear, every conversion, and the transformation of the multitude of lost souls. Her emotions ranged from despondence to delight and from pleasure to pain. Her feet were planted firmly in the perfectly mown sod, unable to move. She folded her arms in an attempt to shield her exposed flesh from the cold. Hattie eventually gave in to the scene. She grew too weary to resist.

The images soon faded from the sheet. The whiteness was now even more apparent than when she first hung it. Time had stood still during the vision. She had no idea how long she had been staring at the sheet. It could have been minutes. It could have been hours. The pain she felt in her knees gave a hint to the length of time she had been standing. She reached out and touched the sheet. It was almost completely dry. The sun was no longer directly above her head. She looked down at the ground and saw her shadow extended across the green grass.

Hattie bent down and retrieved the last towel from the basket. It, too, was almost dry. After hanging it on the line, Hattie made her way to the back steps of her house. She paused on each step, dragging the basket behind her. When she reached the door, she walked inside. "Thy will be done, Lord, on earth just as it is in heaven," she whispered as she closed the door behind her.

***

It had been two days since Gideon first met Danny St. John. In that time he couldn't get the gentle young man out of his mind. Danny was in his thoughts when he drove through the crowded Los Angeles streets. Images of Danny sat across the table from him when he had his morning coffee and muffins.

How could a sweet guy like that get himself involved in a horrible situation like this? he thought as he transcribed notes from his recorded interview with Hattie Williams. Gideon could still smell the distinct scent of sandalwood he had recognized the day Danny cried on his shoulder in the dingy little conference room.

It was nine thirty at night. Gideon sat alone in the office of his home in the Hollywood Hills. The room was a soothing shade of beige, with a white contoured ceiling. There was a sitting area with a couch, two comfortable chairs, and a coffee table, which held a stack of books he had read. His housekeeper had left the room in pristine condition after she had cleaned that morning. A wet bar in the far corner of the room had gone untouched since the day he moved into the house three years earlier.

While sitting at the desk, in front of his laptop computer, Gideon continually stopped and started the recording of Hattie Williams. Half the screen was filled with the haunting words she had spoken.

"There's no light around Samantha Cleaveland," came Hattie's muted voice from the recorder. Gideon rewound the tape and played it again. "There's no light around Samantha Cleaveland." And again, "There's no light around Samantha Cleaveland."

Gideon thought again about Danny as he typed the words on his laptop. *I wish there was something I could do to help him.*

Gideon abruptly stood up from the desk and walked to the window. Laid out before him was the twinkling Los Angeles skyline. The jagged jumble of tall obelisk high-rises were each dotted with lighted windows on every floor. Neon signs blinked over the canvas in an attempt to lure customers in to buy Nikes, big-screen televisions, cigarettes, and malt liquor.

You've got to stay objective, man, Gideon silently admonished himself as he stood at the window. *For all you know, Danny could have killed Hezekiah himself.*

Even in the face of all he had learned as a reporter, Gideon could not stop thinking of how wonderful Danny had felt in his arms. He wanted to protect him.

Protect him from what? he thought. *Protect him from Hezekiah and Samantha. Maybe protect him from himself.*

Gideon had never been in love in his entire forty-five years. He purposefully hadn't allowed himself to get close enough to anyone and had never allowed anyone to get close to him. Every ounce of psychic energy had been reserved for his career. He had known he wanted to be a reporter since he was in the fifth grade at the little Union Elementary School in Texarkana.

His third grade teacher, Mrs. Perry, had recognized Gideon's natural curiosity and desire for finding the "answers behind the answers." She assigned him the task of writing a short article for the school newsletter on the upcoming school election. Gideon had instinctively interviewed all the young candidates, the teachers overseeing the election, and even the school principal. The directness of his questions had surprised some of the adults even then. The attention he garnered from that article was the beginning of his goal to be a news reporter.

He considered emotions like love and fear a distraction. There was no room for distractions in his world.
This was complicated by the fact that all his life he
had been primarily attracted to men. In the 1980s
there was little room for a black journalist at the major
newspapers and television stations and even less room
for a black gay journalist. It was hard enough to get an
entry-level job. He saw his sexuality as an unnecessary
distraction for the white editor or news producer sitting across the desk from him during his many inter-
views after college.

Until he met Danny, the emotions of love and desire
had seemed irrelevant. Over the years he had rarely
acted on his desires for fear of being publicly exposed
as a homosexual. The occasional nameless encounters
with ciphers from the Internet were far less frequent
than the numerous proclamations of love, proposals
for marriage, and other more temporal propositions
he received almost daily from admiring fans, men and
women on the street, other celebrities, and the occasional network executive.

But somehow the sight of Danny St. John two days
earlier in the crowded homeless drop-in center had
reminded him that he was not exempt from the need
to love and be loved just like every other human in the
world.

Gideon tried to resist his feelings for Danny, but the
more he looked into the death of Hezekiah Cleaveland,
the more he found himself looking into the eyes of
Danny St. John. The more he transcribed notes from
church members, the more he remembered Danny.
Whenever he thought of Samantha Cleaveland, his
thoughts would inevitably rush to the fragile young
man who had needed him so deeply for those brief moments after he had confronted him with the e-mails
from Hezekiah.

Gideon felt himself teetering on the edge of an ethical precipice. *A reporter reports the news.* The words of his Journalism Ethics and Standards professor echoed in his head. *Always remain objective, and most importantly, never, ever become part of the story.*

Danny called to him from across the ethical divide. The canons of journalism had served as his bible throughout his career. The words *Professional integrity is the cornerstone of a journalist's credibility* greeted him each day when he turned on his computer and scrolled across the screen each time the computer fell asleep.

Gideon longed to touch Danny's soft skin again. He wanted to feel his body again in his arms. He resisted the urge to pick up his cell phone and dial Danny. "Get a hold of yourself, man," he said out loud. "He's not worth jeopardizing your entire career."

But Gideon's heart said otherwise. *He's so beautiful. He's the most beautiful man I've ever met.* This time the words went unspoken. Gideon walked away from the window and returned to his desk. The white computer screen stared back at him. Of all the words on the screen, the only ones he could see were *Danny St. John.*

How do you fall in love with someone you've only met once? he silently questioned. "It's not possible. Maybe this happens to people who watch too many soap operas," he said aloud. *You're better than that, Gideon Truman. You're stronger than that.*

Chapter 11

Hattie Williams sat in the conference room at New Testament Cathedral. A stack of checks that needed her signature were on the table in front of her. Given that she was one of the founding members, a board trustee, and a longtime confidant to Hezekiah Cleaveland, Hattie's was the second signature required on all checks issued by the church. Like clockwork on each Friday afternoon at three o'clock a black Escalade pulled in front of her modest home. The driver would politely tap on her iron-bar door and say, "Good afternoon, Mother Williams. I'm here to take you to church to sign checks." The driver would then slowly escort her down the front steps and into the rear of the waiting SUV.

"She's too old for this. She doesn't know enough about church business to be a signatory," Samantha had often said to Hezekiah. "Why in God's name don't you make me the second signer? You don't trust me?"

"Of course I trust you, darling," Hezekiah would lovingly reply. "I've told you a thousand times, you and I both can't be signers. We don't want to appear that we are a dynasty. It's just not appropriate."

"But we are a dynasty, and you need to stop pretending we're not. We are the Cleavelands. We're worth millions of dollars. We run one of the largest ministries in the country, yet you still want to run it like some jackleg preacher in a storefront with all his brothers, sisters, aunts, uncles, and cousins as the only members. Grow up, Hezekiah. Whether you want to accept it or not, this is a business, and you need to start running it like a business."

Hezekiah's patience always grew thin at this point in the conversation. "That's where you and I differ. This isn't a business. It's a church. It's a ministry whose sole purpose is to bring souls to Christ. Not to make millions of dollars. And don't you ever forget that."

"I realize that," Samantha would snap back. "And please do not admonish me. You are not in any position to take the moral high road. I am your wife, and I know all your little secrets. You spend their tithes on expensive clothes and your little toys just like I do."

"I don't want to argue about this again, Samantha," Hezekiah would say impatiently. "Hattie is the signatory, and that's how it's going to stay until either she or I leaves this world."

Each Friday Hattie would be greeted in the air-conditioned conference room by an attractive young assistant. "Good afternoon, Mother Williams. How are you today?" she would politely inquire.

"I'm fine, baby. God is good."

As usual there was a stack of checks, a gold pen, a pitcher of ice water, and one glass neatly arranged on the table.

"If you need anything, Mother, just buzz me on the intercom."

"I'll be fine, dear." In the years Hattie had been signing the checks, she had never used the intercom.

Hattie leaned her cane against the large table and settled into the comfortable leather chair at the head of the table. She placed her patent leather purse on the floor, near the heel of her sensible shoe. Utility bills, payroll checks, payments to the many vendors necessary to maintain the mega church, the weekly $3,055.00

check to the florist, each year millions of dollars would pass under her signature. Hattie had only one rule. She would never approve personal expenses for Samantha Cleaveland. The checks to Samantha's dressmaker always went unsigned, until one day they stopped appearing in the weekly stack. Payments to her personal hairdresser, manicurist, and any other person who contributed to her beauty were routinely placed in a separate stack and left unsigned. Those, too, were eventually left out of the pile. No one ever dared ask why she refused to sign them, because everyone already knew.

As Hattie worked her way through the checks, which now displayed Samantha Cleaveland's calligraphic signature, there was a gentle tap on the door. Before she could respond, the door opened.

"Excuse me, Mother Williams," Cynthia Pryce said, peering in. "I know you're busy, but may I have a word with you?"

Hattie looked up from the papers at Cynthia and said, "Come in, baby. I'm about done with these. What can I do for you?"

Cynthia closed the door and sat at the table. "Mother Williams, I wanted to talk to you about Samantha."

Hattie sat the gold pen down and took a sip of cold water.

"May I be direct with you?" Cynthia said, leaning in closer.

Hattie treated it as a rhetorical question.

"Some of the members have been talking, and well . . . we're very concerned about Samantha."

"How so?" Hattie asked calmly.

"It's only been a month since Hezekiah's death, God rest his soul. We are concerned that she may not be giving herself enough time to grieve. She was back in the pulpit only a week after he died, and now she's taken on being the interim pastor. Some of us think we, I mean the board of trustees, may have overestimated how strong she really is. As you well know, it takes time for a woman to get over the loss of a husband. How long did it take for you to get over the death of your husband?"

Again Hattie did not respond.

Cynthia stumbled briefly in the silence but quickly regained her purpose and continued. "I think . . . I mean some of us think, that in the shock of Hezekiah's murder, the trustees may have put too much on Samantha too soon. She needs time to heal, wouldn't you agree, Mother Williams?"

Hattie studied her intently. She could see her glow of intensity. *Too cool of a customer to sweat, but not too cool to hide her true heart.*

Hattie heard the words Cynthia spoke, but even more clearly she heard her heart. She acknowledged there was some truth in the trustees acting too hastily in appointing Samantha as interim pastor. There was also truth in a widow needing time to grieve. But Hattie knew Samantha was not grieving. However, the truth was overshadowed by the vision of Samantha leading the masses of lost souls to God. The poorly veiled entreaty by Cynthia to make her husband, Percy, pastor once again forced Hattie to decide what was most important. Leading souls to Christ or seeing to it that Samantha got all that she deserved.

"Sister Pryce, who do you think should be pastor?"

"I think it's obvious, don't you? Reverend Pryce and I have prayed about this ever since Hezekiah was killed, and with God's help, and your prayers, we are willing to take the position, for the good of the church and for Samantha Cleaveland."

Hattie grew weary of the insults to her intelligence and said calmly, "You mean for the good of Cynthia Pryce, don't you?"

Cynthia's charming and pious facade quickly melted to reveal her heart. Her face grew hard, her jaw clenched, and her eyes tightened. "No, not for me, Mother Williams," she said curtly. "This would be an enormous sacrifice on my part." Cynthia could barely contain the contempt she felt for the old woman who held so much power in her arthritic hands.

A side of Hattie that few rarely had the opportunity to see emerged in full force. "You've been chomping at the bit for years, and now that Hezekiah is gone, you see it as the opportunity to get what you've always wanted—to be the first lady of New Testament Cathedral."

In the face of such candor Cynthia found it impossible to continue the charade. "Okay, Mother Williams," she said coolly. "There doesn't seem to be any point in denying that to you. Yes, I want to be first lady, and I think I'd make a damned good one. But that's not the point. New Testament Cathedral needs someone at the helm who can lead us all through this grieving process. Someone who can give their all to this ministry, and there's no way Samantha can do that now. The woman just buried her husband. She can't focus on saving souls. You'd be doing her a favor by making Percy the pastor."

"I think you underestimate Samantha Cleaveland."

"No, Mother, I don't think I have in this case."

"So, what are you asking me to do?"

"Reverend Davis is going to call a special session of the board of trustees. At that meeting Percy will be nominated for the position of pastor. I'm asking you to support Percy as the permanent pastor of New Testament Cathedral."

***

Danny sat alone in a window seat at the coffee shop a short walk from his apartment in the West Adams District. The room was comfortable, with clusters of cushioned chairs, worn wooden tables, and racks of throwaway neighborhood newspapers and magazines scattered on surfaces. The space was so comfortable, it felt contrived to Danny. The tables, floors, and walls were all made from distressed wood that could not have been as old as some of the magazines scattered around the room.

Must have taken a lot of planning by some West Hollywood queen to make it look this lived in, he thought.

There were only two other customers. An attractive young woman was sitting on a comfy couch in the center of the room. An aqua, orange, and blue scarf was wrapped around her head like a turban, and a bouquet of sandy brown dreads sprang from the top. Brown beads and milky white cowrie shells dangled from the tip of each braid. She wore large round earrings, each bearing the pounded imprint of the jeweler's hammer. Her baggy dress was accessorized with wooden and bronze African bracelets and silver rings with large green and amber stones. She sat alone, with her legs folded under her, reading *Love Poems* by Nikki Giovanni.

Danny noticed her sandals. They were expensive and wrapped her delicate feet with straps of new brown leather. *Third-generation Baldwin Hills,* he thought as he sipped his iced coffee.

The only other customer in the shop was a man who on occasion discreetly tried to make eye contact with Danny. He looked to be in his mid- to late forties. In an odd way he reminded Danny of Hezekiah. But that was not unusual. The mailman, bus drivers rolling by, and even Lester Holt from *The Today Show* reminded Danny of Hezekiah. The man in the coffee shop was tall, with a thick, black, bushy mustache. So thick and so black, Danny assumed he either dyed it or used a mascara brush to make it look so perfect. He wore a black suit and a red tie. He seemed out of place in the casual neighborhood coffee shop, but he was nonetheless comfortable across the room reading the newspaper and sipping a cup of steaming coffee, occasionally glancing in Danny's direction. Danny could see the man from the corner of his eye, but he never looked directly at him for fear of inadvertently initiating an unwanted connection.

The room smelled of freshly roasted coffee beans being brewed by the lone barista. The mournful voice of Nina Simone whispered gently from places unknown.

"There a light
A certain kind of light
It's never shown on me
I want my whole life to be
Lived with you
Lived with you

There's a way
Everybody say
Do each and every little thing
What good does it bring
If I ain't got you, if I ain't got you
If I ain't got you."

Danny wished the song would end. It seemed the music was playing so cruelly just for him, a sad soundtrack to his life.

You don't know
What it's like
Baby, you don't know
What it's like
To love somebody
To love somebody
The way I love you

As Danny looked out the window at the steady stream of cars whizzing by on the boulevard, he heard a gentle tap on the wooden table.

Danny looked up sharply and saw the warm smile of Gideon Truman, who was standing above him.

"I'm sorry if I startled you," Gideon said. "I said your name, but you didn't hear me."

Gideon looked very casual wearing a navy blue jogging jacket over a white T-shirt, denim jeans, and white running shoes.

"I was listening to the music," Danny said without standing. "Such a sad song. It reminds me of my life. Have a seat."

"Let me order you another coffee. What are you having?"

"I've barely touched this one," Danny said, noticing his drink for the first time in the last ten minutes. "You go ahead. Maybe I'll get another one later."

When Gideon retuned, he sat at the table, directly opposite Danny. "Thanks for agreeing to meet with me again," he said, casually placing a freshly brewed cup of coffee and a napkin on the table. The vapor from the cup formed an aromatic partition between the two men. "I wasn't sure if you'd want to see me again after our last encounter."

"What do you mean? You were very kind to me. I have to apologize for getting so emotional. You caught me off guard with those e-mails."

"I should be the one apologizing. It was very insensitive of me to confront you like that. I've been a reporter for so long, I guess I sometimes forget people have feelings."

"Thank you. I realize you're just doing your job."

"That's no excuse. I should have been more aware of how this all must have impacted you."

Danny looked Gideon directly in the eyes and asked, "Have you ever lost someone you loved?"

"I have not. I can only imagine what you're going through, Danny. It must be very difficult for you."

Danny looked again to the window. A cyclist wearing fluorescent yellow biking gear and a bulbous helmet rode by. The number 210 bus, filled with commuters, rolled to a stop on a nearby corner to unload and load more passengers. Stoplights at the intersections flashed yellow, red, and green, and old ladies trying to look invisible in coats too bulky for such a sunny day rolled two-wheeled metal carts filled with a week's worth of groceries home. The world seemed to go on carelessly, oblivious to Danny's pain.

"Some days I don't think I can get out of bed, it hurts so much," Danny finally responded. "It's as if it was me who was shot that morning. Sometimes I wish it had been me. Then at least I wouldn't have to live with this pain."

Gideon resisted the urge to reach out and touch Danny's hand. Instead, he motioned to the barista behind the counter to bring another glass of iced coffee for Danny.

"I know it feels like your life has ended, but it's true that time heals wounds. Give yourself permission to mourn. It's all part of the healing process."

Danny looked again at Gideon but did not respond. In the midst of the silence, the barista arrived with a tall glass of cold coffee. The ice cubes clinked against the sides of the glass as he placed it in front of Danny.

"Thank you," Danny said to the young man, seeing the tattoo of a snake wrapped around his arm.

"Do you have anyone in your life you can talk to about how you're feeling?"

"Hezekiah was my confidant. I've only told one person about him. I was too afraid he would get hurt if someone knew about us. He had always warned me if anyone found out about us, it would destroy him. Ironic, isn't it? Before he died, he told me about a reporter who had found out about us. The reporter who was found dead in his home two days after Hezekiah was killed."

"Do you think their deaths are related?"

"I didn't think that until you showed me the e-mails. Now it feels out of control. I don't know how many people out there know about me. Are you going to tell me who gave you the e-mails?"

"I'm sorry, Danny. I can't."

It hurt Gideon to hold back the information from Danny. He wanted to tell him everything, everything he knew about Hezekiah, but more importantly, everything he knew—and those things he didn't know—about himself. When he looked in Danny's eyes, he sensed Danny could tell him things about himself that he didn't know. It was the exact sense of vulnerability he had felt in the presence of Hattie Williams. He felt Danny could see into his soul and tell him secrets he had kept from himself.

Gideon felt exposed and in dire need of a diversion. "Who do you think killed Hezekiah?"

Danny did not hesitate in his response. "I know who killed him. She may not have pulled the trigger, but I know she had something to do with it."

Gideon looked surprised. "*She?* Who are you talking about?"

"His wife, Samantha Cleaveland." When Danny said her name, he felt a sense of relief. By saying it to Gideon, the knowledge was no longer his burden to bear alone. He didn't know why, but he trusted Gideon. Not to keep a secret, but to be sensitive enough to know which facts were important enough to share and those that were best kept private because they might harm someone unnecessarily.

"Did she know about you too?"

"Hezekiah told her a few weeks before he died. On the morning he was killed, he had planned to announce that he was stepping down as pastor."

"How do you know that?"

Danny had a puzzled look on his face. "He was my lover for two years. We talked to each other about everything. We didn't have secrets from each other. I didn't want him to give up everything for me, and I tried to talk him out of it. But his mind was made up. It wasn't only me he was leaving the church for. He was leaving it for himself too. He felt his life had been a lie up until that point. He felt he . . ." Danny stopped mid-sentence. "I don't know why I'm telling you all this. Are you going to report this on your show? I guess it would make you an even bigger reporter than you already are."

Gideon had forgotten he was a reporter until Danny reminded him. He felt more like a man helping someone he loved through a difficult time. At that moment Gideon was embarrassed he was a reporter, and wanted to apologize for the profession he had chosen.

"Danny, I want you to know I would never do anything to hurt you. If you tell me something that you would prefer be kept between you and me, then you have my word it will go no further than us."

Danny looked into Gideon's eyes and said, "For some reason I believe you. Maybe it's because I *need* to believe you."

"I wouldn't lie to you, Danny. I respect and like you too much to lie to you."

"Why not? You're a reporter. I thought you guys would do or say anything to get a story."

Gideon was embarrassed again. His face was flushed beneath the sun-bronzed skin. He needed to convince Danny that he could be trusted. "I won't deny I've said and done some things in my career to get a story that I'm not proud of, but for some reason I want you to trust me. For some reason I feel the need to earn your trust."

"Why is that?"

"I don't really know. Maybe because deep down I'm the one who really needs someone to trust."

"I understand that. Hezekiah and I came to the same conclusion. He once told me he loved me so deeply and gave his love unconditionally because he needed me to love him. He felt I was the only person who could truly love him. I felt the same way about him. The more I loved him, the more he seemed to love me in return."

Gideon resisted the urge to touch Danny's face. He understood how Hezekiah could fall so deeply in love with this gentle soul that sat across the table from him.

"So, what makes you think Samantha had something to do with his death?" Gideon asked, again needing a distraction from his raw emotions.

"Have you met her?"

"Yes, only once."

"I suspect once is enough if you're able to look beyond that thin veneer of piety. She's an evil woman. I know that sounds dramatic, but I also know it's true."

"But she loved him?" Gideon asked with genuine naïveté.

"Samantha Cleaveland only loves herself. It's obvious. If the world had found out Hezekiah was gay, she would have lost everything. The church, the television ministry, the house and, most importantly, the power. She ran New Testament Cathedral when Hezekiah was alive, and now that he's out of the way, she doesn't have to stand behind him anymore. With him dead, she gets to play the brave grieving widow and keep everything. She's the only person that benefits from his death. I warned Hezekiah she would do anything to stop him from leaving her, and she did. He didn't believe me."

Gideon sat in disbelief. "Can you prove any of this?"

"I can't prove anything. I don't care what happens to Samantha Cleaveland. I just want to move away from this city and put this behind me. I feel like that's the only way I'll ever survive this."

"But you can't just let her get away with it. If what you're saying is true, don't you think she should be held accountable?"

"She will be," Danny replied calmly.

Danny looked again to the window. He could see Hezekiah's reflection looking back at him in the glass. The man he had loved so deeply was now reduced to a faded image in a window plastered with flyers for the next local spoken-word competition, workers' comp attorneys, and car-detailing discounts.

Gideon continued, "Have you considered, Danny, that you might be in danger? If she killed once, who's to say she wouldn't do it again?"

"Of course I've considered it. I'm awake half the night thinking about it," Danny said sharply. Hearing Gideon speak the words made the threat more real and frightening. "If you were able to find me, I'm sure she's already done so by now."

"All the more reason for you to come forward about your affair," Gideon said, leaning over the table that separated them. "If no one knows about the connection between you and Hezekiah other than Samantha and possibly the person who killed him, then if something happens to you, she would have no fear of it being linked to Hezekiah's murder."

Gideon's voice grew louder as he spoke. Danny scanned the room for prying ears. The man in the suit had left. The attractive young earth woman was still engrossed in her book, but now with the addition of earbuds. The tattooed barista was distracted by the grind of roasted Sumatra coffee beans.

"Don't you see?" Gideon continued, lowering his voice to a whisper. "If you spoke publicly about it, I don't think she'd be stupid enough to touch you, for fear of both trails leading back to her. The longer you hide, the longer you're in danger."

"And, more importantly, you would get another salacious story to add to your already impressive credits," Danny said sarcastically.

Gideon flinched from the directness of the comment. The fragile young man had somehow made him forget again that he was a reporter. There was no denying the outing of Pastor Hezekiah T. Cleaveland would launch his already enviable career into the stratosphere. But while he was sitting in the little coffee shop with Danny, the thought had never entered his mind. Instead, he had become consumed with figuring out how he could come to Danny's rescue.

"I can understand how you could think that," Gideon said after recovering from the blow. "But that was not my motivation for suggesting you come forward."

"Then what is your motivation, Mr. Truman?" Danny asked suspiciously.

Faced with the blunt question, Gideon was reminded of how he felt whenever he was confronted by one of his many obsessed fans: the marriage proposals from women who believed their union was destined by God; the neatly wrapped packages of homemade cookies, which were immediately tossed into the garbage; the woman who had professed her eternal love for him every morning and every evening at the studio gate, forcing him to file a restraining order against her. *If he knew how I felt about him after only meeting twice, he would file a restraining order against me too,* Gideon thought.

"I'm suggesting it because I don't want to see another person hurt," Gideon finally said. "You may think I'm an opportunistic talking head, and I can understand how you could come to that conclusion, but I'm not. I don't like to see bad things happen to good people, and if I were in your position, I would hope someone would care enough about me to give me the same advice."

"Well, you're not in my position, are you?" Danny said coldly. "And I don't believe for a second that you're not interested in exploiting me to benefit your own ca-reer. It's because of people like you that Hezekiah and I had to look over our shoulders for two years. You're no better than the reporter who found out about us. He was willing to destroy anyone and anything in his path to get a headline, and I have no reason to believe you would not do the same."

Danny stood up abruptly. His chair scraped the wood floor, sending a screeching reverberation through the room.

Without looking at Gideon, he calmly said, "You don't seem to understand that if I came forward, I'd be placing myself in even more danger than if I stayed silent. At least this way I won't have to deal with the wrath of the whole country for defiling their beloved pastor Cleaveland. It would be like putting a target on my back. This meeting is over, Mr. Truman. I'm sorry I agreed to meet with you and that I wasted your time."

Danny moved swiftly toward the door.

Gideon stood and shouted, "Danny, wait!" But it was too late. The front door had already closed behind Danny. Gideon could see him walking past the window and jaywalking across the street.

The young woman, still reading love poems on the couch, resisted the urge to look in his direction. *Hope they work it out,* she thought. *They make a cute couple.*

"And we're on in five . . . four . . . three . . . two and . . . "

"Good evening, America. I'm Gideon Truman, and welcome to *Truman Live.*"

Four cameras were pointing at Gideon from different vantage points in the television studio. Each capturing a side more attractive than the one before. He was framed by an electric blue backdrop that made him resemble a living Andy Warhol painting hanging in a Manhattan gallery. He was bathed in blistering studio light. Crew members pushed buttons, moved hefty electrical cords, and focused lenses as Gideon read from the scrolling teleprompter just below the camera in front of him.

"We are continuing our coverage this evening of the brutal murder of Reverend Hezekiah T. Cleaveland, pastor of New Testament Cathedral and head of the worldwide television network."

The key to Gideon's popularity was his ability to make each viewer believe he was talking only to him or her. The viewers felt that they were having a quiet chat with an old friend in their living room or bedroom. A fact he himself didn't even realize.

"Less than a month ago, Reverend Hezekiah T. Cleaveland, the pastor of New Testament Cathedral in Los Angeles, was brutally gunned down during a Sunday morning service in his fifteen-thousand-seat mega church."

As Gideon spoke, images of the mayhem that followed Hezekiah's death that Sunday morning flashed on the screen. Camera crews had captured the reactions of members of the congregation who witnessed the assassination. A woman in a pink suit with an equally pink hat wept in her husband's arms. Children clung to their mothers' waists, and police scurried about, looking brave for the evening news.

"My guests this evening are well-known ministers in their own right," Gideon continued. "First, we have Pastor Maurice Millier joining us via satellite from his mega church, Good Shepherd Ministries, in Atlanta, Georgia."

The screen split, and suddenly Gideon was joined by a smiling man with a receding hairline, wearing a black-and-white pin-striped suit. He didn't have the benefit of Gideon's gifted and devoted makeup artist. Instead, his forehead glowed like a fallen halo.

"Welcome, Pastor Millier. Also joining us is Dr. Joyce Goodhart. Dr. Goodhart is a professor of theology at Fuller Seminary in Southern California. Thank you for being with us this evening."

Dr. Goodhart had a sour, yet somber expression. Her pageboy haircut, which she had worn since high school, gave hint to her precise and logical mind.

"And, finally, a very dear friend of Pastor Cleaveland," Gideon continued. "Reverend Richard Johnson, pastor of First Bethany Church of Los Angeles. I want to thank you all for being here this evening."

The screen now contained their four images. Gideon, as the host, dominated the upper screen. The three guests shared the lower third. Snippets of the daily news stories scrolled beneath their stern faces. Viewers were once again given their nightly free front row seat to the *Truman Live Show*. Gideon wore a sleek black suit with a bold plaid red and white shirt. His tie was white with yellow and red stripes that seemed to twirl like a barber's pole every time you blinked your eyes.

"Why don't we start with you, Reverend Johnson? You and your wife, Victoria, were very close friends with the Cleavelands. How is Pastor Samantha Cleaveland doing since her husband was so brutally slain?"

"Thank you for having me, Gideon," Reverend Johnson blustered. An expensive toupee was perched precariously on his head. His necktie formed a puddle on top of his round belly and then made a dramatic slope to this belly button. "Let me first say to your viewers that my church, First Bethany Church of Los Angeles, is celebrating our twenty-fifth anniversary this Sunday, and everybody is welcome to come out and celebrate with us. To find out more information, just go to our Web site at www.newbethany—."

Gideon looked confused and cut in tactfully. "Congratulations, Pastor, on twenty-five years, but our viewers would be interested to hear how Pastor Samantha Cleaveland is doing after her husband's murder."

"Well, Gideon, as you said, my lovely wife and I have known the Cleavelands for years now," Reverend Johnson said reverently. "Our daughters went to school together. My wife and Samantha often meet for lunch and to pray together. This tragedy has rocked the very core of religiosity in our country." Reverend Johnson leaned in toward the camera and then pointed at it. "America needs to repent. When something like this happens to one of our great black leaders, it's a sign that we as a country have lost our way. The government doesn't want people like Hezekiah Cleaveland to have that much power. Especially if he is a black man. Martin Luther King, Jr., and now Hezekiah Cleaveland. This is a sign of the end times, America. Come to Jesus while there's still time."

Gideon diplomatically tried one last time. "Have you talked to Samantha Cleaveland since this happened?"

"I did briefly, but the poor woman was so grief stricken, she hung up on me. I can tell you, though, that Samantha is devastated by this tragedy."

"Let's hear from our other guests," Gideon said, moving on quickly. "Dr. Goodhart, what do you think about what Pastor Johnson just said? Is this a sign of our country's moral decline?"

Dr. Goodhart gave a slight but sarcastic smile for the camera. Her face became the sole image on the screen. "Though this is without question an almost unimaginable tragedy, I think it might be a slight overgeneralization to say it is indicative of some larger moral descent in our country. Let's remember this was the act of one deranged person."

The screen then split, and now Reverend Johnson shared half the spotlight. "That's what they said about Martin Luther King, Jr., but we all know the truth about that," Reverend Johnson smirked.

"Martin Luther King was assassinated by James Earl Ray, not the government," Dr. Goodhart blurted out.

"All I'm saying is that when a black man in this country gets too powerful, he somehow gets conveniently eliminated," Reverend Johnson said, leaning back in his chair with his hands clasped, forming a steeple at the top of his belly. "Millions of people around the world were devoted followers of Pastor Cleaveland,

and I think people in high places felt threatened by that," he said with an air of wisdom and insight, parting his hands and then returning them to the steeple formation when he concluded.

Dr. Goodhart's stone face smirked at the last comment.

"What do you say about all this, Pastor Millier?" Gideon asked. "Is Hezekiah Cleaveland's death a symptom of something more sinister happening in our country?"

Pastor Millier was an elegant man with a hint of gray at his temples. His glasses framed penetrating, yet gentle eyes, which had seen more than most. He'd survived only by closing them and looking inward.

"With all due respect to my colleague, Pastor Johnson, I absolutely don't think this tragedy is a sign of the end of the world or that it's linked to any government conspiracy."

The camera showed the slightly betrayed look on Reverend Johnson's face.

"I must agree with Dr. Goodhart," Pastor Millier continued. This is a tragic but, nonetheless, isolated incident perpetrated by a very sick individual. It's our job as Christians to hold up the members of New Testament Cathedral in our prayers and for us as pastors to show our love and support to Samantha Cleaveland."

"Well, that brings me to my next question," Gideon said. "Samantha Cleaveland was recently selected by the church's board of trustees to replace Hezekiah as pastor. What do you think of that? Is it too soon, considering she just lost her husband? Should they have selected someone from the outside, and do you think she is the best person to get the ministry through this crisis? Dr. Goodhart?"

"I've never met Samantha Cleaveland but—"

"Well, I have met her," Reverend Johnson inter-rupted, "and I feel that if anyone can lead New Testament Cathedral, Samantha can. Now to the question, is this too soon? I have to be honest, I was surprised when I heard she was taking over. Now, don't get me wrong. I have all the love and respect in the world for Sister Samantha, but I'm not convinced that that was the best decision on the part of the trustees."

"What do you think they should have done?" Gideon asked provocatively.

Reverend Johnson responded with gusto. "Well, I think they should have possibly considered combining their church with another, similar church."

"Similar in what way?" Gideon goaded.

"Similar in size and teachings . . ."

"You mean like your church."

"Well, my church, First Bethany Church of Los Angeles," Reverend Johnson said, looking directly into the lens of the camera, "is only half the size of New Testament Cathedral, but I think that would have been the logical and responsible thing to do. It would keep their church members together but also give poor Samantha some time to grieve and to decide if being the pastor is really what she wants to do."

"What do you think, Pastor Millier? Was it a mistake to place her in the leadership role so soon after her husband's death?"

"From what I've seen of Samantha Cleaveland, I be-lieve their board of trustees had no other choice but to name her as pastor."

"What do you mean?" Gideon asked probingly.

"I mean that she is a dynamic leader, a gifted teacher, and has always been the backbone of their ministry. She, more than anyone else, is best suited to lead

New Testament Cathedral through this crisis and to continue the good work and teachings of her late husband."

Again, the look of betrayal was hard for Reverend Johnson to conceal, and Dr. Goodhart slowly faded into the background.

"Let me direct my next question to you, Pastor Johnson. Often when a well-known person dies, skeletons from their past seem to surface. You knew Pastor Cleaveland better than most people. Should we be bracing ourselves for a mistress or maybe an illegitimate child or some other scandal to surface involving Pastor Cleaveland?"

Reverend Johnson leaned forward confidently and said with all the Sunday morning religious fervor he could summon, "I've known Hezekiah for years. I was his confidant, and he was mine. I can assure you that he loved his wife more than anything in the world. He would never have cheated on her, and I know for a fact that he never did. Sure, like any other man, he was tempted occasionally by a beautiful woman, but he never gave in to temptation. If anybody comes forward with a lie like that, you can believe it's for only one thing—money."

Samantha sat comfortably in the rear of the Escalade as it glided through the streets of Los Angeles. She was scheduled to meet her friend, Victoria Johnson, the wife of Pastor Richard Johnson, for dinner. The two had not seen each other since Hezekiah's funeral. The sun was setting over the city, and the streetlights slowly flickered on, unnoticed by pedestrians and drivers. Dino guided the vehicle with trained precision through the remains of the city's rush-hour obstacle course.

Samantha checked her watch. It was 6:40 P.M. She was already late for dinner. Samantha lowered the tinted-glass partition she had had installed between the front and rear of the car to shield her from the prying eyes and ears of drivers and security personnel. "How much longer, Dino? I'm already late," she inquired with a hint of irritation.

"Ten minutes," Dino replied over his shoulder as the partition glided closed.

Victoria was one of Samantha's closest confidants. She was the only other pastor's wife in the country whom Samantha never attempted to outshine. Victoria was her equal in every way—wealth, power, beauty—and both were more ambitious than their successful husbands.

The women were there for each other whenever one needed a shoulder to cry on over her husband's many affairs. They knew all of each other's secrets except one. Victoria was not privy to Samantha's shame over the Danny St. John affair.

As the car hurtled along, Samantha's cell phone rang. She retrieved it from her purse. The telephone screen read NO CALLER ID. Only five people had the number to her private cell: her personal assistant, Dino Goodlaw, Etta Washington, Hezekiah, and her daughter. If anyone wanted to speak to her on that phone, they would have to go through one of those five people. It wasn't Dino. She knew neither Etta nor her assistant would dare call her from a phone other than the one at the house or the church, and she doubted Hezekiah would be calling from the grave. That left Jasmine. *God, please don't let her be in jail again,* she thought. *Or even worse, the hospital got my number from her phone to call about another overdose like the one she had just after Hezekiah was killed. Poor little thing almost died that time.*

After the third and final ring Samantha pressed the TALK button. "Hello," she said curtly.

No one responded.

"Hello," she said again.

She could now hear someone breathing on the line. "Who is this?" she said cautiously.

The breathing continued. Not heavy like the precursor to an obscene call, but natural breaths.

"Jasmine, is that you? Where are you?" she said, growing irritated.

After a moment's silence she heard, "Is this Samantha Cleaveland?"

"Who is this? How did you get this number?" Samantha asked, furious at the idea of having to change her private number again.

"I'll ask the questions," came the breathy response. "Is this Samantha Cleaveland?"

Samantha removed the phone from her ear and pressed the DISCONNECT button. The phone rang again before she could return it to her purse.

NO CALLER ID, glowed from the screen again. Samantha dropped the phone in her purse. After the third ring there was a pause, and then it started again.

The Escalade pulled into the artificially lit circular drive of the restaurant. Yellow lights positioned on the ground shone up on palm trees and dense shrubs encircled by the driveway. Women in sleek summer dresses and glittering jewelry stood near the edge of the driveway with their black-suited escorts, waiting for red-vested valets to retrieve Bentleys, Maseratis, and Ferraris.

The phone rang again as Dino slowly rolled toward the drop-off point. Samantha snatched the phone from her purse and asked, "Who is this?"

"Hang up on me again and you'll regret it," came the breathy reply. "Now answer my question. Is this Samantha Cleaveland?"

"Yes, it is," she said calmly. "What do you want?"

Samantha heard a tap on the window. She didn't unlock the door. Dino knew not to disturb her if she did not respond to his tap. Instead, he stood at the ready by her door, in front of the main walkway to the restaurant entrance. Other patrons looked discreetly from the corners of their eyes to see who would emerge from the car guarded by the hulking man. Was it a rapper perhaps, or maybe a movie star?

"I know about Danny," the voice said, waiting for a reaction.

"Who is Danny?" she asked impatiently.

"I think you mean, who was sleeping with Danny? And we both know what the answer is. Pastor Cleaveland."

"Look, whoever you are, I don't have time for this bullshit. Either get to the point or I'm hanging up and calling the police," she said.

"Such a filthy mouth for a pastor," the caller said sarcastically. "Did you suck your husband's holy dick with that mouth? I know Danny did with his."

"I'm hanging up. Don't call me again, or I will call the police."

"If you hang up this phone," the voice said urgently, "I'll be forced to turn over evidence to the press that shows before your loving husband died, he was in love with a very handsome young man."

Samantha leaned forward in the seat. "What evidence?" she said. "You're crazy. My husband wasn't gay."

"To start, I've got a stack of e-mails full of language so graphic, it would make even you blush. There's some in there that even prove you knew about it."

"You're lying."

"Don't call me a liar again, bitch, or this time next week you and your dead husband will be on the cover of every tabloid in the country," the voice said angrily.

"How dare you threaten me? I just buried my husband. What kind of monster are you?"

"You can save the grieving widow routine for your Sunday morning sermon. I know you were glad to get rid of him. His dick almost cost you millions. I wouldn't be surprised if you had something to do with his death yourself."

Samantha froze after hearing the last words. With lightning speed and cold logic, she weighed the cost of either revelation surfacing in public and decided she could not risk even the rumors being discussed.

"What do you want from me?"

"Now, that's what I like, a woman who knows when she's been screwed."

"There's no need to be vulgar," Samantha said coolly.

"You're not in a position to preach to me. In this relationship I'm the preacher. You do what I say. Got it?"

Samantha was silent. During the conversation the well-heeled patrons in front of the restaurant came and went, many without benefit of seeing who occupied the black Escalade. Dino stood firmly at the rear door, unfazed by the irritated valets, who were forced to maneuver around the car in the narrow drive.

"I want one million dollars, cash. You have seventy-two hours to make it happen. That gives you until Saturday night to come up with the money."

"A million dollars, you're out of your mind," she said.

"Maybe I am. Then I guess I should hang up and let Gideon Truman decide if I'm crazy."

"No, wait," Samantha said quickly. "Don't hang up. I don't have that kind of money."

"Bullshit," the caller said loudly. "You collect three times that much every Sunday morning. Why don't you take up a special offering this Sunday? Tell them it's for your favorite charity."

"There is no way I can come up with that much cash on such short notice."

"Every time you lie to me, the price goes up five hundred thousand. It's now one-point-five million."

"You can't prove any of this. My husband was not gay," Samantha said emphatically.

"Two million," the voice said calmly.

Samantha paused to regain her composure. "What will you give me in return?" she finally asked.

"My word that you will never hear from me again," the voice said sincerely.

Samantha scoffed. "The word of a blackmailer . . ."

"I prefer to think of myself as a keeper of secrets."

"I'll need more time," Samantha said hesitantly.

"You don't have more time. I will call you in two days with instructions. If you contact the police, I will immediately send copies of every e-mail in my possession to all the major news outlets in the country. I know this all sounds like such a cliché, but trust me, Samantha, this is real life," the voice said with a slight chuckle and disconnected the line.

Samantha sat momentarily dazed. She could see Dino through the darkly tinted window. The cell phone was still warm in her hand.

Two million dollars, she thought. *I'll kill the son of a bitch before I give him two million dollars.*

Samantha released the lock, and on cue Dino opened the door. Her slender calf emerged from the rear of the vehicle. The curiosity of the onlookers waiting for their cars to be brought around was fully satisfied as the beautiful woman emerged from the rear of the vehicle. The heels of her Dolce & Gabbana brown suede pumps gently clicked on the cobblestone path as she walked under a long green awning toward the glass double door entrance. The brown silk dress she wore flowed like water around her thighs as she made her way through the bedazzled onlookers.

Even for those few in the crowd who didn't know exactly who she was, her carriage, her stunning beauty, the exquisite liquid dress, and the sparkling diamonds that encircled her wrist immediately elevated her in their eyes to the status of celebrity. Samantha hated making eye contact with empty faces in a crowd, and tonight was no exception. She ignored the awestruck gasps and such whispers as "That's Samantha Cleaveland," from envy-stricken women and such replies as "My God, she's stunning," from their ogling male companions.

She was greeted by the tuxedo-wearing owner of the restaurant, who eagerly swung the doors open to welcome her. "Good evening, Pastor Cleaveland. We're so pleased you decided to dine with us this evening. I am so sorry for your loss. He was a very good man."

Samantha extended her down-turned hand, which the well-dressed man lifted and kissed gently. "Your dinner companion is waiting for you at our best table in the house. Please follow me," he said with his most impressive French accent.

Samantha, however, was not impressed. The words *two million dollars* continued to ring in her four-carat-diamond-studded ears. As she made her way through the restaurant behind the owner, other diners craned to see her entrance. Samantha raised the bar in the restaurant, which catered to the city's wealthiest and most beautiful citizens. Conversations paused as she walked by. The nibbling of escargot, foie gras, and Almas caviar stopped mid-chew when her presence was felt seconds before she was seen. Everyone felt someone important had entered the building. If she had been the wind, the room's temperature would have dropped twenty degrees, tables would have been toppled, and freshly coiffed hair would have been left in ruins.

Victoria stood as Samantha approached. She wore a tight-fitting cream pantsuit. Her signature diamond broach shaped like a butterfly twinkled on her lapel. One hand was still gloved in sleek buttery-cream-colored leather.

The owner stepped to one side and, with a sweep of his hand, presented to Samantha a perfectly appointed table filled with crystal, silver, and white linens. A single candle flicked in the center. He waited patiently behind a chair he positioned for Samantha as the two women exchanged air kisses.

"*Bon appétit*, ladies," said the owner, who was honored to be dismissed by Samantha.

Before the women could settle into their comfortable chairs, a tall man with a chiseled face and wavy black locks tucked behind his ears approached. "Good evening, ladies. I am Rancor, your sommelier."

"I don't care who you are, handsome," Victoria snapped. "I've been sitting at this damn table for the last ten minutes with nothing to drink. Bring us a bottle of nineteen-sixty-six Dom Pérignon."

"I thought you were trying to cut back," Samantha said.

"I am, dear. I'm only having one bottle tonight," Victoria replied, removing the last glove. "Don't start lecturing me again, girl. I'm a grown-ass woman."

"I know you are. I wasn't lecturing, just asking."

The sommelier vanished, unnoticed by the women. Word slowly spread through the gold-lit dining room as to who the two beautiful women were.

"Who is the woman dining with Pastor Samantha Cleaveland?" a man in a party of six at a nearby table asked his waiter.

The waiter bent down. "That is Victoria Johnson," he whispered. "Her husband is the pastor of another mega church."

"I must find out who Samantha's designer is," a stylishly dressed French woman at another table said to her tanned and toned husband. "That dress is fabulous."

"Oh shit, I'm sorry, honey. I forgot about Hezekiah," Victoria said loudly, causing even more heads to turn. "I haven't seen you since the funeral. So you finally went ahead and did it?" she said, laughing.

Samantha leaned in and looked at her hard. "Keep your voice down. What do you mean, did it?"

"Killed that prick. I didn't think you had it in you, girl. I told you to break his legs, not kill him." Victoria laughed out loud again. "Where is that gay-ass waiter with my champagne?" she said, craning her neck, which caused the diamond butterfly on her lapel to flicker in the candlelight. "At least you know he won't be fucking around on you anymore."

Samantha's hand trembled slightly. "That isn't very funny, Victoria. You know I didn't kill him," she said angrily.

"Calm down, girl. I was only joking," Victoria said, reaching across the table to touch Samantha's trembling hand. "Sammy, what is wrong with you? You're shaking. Are you all right?"

At that moment the sommelier arrived, placing a pedestaled ice bucket next to the table. Victoria reached for the crystal flute before he could fill it completely.

"That's enough, thank you," she said curtly. "What do you think I am? A drunk?"

"No, ma'am. I'm sorry. Your waiter will be with you shortly. Enjoy your meal."

Victoria took a long sip and continued. "Now, what is going on with you? I know this isn't about Hezekiah. Shit, I wish some crackhead would kill Richard. Hell, I'd pay him myself."

Samantha was silent and took a sip of champagne.

"Come on, girl. I don't like seeing you like this. Did I upset you with my big mouth?" Victoria said softly. "You know better than to take me too seriously."

"No, no, it's not that. I just got a frightening telephone call on the way here."

"From whom?"

"I don't know," Samantha said.

"What was it about?"

Samantha took another sip of champagne and said, "Blackmail."

Victoria choked on her drink when she heard the word and coughed loudly, again drawing attention to the table. "Blackmail?" she blurted. "What do they want?"

"Please keep your voice down," Samantha said firmly. "A ridiculous amount, two million dollars."

Another choking cough escaped from Victoria's red lips. "Oh, shit," she said, this time in a whisper. "What the fuck for?"

"Hezekiah, of course," Samantha said scornfully.

Samantha surveyed the room to ensure their conversation could not be overheard. She hesitated, but Victoria prompted her to say more with a swipe of her hand.

"I never told you this, Victoria. I guess the indignity of it was much too embarrassing for me, but Hezekiah was having an affair with . . . with a man before he was killed."

Victoria's jaw fell open. She cupped her mouth to prevent a gasp from escaping. There was silence at the table while the two women looked desperately into each other's eyes.

"Oh ... my ... fucking ... God," Victoria finally said, pausing after each word. She reached for the bottle of champagne, filled her glass to the rim, and took two long gulps. "Sammy. Honey, this is un-fucking-believable. Sleeping with every whore he could stick his dick into wasn't enough. The bastard had to have dick too. Un-fucking-believable."

"I don't know what I'm going to do," Samantha said softly.

At that moment the waiter appeared mysteriously at the table. "Good evening, ladies. Welcome to Le Cheval. My name is—"

Victoria immediately held up her hand. "I don't need to know your name," she said without looking in the shocked man's direction. "Could you please give us a moment?" she said sharply. "We'll let you know when we're ready."

The stunned waiter vanished without another word.

"Honey, you need to call the police."

"I can't do that, and you know it," Samantha said. "If this gets out, I'll be a laughingstock. I could lose everything."

"What are you talking about? People won't blame you if your husband was a faggot. If anything, they'll feel sorry for you."

"That's exactly the point. I don't want people feeling sorry for me over some dumb bullshit like this," Samantha said angrily. "It's bad enough I have to hear, 'I'm so sorry for your loss,' from every asshole I talk to. And the timing could not be any worse. I've got the board of trustees and that bitch Cynthia Pryce watching my every move. They're just looking for a reason to not make me permanent pastor. A public scandal like this would be just enough for them to kick my ass to the curb."

As she said the words, a couple appeared at the table. The woman was close to six feet tall and wore a slinky yellow silk dress. Her hair was ribbons of golden locks that cascaded around a model's face. Her companion seemed almost half her height. A Rolex watch weighted his arm down to his pudgy side.

"Pastor Cleaveland," he said, extending his hand. "We don't mean to disturb you, but we wanted to extend our condolences for your loss. I met your husband a few times, and he was a great man."

Victoria let out an irritated huff in response to the interruption.

Samantha lit up as if she were on television. Her back straightened, and she flashed her signature smile. "That is very kind of you," she said. "May I introduce you to my friend Victoria Johnson?"

Victoria grimaced in the couple's direction but said nothing.

"Again, we're sorry to bother you. We just wanted—"

"We got it. You're sorry. Condolences, blah, blah, blah," the champagne said on Victoria's behalf. "Now, could you please leave us alone?"

"Victoria," Samantha said sharply. "You'll have to excuse my friend. She just got a bit of bad news. Thank you very much for your kind words."

The wounded couple slipped away silently.

"That was unnecessary, Victoria."

"I don't care about them. I'm more worried about you right now. What are you going to do?"

Samantha leaned back in her chair and placed a napkin in her lap. "I don't think I have a choice. I can't let even a rumor like that get out. I've got to pay him."

"Do you have that kind of money?"

"Of course I do."

"How the hell are you going to explain that to your accountants?"

"I won't have to. I have offshore accounts that not even Hezekiah knew about," Samantha said dismissively. "It's not a question of the money. I'm just so mad at this son-of-a-bitch. I don't like to be manipulated like this," she added, clenching the champagne flute almost to the point of breaking it. "If I ever find out who he is, I swear I'll . . ." Samantha stopped mid-sentence.

"I told you, girl, I know people who specialize in shit like this. They can make this whole thing disappear if you want. It'll be expensive, but nowhere near two million dollars," Victoria said wickedly.

"Thanks, girl. I knew I could count on you," Samantha said, shaking off the fear that had gripped her since the telephone call, "but I think I can handle this on my own."

"Are you sure, girl? This could be some psycho. How do you know it's not the same nutcase that killed Hezekiah?"

"I don't know that," Samantha said, avoiding eye contact. "It did cross my mind when I was speaking to him."

"Are you sure you don't want me to make a call for you? Believe me, these boys will root out the motherfucker in a day, and that will be the last anyone will ever hear from him."

"If I can't handle it, you'll be the first person I'll call."

"All right, honey. But you better be fucking careful," Victoria said, reaching across the table to take Samantha's hand. "I don't want to go to any more Cleaveland funerals this year."

***

Gideon knocked on the heavy wire-mesh security door at Danny's apartment. His button-down downy white shirt, perfectly pleated khakis, and brown Gucci loafers seemed out of place in the respectable yet edgy neighborhood. The pounding made a familiar tinny rattle that was often heard in neighborhoods where barred doors and windows were required for relatively intruder-free living. He pounded harder the second time. The building was a two-story, 1920s fourplex splattered with bubbly beige stucco and bold wooden trim around the windows and doors. The front yard was neat, with freshly mown grass, recently pruned pine trees, and large wagging elephant's ear plants. Oversize ferns nestled under the windows and around the porches of each of the four units.

Gideon saw a cat lounging on the windowsill in Danny's apartment. The scraggly gray cat seemed oblivious to the pounding on the door. Then, suddenly, the preoccupied cat casually lifted his head and looked over his shoulder into the apartment. Gideon saw the drape move slightly, and Danny appeared in the window.

Gideon waved and held up a small box tied with a red ribbon. Danny looked blankly at Gideon and was clearly deciding whether to open the door to the uninvited guest or simply to ignore him.

Danny disappeared from the window, and the lazy cat rested his head on the sill again. Gideon then heard the dead-bolt locks on the wooden door behind the security screen turn, and the door opened. He could see only the silhouette of Danny through the security screen.

"What do you want?" Danny asked coldly.

"Hello, Danny," Gideon said. "I wanted to apologize for the other day. I didn't mean to offend you."

"Apology accepted. Is there anything else?"

Gideon held up the box. "This is for you."

"I don't want any gifts from you."

"It's not a gift exactly," Gideon said sheepishly. "It's more a peace offering. I felt bad that I had hurt you. You don't need any more hurt in your life, and I was devastated to think that I had caused you any additional distress." Gideon extended the box toward the door and said, "Please. I don't expect anything in return, other than assurance that you accept my apology."

Danny stood with his feet planted firmly on the hardwood floor in the entry hall. Gideon couldn't see the suspicious expression on his face through the black screen; then suddenly he heard the metallic churning of another lock, and the prison door swung open. Danny stood shirtless in the threshold. Gideon immediately noticed his well-defined torso. He had a swimmer's build. His skin was like brown whipped butter spread over a perfectly flat stomach, moderately muscular shoulders and chest. He wore a pair of baggy, faded blue jeans that sagged just below the waist, exposing the red elastic band of his boxer shorts.

"You can come in only on one condition," Danny said flatly.

"What's that?" Gideon asked, slightly raising his eyebrow.

"You have to swear you won't involve me in any way in your investigation. It's too dangerous, and I don't want to live the rest of my life looking over my shoulder for that horrible woman."

Gideon, without hesitation, raised his right hand and said, "I don't want you to live in fear, either. I promise."

Danny looked him in the eye, as if attempting to discern the sincerity of his promise. Without saying a word, he slowly stepped aside and allowed Gideon to enter. Gideon followed Danny into the living room.

"How did you find out my address?" Danny asked in a softer tone.

Gideon smiled and said, "You forget I'm a reporter. We have our ways."

"That's the problem. I can't forget you're a reporter. Sometimes I think you wish I would. You want a cup of coffee or tea?"

"Sometimes I wish I could forget myself," Gideon said as he instinctively surveyed the room. "Coffee would be nice, if it's not too much trouble."

"I just made a pot. Hope decaf is okay. Have a seat," Danny said, disappearing down the hall toward the kitchen.

"That's fine," Gideon called out to his well-defined back.

Gideon sat on the edge of the couch under the bay window and placed the box on the coffee table. The cat purred and licked his paw on the sill, unfazed by his presence. His reporter instincts immediately kicked in, and the deductions quickly mounted.

Not many pictures on the walls, he thought. *He's not comfortable here. This isn't home to him. Only a couch, and no chairs. Doesn't get, or want, many visitors. Stack of newspapers all folded to stories about Hezekiah. He's still looking for answers. The plants are wilting. Hasn't, as of yet, gotten back into a routine since Hezekiah's death.*

"Do you take sugar and cream?" Danny called from kitchen.

"Two sugars," he responded

The apartment is neat, but a faint layer of dust is evident on the coffee table. Gideon's observant mind continued without his consent. *He can manage some chores, but that's limited to those that make his life bearable. Less pressing ones are dismissed.*

He looked for signs that Hezekiah had been in the room, a Bible perhaps, or an expensive piece of art out of place amid the neat but thrift-store decor. But there was nothing: no photographs of the handsome pastor, no coat that looked too large for Danny hanging on the coatrack, no gold pen on the desk, no hint of a wealthy ecclesiastical presence ever having been in the room.

Danny returned with two steaming mugs and placed them on the coffee table. While away, he had put on a white T-shirt that did little to conceal his chiseled frame. Danny sat at the opposite end of the couch.

"Thank you," Gideon said, reaching for the mug. "What's his name?"

"What's whose name?" Danny asked suspiciously.

Gideon pointed over his shoulder and said, "The cat."

"Oh . . . that's Parker."

Gideon reached over his shoulder and scratched Parker behind his ear. The cat purred even louder. After several rubs he stood, stretched, and climbed down the back of the couch and found a place on Gideon's lap.

"Parker, get down," Danny commanded.

"No, he's fine. I like cats."

The cat ignored the human exchange, curled, and twisted until it found just the right position.

"You haven't opened the present," Gideon said. "I hope you like it."

"You don't have to give me anything. I believe you. I believe you're not trying to use me to get your story."

"Thank you," Gideon said with obvious relief. "But I'd feel even better if you accepted it." Gideon reached for the box, being careful to not disturb Parker, and handed it to Danny. "Please take it. It's really nothing."

Danny reached across the space between them and took the box. "What is it?"

"The best way to find out is to open it."

Danny pulled the ribbon on the small black box and lifted the hinged lid to reveal a Slate Serti Rolex watch. It was two toned, with a circle of cobalt blue around a champagne-gold face. The shiny metal band was silver with a gold strip running down the center. The second hand ticked proudly, as if it knew exactly how much the little time machine cost.

Danny immediately shut the box lid. "I can't accept this," he said, handing the extravagant gift back to Gideon. "Gideon, you don't give expensive gifts like this to someone you just met," he added in a firm but sympathetic voice.

He had read the rumors about Gideon like everyone else in the country. TMZ had speculated endlessly about his sexual orientation. The tabloids contained weekly pictures of the handsome Gideon Truman in restaurants or walking to his car, with titillating headlines such as IS HE OR ISN'T HE? and GAY'DEON TRUMAN?

Danny could sense the handsome man's dejection and embarrassment.

"I've done it again. Danny. I'm so sorry. I didn't mean to offend you. It's just . . ."

Danny laughed softly and said, "You didn't offend me. It's just, well, a little inappropriate, don't you think?"

"I've never been any good at this. I inevitably say or do the wrong thing," Gideon said, resting his head on the back of the couch.

"Good at what?"

Without lifting his head, Gideon turned toward Danny at the opposite end of the couch and said shyly, "Letting someone very special know that I care about them."

"So, it's true," Danny said softly.

"Yes. Most of what you've read or heard is true."

"So, I'm assuming you don't get much practice at this," Danny said with a gentle smile.

"Nope," he replied, rolling his head from side to side on the back of the couch. "Actually, I get none at all."

"That is very sad. I'm sorry."

"No, don't be. I was actually fine until I met you," Gideon said, looking at the circa 1970 light fixture dangling from the ceiling. "I understand why Hezekiah loved you. You are the gentlest, most centered person I've ever met. I feel grounded when I'm around you, and I would give anything for you to feel safe with me."

Danny sat back on the couch, his position matching Gideon's. The two men gazed up at the light fixture, and Parker continued to purr on Gideon's lap. Gideon continued to rub Parker's soft head with his right hand. Without looking in Danny's direction, Gideon laid his left hand, palm up, halfway between them on the center cushion. Except for Parker's little revving motor, the room was silent.

Danny longed to feel safe with someone again. His world had become so dark and lonely. A stark and devastating contrast to the two years he had spent with Hezekiah. There was never a lonely moment when they were in the world together. Even during the times when they weren't in each other's presence, they each knew the other was very near. They called each other two, sometimes three, times a day and e-mailed or texted even more frequently. They each seemed to instinctively know when the other needed to hear their voice. In moments of impending despair, fear, or fatigue, the telephone would ring at just the right time.

"I was thinking of you," either of them would say, "and wanted to tell you how much I love you." The looming despair, fear, or fatigue would dissipate. Or, Are u all right? the text would read. Just got a funny feeling that u needed 2 hear from me. The reply would inevitably be, I did need 2 hear from u. much better now. Will call ASAP. XOXO.

Then one day the telephone calls suddenly stopped. The e-mails didn't come. The text alert that had provided two years of sweet music to his ears didn't chime. That was the hardest part for Danny. His world had gone silent in the time it took the bullet to leave the gun, cross the expanse of the sanctuary and enter Hezekiah. Now the quiet seemed to taunt him. Danny had instinctively checked his iPhone for messages from Hezekiah for weeks after his death, even when he knew there would be none. Somehow the act of sliding the screen awake and tapping the messages icon provided him a bit of comfort, and he welcomed the comfort, no matter how small, wherever he could find it.

Gideon's hand remained extended between them on the sofa cushion. He hadn't realized how empty his life had become until he met Danny St. John. Parties in Manhattan with six-foot Nubian goddesses on his arm; holding court at the finest restaurants in Los Angeles, San Francisco, London, and Paris, with A-list celebrities, politicians, and corporate moguls competing for the pearls that fell from his lips, all felt empty. Each evening, when the parties were over and all the autographs had been signed and the models had been sent home in cabs, Gideon was alone. The void had never been apparent, because there was always another party the next night. The frantic motion of his life served as the lush green camouflage that covered the pit that ambition, fame, and wealth had dug.

Somehow Danny had removed the brush and exposed the gaping hole in his soul. It was so dark and deep that he couldn't see the bottom. When he spoke, his words echoed against the walls of loneliness. When he cried, his tears fell and never touched the floor of the bottomless pit. Today, sitting on the couch with the cat purring in his lap, he needed someone to catch his tears. He needed someone to hear his words in the pit to make them real. He needed to love someone other than himself and nourish something other than his career.

Just as Gideon was preparing to accept rejection and pull his hand away, he felt the warmth of Danny's gentle touch on his palm. The touch sent a vibration through his entire body. He felt like a tuning fork that had been tapped with a delicate silver mallet. The two men remained hand in hand at opposite ends of the couch, still and silent, for the next half hour.

Chapter 12

"I'm leaving you, Scarlett. I want a divorce."

"David, why are you doing this?"

"Our entire marriage has been a lie. It's over."

David stood firmly in the doorway to the kitchen. The house smelled of freshly brewed coffee. He was fully dressed for the day in a chocolate-brown suit that molded perfectly to his frame, a banana-yellow silk necktie, and a powder-blue shirt. He clutched a briefcase in one hand and car keys in the other.

The two had not spoken in days. Neither of them had made an attempt to reach out to the other. They each had their own reasons. In between shedding tears for Hezekiah, Scarlett had only enough energy left to care for Natalie. Combing her hair in the morning and preparing her lunch for school left her exhausted. She didn't have the strength to worry about David and hated herself for not caring.

David was still reeling from the passionate love he and Samantha Cleaveland had made on her living room floor. He could still smell the sweetness of her perfume. The thought of her touch only made him long for more. She had possessed him and now owned his soul, which he willingly gave.

"Can't we talk about this? I've told you I wasn't in love with Hezekiah. I love you. Why can't you just accept that and allow us to move on?"

"This isn't about you for once, Scarlett."

"I told you I lied to you for Natalie, not for myself."

"I don't believe that, and on some level, I don't think you believe it, either," David said coldly. "You lied because you wanted to cover your tracks and preserve the ridiculous victim routine that you've used your entire life. You slept with Hezekiah because you wanted to. He didn't rape you. You were an adult. I don't buy for a minute your 'young and naive' excuse. You knew exactly what you were doing. You wanted him, and Samantha called your bluff and put you back in your place."

"How dare you? I was the victim. I walked away on my own because I didn't want anything from them," Scarlett replied indignantly.

"Correction, darling, you walked away because you knew you couldn't get the one thing you wanted—Hezekiah. Then the wounded little girl nonsense was the perfect cover for your being slapped back into reality by Samantha. It didn't matter that I or anyone else didn't know about Natalie. The important thing was that you knew and you could feel like the victim back in your safe little cocoon of self-pity, and since then you've been alone."

Scarlett raised her hand and slapped David hard on the cheek. His head turned from the blow, but his body remained firmly planted.

"I suppose now I'm supposed to slap you back. Is this a page from your battered wife script?" he said, rubbing his stinging cheek. "I'm afraid you'll have to remind me what my next line is. I don't seem to remember this scene."

Scarlett was unprepared for his lack of emotion and his painfully pointed words. His cold demeanor was completely unexpected and left her at a loss. His words swirled in her head, almost making her dizzy. Was she the perfect victim? Did the world, in fact, revolve around her and not Natalie? Was there some twisted desire to be abandoned and left alone with her scars and wounds? Was this the monster she'd created?

She slapped him again and waited for a response. But she was greeted only with a questioning stare.

"I hate you," she finally said in almost a whisper.

"You don't hate me. Scarlett. You hate the truth about yourself."

Scarlett looked puzzled. The words stung. Her entire life she felt she had sacrificed her happiness for others. But in the face of such a damning statement, she slowly began to realize that in fact she had made all the sacrifices for herself. She needed to be the victim. It was all she knew. It was familiar and was where she felt safe and, ironically, in control.

"You're a coward to leave me for this," she said, turning her back to him and walking to the sink. "I thought you were a better man than that."

"That's where you're wrong again," he said with a hint of irony. "I'm not leaving you because you're a liar. I'm not even leaving you because you're delusional."

Scarlett turned from the sink to face David. He had not moved from the threshold. Now the span of the room divided them. Steam from the coffeemaker on the marble island formed a mist between them. "Then why?" she asked, her question tinged with a dare.

"I'm leaving you for Samantha Cleaveland."

"Pastor Cleaveland," came the voice from the intercom in Samantha's office. "I'm sorry to disturb you, but you have a call from someone who says he's a business acquaintance. He's very insistent on speaking with you."

"Who is it?" Samantha asked, placing her reading glasses on the desk.

"He refused to give his name. He said it is urgent that he speak with you now. He said to tell you it's about Danny boy."

Samantha immediately snatched the telephone from its cradle and snapped, "Put him through."

"Good morning, Samantha," the calm voice said. "It's a beautiful day, isn't it?"

Samantha cringed when she heard her name in the receiver. She resisted the urge to insist she be called Pastor Cleaveland and said, "Why are you calling me here? You have my cell number."

"It was a little test. I wanted to see if you would take my call at church. And look at this. You did. You must really like me," the voice said sarcastically.

"No, I don't like you," she said without emotion. "I pity you."

"And why is that, Samantha?"

"I pity any man who would blackmail a widow. Your mother must have fucked you up pretty bad."

"Holy shit," came the amused reply. "Do you pray for your flock with that filthy mouth?"

"Look, asshole, I have the money. Where do you want me to leave it?"

"Now, that's a good girl. Who else have you told about this?"

"Who am I going to tell? You asked for the money. I got it. Now, stop wasting my time and let's get this over with. Where do you want to meet me?"

"Griffith Park. Tomorrow, Saturday night. At midnight. At the entrance on Western Avenue drive up the road to the first parking lot. Park, turn your lights off, and wait for me."

"How will I know you?"

"I'll be the man you hand the money to. And remember, come alone. No driver and no police. If I see anything or anyone that looks suspicious, I'll leave and go straight to Gideon Truman. You know Gideon, don't you, Samantha?"

"Yes, I know him."

"I think he'd be very interested in who your late husband was sleeping with, don't you?"

"I'll be alone, but let me warn you, my friend. I'm holding up my end of this, and I expect you to hold up yours. I don't want to hear from you ever again, and you'll forget about Danny St. John. If you don't you will be very sorry you ever fucked with me," she whispered. "I won't mind losing everything I have to hunt you down like the animal you are and kill you myself."

"Don't worry. After this is over, you'll never hear from me again, Until tomorrow, then, Pastor."

Samantha heard the dial tone. The office was still. Sun poured through the windows, offering a bright and cheery contrast to the blackness she felt in her soul. A leather-bound Bible on her desk was opened to 1 Chronicles 16:22.

Saying, Touch not mine anointed, and do my prophets no harm.

It was the text she had chosen for the Sunday morning sermon. Samantha reached under her desk and retrieved a black leather duffel bag. She walked across the room to a glass console that held a crystal decanter filled with water, a set of six etched Waterford glasses on a silver tray, and a spray of exotic purple, pink, and red flowers. The 450-year-old painting of Madonna and child, *A Sacra Conversazione,* hung above the table. Samantha had bought the painting at Sotheby's only months before Hezekiah was killed.

The three darkly clothed figures in the massive oil masterpiece fawned over a squirming cherubic infant as Samantha reached behind the gold-leaf frame and released a latch. The painting slowly glided up the wall toward the twenty-foot-high glass and steel-beamed ceiling, exposing a small, cold gray vault embedded in the wall.

Samantha unzipped the duffel bag and placed it on the console, rattling the delicate glass arrangement and causing the flowers to shudder. With perfectly manicured fingers she gently manipulated the tumbler. At forty-three the dial emitted a gentle click. The second click came at thirty-nine. When she spun the dial to fifty-four, the heavy metal door gave a double click and obediently succumbed to the expert touch of the only person on earth who knew the sequence to its heart. It was simple for those who knew. The numbers were the first two digits of her, Hezekiah's, and Jasmine's cell phone numbers.

The metal box was filled with only a fraction of the Cleaveland fortune, one of several fractions that Hezekiah had known nothing of. A single-strand pearl necklace once owned by Marie Antoinette was nestled in a purple velvet box. A flawless 6.04-carat black diamond from South Africa sat uncased on a stack of stocks, bonds, and deeds to commercial properties in Milan, Santa Monica, and New York, to a villa in Saint-Jean-Cap-Ferrat, a Brazilian horse ranch, and a penthouse in Hong Kong. Her prize possession, however, sat in the front of the metal cave. It was a simple silver cross and chain that she had removed from her husband's neck as she cradled his dead body in her arms in the pulpit on the day he was murdered.

Samantha picked up the cross and ran the smooth, cold chain between her fingers. It served as evidence that she alone was the master of her fate.

In the rear of the vault were stacks of hundred-dollar bills. Each stack contained fifty thousand dollars, held together by a single white paper strip. Samantha retrieved forty of the stacks and tossed them indiscriminately into the duffel bag. The cross swung from the chain in her hand each time she threw another bundle into the bag. Their absence left only a small dent in the remaining piles of money.

The final item she pulled from the vault was a small matte black Smith & Wesson Centennial 442 snub-nosed revolver. She held the gun in the same hand as the cross and looked at it as one would an old friend or trusted ally. She expertly spun the cylinder to ensure all five cartridge chambers were filled and ready. Samantha gently placed the gun on top of the disheveled bundles of money and zipped the bag.

Samantha returned the cross to the front of the vault and closed the door. With a click of the switch on the wall, Madonna and child descended from the heavens and covered the evidence of Samantha's true heart. The cash, jewels, stocks, deeds, and bonds no longer existed. There was only the most virtuous of mothers cradling the squirming infant in her loving arms.

Samantha walked to her desk with the duffel bag swinging at her side. The extra weight caused her heels to dig deep into the plush white carpet. The door to her office flung open, and David Shackelford stormed in with a frantic assistant at his heels as Samantha returned the bag to its place under her desk and sat down.

"Pastor Cleaveland, I'm so sorry, but he just barged past me. I couldn't stop him," the nervous woman said.

"I told you it's all right," David said, blocking the woman. He moved quickly toward Samantha. "She will want to see me. Samantha, I need to talk to you now."

"Pastor Cleaveland, would you like for me to call security?" the woman called out over David's shoulders.

Samantha stood from her desk and said, "No, Amber. This is Brother Shackelford. He's a friend of the church. You can leave us alone. Thank you."

"Are you sure, ma'am? I can—"

"I said leave us alone," Samantha snapped.

The young woman walked backward with the two in her sights until the door was closed.

"What do you want, David? This is not a good time for me. I was on my way out."

David walked behind her desk, placed his hands on each of her shoulders, pulled her close, and pressed his lips to hers.

Samantha pushed him away and said, "What the hell are you doing? Are you crazy? Someone could walk in."

David kissed her hard again and said, "I don't care if someone comes in," as he nuzzled her neck.

Samantha struggled to break free. "Let me go, David. This is not the place for this."

"I love you, Samantha," David panted breathlessly. "You're all I've been able to think about. Make love to me now. Right now!"

"David, honey, stop. Stop, baby," she said, pushing him away. "There'll be plenty of time for that later. But not now, damn it. I've got a major problem I have to deal with."

David tried again to remove the distance between them, but Samantha held up her hand.

"If you have a problem, let me help. I'm here for you now, full-time."

"What do you mean, full-time?" Samantha asked suspiciously.

"I mean I've left Scarlett."

"You did what?" Samantha asked coldly. "Why on earth did you do that?"

"Because I'm in love with you, Samantha Cleaveland. I want to be with you."

"Don't be ridiculous, David. Go back to your wife. I don't want you. I don't want anyone right now. For Christ's sake, I just buried my husband."

"That's all the more reason for you to be with me. You need me. A woman like you needs a man in her life. What is the problem you're dealing with? Tell me about it. Let me help."

Samantha looked David in the eye. She could see the desperation and longing. She could also see the tent in his expensively tailored slacks.

"I don't think you can help me, David. I don't think anyone can," she said and walked to the desk and sat down.

"Try me, baby. I'm here for you." David walked to her and placed his hand on her shoulder. "Tell me. What's going on? Do you need a lawyer?"

"No, no, I don't need a lawyer. I've already got lawyers coming out my ass."

"Then what is it? Tell me."

Samantha sighed, as if exhausted. She looked toward the window and said, "All right, David, I'll tell you. I'm being blackmailed."

"Blackmailed?" David shouted. "By whom? For what?"

"I don't know who it is. It's about Hezekiah." Samantha pulled a silk handkerchief from her purse and dabbed a nonexistent tear from her eye. "It's horrible, David. Hezekiah was . . ." Samantha paused. "Hezekiah was involved with a man for two years before he died."

"What do you mean, involved?"

"Sexually. Someone found out about it. They can prove it."

"How much do they want?"

"The first payment is two million dollars. He said he'd keep coming back for more every year. There's no end to how much he'll demand."

"Oh my God. Have you called the police?"

"I can't get the police involved. I'd be ruined. The church would be ruined. New Testament could never survive a scandal like this. If it came out, that would be the end of the entire ministry, and there's more."

"More? What else?"

"He's threatened to kill me if I don't pay."

David kneeled down in front of her. "Kill you? What did he say?"

"He said if I didn't pay him every time, he would contact the media and then hunt me down like an animal and kill me."

"Baby, this is horrible," David said, squeezing her hand. "What are you going to do?"

"I don't have a choice. I have to pay him, and I'll have to keep paying him every time he asks. David, I'm so afraid."

"Maybe I should talk to him."

"And say what? 'Please don't do this anymore'? It won't work, David. There's nothing you or anyone can do. I'm going to meet him tomorrow night and give him the money." Samantha reached under the desk and slid out the duffel bag. "Here it is," she said, unzipping the bag to reveal the piles of cash and the revolver.

"What is that for?" David asked, looking at the gun.

"I told you he said he'd kill me. I want to be able to at least protect myself if necessary."

"Samantha, you can't go out there alone. It's too dangerous. You don't know what kind of psychopath this guy is. I'm going to come with you."

"No," Samantha said, standing and walking to the window. "He said I had to come alone."

"Then I'll follow you from a distance. Give me the gun. If it gets out of hand, I'll be right there."

Samantha smiled. "You are such a sweet man. I don't want to get you involved in this."

David walked behind her and placed his hands on her shoulders. "I'm in love with you, so that automatically gets me involved."

Samantha leaned back into his arms. "Have you ever shot a gun before, David?" she asked, staring out over the construction site of the new cathedral. "Do you think you could actually kill a man?"

She could feel David's heart pounding in his chest. He did not respond. Samantha leaned farther back and pressed her waist against the mound that was growing in his pants. She twisted slightly from side to side and whispered again, "Do you think you could kill a man?"

David could smell the sweet aroma of her perfume. Her warm breath sent an intoxicating bouquet to his nostrils. Before he could think, he heard the words slip from his lips into her ear. "For you I would kill a man."

Scarlett clumsily rummaged through the mirrored medicine cabinet in her bathroom. She pushed hairbrushes, bottles of lotion, and shaving creams aside, causing a container of dental floss to tumble to the counter, with minty string trailing behind. Her hands shook as she searched frantically for her Zoloft prescription. She finally found it behind two plastic bottles of peroxide. She shook the bottle, but she had taken so many after Hezekiah's death, it was empty. Next to it, however, was her prescription for Xanax, and behind that a full bottle of Prozac.

Over the years her therapist had prescribed a variety of antianxiety potions and notions to deal with the stresses that had defined her life. Zoloft was her favorite, but today she would settle for a Xanax. Scarlett swallowed the pill without water. Her knees wobbled as she made her way into the living room. Her head had not stopped spinning since the startling announcement from her husband earlier that day.

It's happening again, she thought as she stumbled to the sofa in the center of the room, blanketed in pink, green, and purple pillows. A pristine brick-framed fireplace, which had never known fire, served as the focal point of the room. Most notably there were no photographs on the mantelpiece, or anywhere else in the room, of Natalie, David, or herself. Large potted plants flanked a sliding glass window that opened to a paved patio and a modest backyard. In the center of the window was a small lemon tree, whose fruit no one in the home had ever tasted.

Scarlett ran her trembling fingers through her disheveled silky hair. She had long since given up on trying to stop the tide of tears that had been flowing since David left the house.

She's doing it again, she thought as she looked at the tree sagging from bulbous lemons on the verge of bursting and falling to the ground to rot. *Why does she have to destroy everything I love?*

The telephone on a table next to the sofa rang as she pondered the mysteries of her life. She didn't answer. On the third ring she heard, "Hello, Scarlett. This is Cynthia Pryce. When you have a moment, could you please call me? I need to talk to you about Samantha Cleaveland. My number is seven-six-one—"

Scarlett lunged across the sofa and grabbed the receiver. "Cynthia," she said with no hint of sorrow.

"Hello. I was in the garden, picking lemons from my tree, and didn't hear the phone. How are you?"

"I'm doing well. Do you have a few moments to talk about a church matter?"

"I do, but could you hold on for just a moment? I need to put these lemons in the sink."

Scarlett put the telephone on mute, wiped her wet cheeks with the sleeve of her blouse, and took three deep breaths. The little pill had begun to work its magic. Her hands had stopped shaking, and the pain from the thought of her husband leaving her was reduced to only a dull, throbbing ache. She longed for her Zoloft. One pill and she would have been completely numb by now.

"Cynthia, I'm back. I'm making lemonade for David and Natalie. Now, how can I help you? You said something about Samantha Cleaveland."

"Yes. Scarlett, this is kind of a sensitive topic. I hope I can count on your discretion."

"Of course. Now, what is this about?"

"Percy and I were approached by some of the other trustees. Now, understand if it were only one, we wouldn't have paid much attention to it. But we've been approached by a number of them."

"About what?" Scarlett asked impatiently.

"About Samantha Cleaveland. You see, dear, some of the trustees feel they may have acted in haste by naming her as interim pastor so soon after Hezekiah's death, God rest his soul. We were all terribly devastated by Hezekiah's death, and obviously not thinking clearly. They feel we put the needs of the church before her needs. As I'm sure you will agree, the pain a woman feels after the loss of a spouse is second only to the loss of a child. The poor woman has just lived through one of the most traumatic things a woman can experience, and here we are, thinking about ourselves and the church. It's terrible, just terrible, and some of the trustees feel they've made a mistake by acting so quickly."

Scarlett listened intently to the woman's rambling. She easily detected the tinge of deceit in her voice. Cynthia had never been able to fully conceal her contempt whenever she spoke of Samantha Cleaveland, no matter how hard she tried.

"Hello . . . ? Scarlett, are you still there?" Cynthia asked into the silence.

"I'm here. Go on," Scarlett said.

"Well, as I was saying, people feel we really must act quickly to correct this lapse in our judgment . . . for Samantha's sake."

"What trustees said this to you?"

Cynthia answered quickly, "I really can't say, dear. They've all spoken to me, us, in the strictest of confidence. But trust me, it's more than a majority of the trustees."

"So why are you telling me this?"

"Well, dear, as a member of the board of trustees, and as a woman, don't you think you have some responsibility to Samantha, as well? Surely you must see that action must be taken to protect her and give her time to heal, don't you?" Cynthia asked.

"So what are you proposing?"

"I'm not proposing anything, dear," Cynthia said innocently. "Rather your fellow trustees are proposing that Samantha be relieved of the awesome burden of pastor, at least for the time being, and be allowed to properly mourn the loss of her husband."

"And who do the *trustees* propose to replace her with?" Scarlett asked, already knowing the answer.

"Isn't it obvious? Percy," Cynthia said, barely concealing her arrogance. "It will completely turn our lives upside down, but Percy has convinced me that it is the right thing to do for Samantha and for New Testament. Believe me, dear, it is the last thing I want for my life right now, but I do feel some responsibility to my sister Samantha and to the memory of Hezekiah. I've spent many nights praying about this, and the Lord told me that my husband is right."

Scarlett wasn't offended by the woman's transparent attempt to deceive her. Neither was she insulted at being considered so naive as to believe she wouldn't recognize a blatant power grab. Instead, she was pleased that someone else had taken it upon themselves to challenge Samantha Cleaveland's absolute and unbridled power over New Testament Cathedral and, more importantly, her life.

"You know, *dear*," Scarlett finally said, "I've never really thought of it in those terms. I'm not sure what we were thinking. I guess it was as you said. We must have all been so traumatized after Hezekiah's death, God rest his soul, that we never considered how this would affect Samantha. The poor woman must be going through hell right now, and all we could do was think of our own needs. I feel just terrible about this."

"We all do, dear. We all do. I'm so glad you agree."

"So how are the *trustees* proposing we reverse the vote?"

"There will be a special meeting of the board of trustees where Percy will be nominated to serve as the pastor. Can I . . . I mean can New Testament and Samantha count on your vote?"

Scarlett did not hesitate with her response. "Definitely, Cynthia. I have always felt Percy would make an excellent pastor. I'm sure Samantha will be relieved. You, I mean New Testament Cathedral and Samantha, can count on my vote."

* * *

Samantha sat directly in front of Gideon Truman in a seventeenth-century Gothic throne-like chair in the living room of her estate. The top edge of the ornately carved back of the dark walnut seat hovered just above the top of her satin hair. A wall of French doors served as the backdrop, revealing the perfectly maintained grounds of the estate. Light poured into the room, enveloping Samantha in a warm glow. On occasion a pair of preening peacocks could be seen through the window, strolling across the freshly mown lawn.

The idyllic scene was, however, upstaged by Samantha Cleaveland's presence. Her skin took on the rosy hue of the spray of flowers in an etched Lalique crystal vase placed on a glass table next to her. She wore a peach floral silk blouse that revealed only enough cleavage to hint at her perfect, full breasts.

Two cameramen positioned themselves at angles to Samantha to capture her left and right, and two others pointed theirs to Gideon. He wore a black suit and his trademark plaid shirt with a blue and red striped necktie. Bright lights mounted on tripods were directed at them just beyond the cameras' view. The first thing he had noted when he entered the home was that both Picassos had been replaced by nondescript pieces of abstract art.

The other person in the room was Gideon's producer, Megan, a fresh-faced brunette who was the daughter of a faceless network executive. Megan handed Gideon large index cards containing the questions America had for Samantha Cleaveland, and provided final directions and assuring comments to Samantha.

"Pastor Cleaveland, just be natural. If you make a mistake or get confused, don't worry about it. We can edit it out later." Megan turned to Samantha when she

spoke and slightly brushed against the table holding
the vase and flower arrangement.

"I don't get confused or make mistakes," Samantha
said coldly. "Would you please be more careful? That
vase probably cost more than your house. Are we ready
to start yet? I'd like to get this over with."

"Yes, ma'am," Megan said with a stammer. "We are
ready whenever you are."

"I was ready when you invaded my home two hours
ago," Samantha responded with an irritated gesture of
her hand and a raised eyebrow.

Megan retreated sheepishly to her place behind a
monitor just beyond the eyes of the cameras and said,
"Okay, everyone, we're rolling in five . . . four . . . three
. . . two . . . and . . ."

"Good evening. I'm Gideon Truman, and welcome
to *Truman Live*." Gideon's face filled the monitor. His
eyes sparkled, and he flashed the smile that made people all over the world welcome him into their homes.

"Tonight we are honored to have a woman who until
recently was one half of a power couple who for years
has captivated the hearts of people around the world.
Her recent tragedy made national and international
headlines and rocked the religious world to its core.
Please welcome Pastor Samantha Cleaveland of New
Testament Cathedral in Los Angeles. Good evening,
Pastor Cleaveland, and thank you for inviting us into
your lovely home."

Samantha came to life when the camera was rolling.
Her skin captured the light around her and sent it back
to the world brighter than it had come.

"Thank you, Gideon. It's my pleasure."

"I'm sure I speak for millions of people when I say
how sorry I am for the tragic loss of your husband, Pastor Hezekiah Cleaveland."

"Thank you," she said with a gracious nod of her head.

"Let me start by asking, are the police any closer to finding out who assassinated Pastor Cleaveland?"

"The Los Angeles Police Department has been amazing throughout this entire ordeal," she said as if by rote, "but unfortunately they are no closer today to finding his killer than they were the day it happened. A part of me feels we may never know who killed Hezekiah. The important thing, however, is that this person will have to answer to God either in this life or the next."

"You are a woman with strong religious beliefs. Are you in any way able to forgive the man or woman who did this to you, your family, and all the people who love you?"

"I'm so glad you asked me that question." Samantha looked Gideon directly in the eye and continued, "I have already forgiven him. This has caused me and my daughter immense pain and anguish. There were days when I didn't think I could go on without him. But you know, Gideon, God promised us all that he would never give us more burdens than we could bear. And with that knowledge I was able to get up one morning a few weeks after it happened, put on my makeup, and face another day. Don't get me wrong, though. I still cry every day, and I miss him more than you can imagine, but life must go on, and every day I grow a little stronger."

"You mentioned your daughter, Jasmine. How is she handling the loss of her father?"

"Jasmine took her father's death very hard. They were very close. She was daddy's little girl," Samantha said with a smile. "They were inseparable from the day she was born until the day he died. She couldn't bear to be in the house after he was killed, so she's staying temporarily with very dear friends of our family in Malibu. I speak with her every day, and we pray together on the telephone every evening, before she goes to bed. God and time heals all wounds, and every day she becomes stronger. As painful as this has all been, I know that someday she will come to understand that this is all part of God's master plan."

"Can you think of any reason anyone would want to kill your husband?"

Megan looked away from the monitor and scanned her copy of the questions they had developed together. Gideon's last question was not on the list.

Samantha's suddenly dilated pupils were the only visible reaction to the unexpected question. "I've thought a lot about this and have had multiple conversations with detectives, who wanted to know the same thing. Everyone loved Hezekiah. He was the kind of person that would give you his last dollar if you needed it. I've never known him to make an enemy. I can't think of anyone who would have wanted him dead."

"New Testament Cathedral is the sixth largest church in the country. Your television ministry generates millions each year. Do you think jealousy may have played into this?"

"I would hate to think jealousy was a factor, but anything is possible," Samantha said languidly. "There are many troubled people in the world. We may never know what motivated this person to do what he did."

"Do you think you may have factored into his death in any way?"

Megan swiftly removed her glasses, stood up, and took a step toward Gideon. Samantha saw her from the corner of her eye and held up her hand, issuing the universal sign for "stop."

"I'm not sure what you mean," Samantha said. Her eyes were a centimeter tighter than before.

Gideon saw the almost imperceptible shift in her demeanor. He pressed on, unfazed by the icy glare from his guest or the rustling of the producer behind his shoulder. "What I mean is, could you have done something to contribute to the murder of your husband, inadvertently, of course?"

Megan clutched her mouth to prevent a gasp from escaping. The four cameramen looked nervously at each other, then zoomed in on Samantha's stone face.

"Anything is possible, of course. I'm sure I've made decisions in the ministry that may have possibly upset some people, but I honestly don't think I've done anything to anyone that would elicit such an extreme response as this. What your viewers need to understand is that for the most part the world is filled with people who have no desire to hurt anyone.

"I've traveled all over the world and met so many people from different cultures, and I'm always amazed to find people just like you and me, all believing in the same God, but maybe calling him by a different name, who simply want to live their lives without doing harm. There are, however, a small minority of people out there who don't have God in their lives, and unfortunately, they sometimes make misguided decisions that hurt other people."

Gideon pushed a little harder. "I find it difficult to fathom that a man as powerful as Hezekiah Cleaveland, one of the most high-profile and wealthiest ministers in the country, didn't have any enemies. So do you think this was a random shooting?"

"My husband was human like everyone else. He made mistakes, and like us all, he did things that, if he were alive, I'm sure he wouldn't be proud of. But I'll say it again. I don't think he ever did anything that would warrant him being killed. If that were the case, we all would have to walk down the street looking over our shoulders."

"Let's talk about New Testament Cathedral," Gideon said, flipping the index cards. "Shortly after Hezekiah's death you were installed as pastor. How has the transition from first lady to pastor been for you?"

"I believe it was a blessing for me. The appointment was totally unexpected. I didn't even know I was being considered for the position until I received a call from the president of our board of trustees," Samantha said, batting her mink eyelashes.

She went on. "I, of course, was honored and a little concerned about whether it was too soon after losing my husband. However, the trustees had faith in me and were insistent that it was the best thing for New Testament Cathedral. Initially, I said no because I felt I needed more time to mourn my loss. But my daughter said something that changed my mind."

"What did she say?" Gideon asked.

"Something very simple. She looked me in the eye and said, 'Mommy, Daddy would have wanted it that way.' So I prayed through my tears and through my grief and God . . ." Samantha paused and gingerly dabbed the corner of her eye with the tip of her finger. "God spoke to my heart late one night and said, 'Samantha, this is my will. With me you can do all things.' After I heard that, I knew I had to either live what I've been preaching all these years or just walk away. I decided I would stand by God's word."

Gideon looked down at the index cards so the camera could not catch the smirk on his face. An image of Danny flashed in his head as he pondered his next question. He resisted the urge to ask, "Were you aware that your husband was involved in a homosexual affair for two years with a man named Danny St. John?" Or,

"How do you think the millions of people who send you their hard-earned money every year would feel if they knew about it?" And his knockout punch, "If the public found out that one of the most loved ministers in the country was gay, it would have cost you millions. What did you do to Hezekiah when you learned of the affair?"

Suddenly Gideon's hand felt warm from the memory of Danny's touch. He remembered the fear in his voice and the worry in his eyes.

Megan braced herself for the next unscripted question, and the cameramen stood in anticipation, with the lenses zoomed in on the hunter and his prey.

"Pastor Cleaveland," Gideon said, looking up again. "I think your board of trustees made an excellent decision."

An audible sigh of relief could be heard from Megan in the background.

For the remainder of the one-hour interview Gideon stuck to the script, asking one softball question after another, each skillfully spun by Samantha to solidify her image as the brave grieving widow who set aside her own needs for the good of the church.

"Pastor Cleaveland, it has been a pleasure speaking with you today. I now see why America has fallen in love with you. I wish you, Jasmine, and New Testament Cathedral the best."

"It's been my pleasure."

The cameramen stood up straight and deeply exhaled. Megan dashed from behind the monitor to Samantha and said, "Pastor Cleaveland, that was brilliant. You looked beautiful on the screen and . . ."

Samantha stood up, removed the mike from her blouse, and walked past Megan before she could finish the sentence and said, "I want you all out of my house and off the property in ten minutes."

Gideon, Megan, and the cameramen stood frozen as
Samantha left the room.

"What the fuck were you doing, Gideon?" Megan
finally said. "You practically accused her of killing her
husband. Why didn't you stick to the questions we
agreed on?"

"They were softball, bullshit questions," Gideon said
defensively. "Trust me, I had tougher ones I could have
asked, but I restrained myself. The whole fucking interview was like a Samantha Cleaveland infomercial. I feel
like a goddamned idiot."

"So you think that's why she stormed out of here in a
puff of smoke like Endora?" Megan asked sarcastically.

The cameramen wasted no time in packing the equipment, rolling up cords, and returning the room to the
perfect state it was in when they arrived.

Gideon and Megan continued their discussion while
the four men worked frantically to meet the ten minute
deadline.

"Gideon, do you know something you're not telling
me? What is this about?"

"I don't know anything. I just don't like that phony
bitch."

"So you accuse one of the most popular women in
the country of being involved in her husband's death
just because you think she's a bitch? Have you forgotten about professional detachment?"

Gideon could not deny that his emotions had caused
him to straddle the fine line between the television
ratings game and good journalism. But for the love of
Danny, he had stayed in the shallow waters of compli-
ments, sympathy, and scripture-laced sound bites.

"How do you think viewers are going to react when
they see you insinuate that Samantha Cleaveland caused
her husband's death?" Megan continued. "You're going
to look like an asshole."

"I don't care what I look like. I've got more important things on my mind."

Cynthia Pryce abruptly turned off the big-screen television in her bedroom. Gideon's interview with Samantha had just aired for the third time since the taping.

"The coward, the fucking coward," she said out loud, throwing the remote control across the bed. "He didn't even mention any of Hezekiah's affairs."

Cynthia reached for her cell phone and dialed Gideon's number.

"Hello. This is Gideon Truman."

"What the fuck was that all about?"

"I beg your pardon. Who is this?" he said, immediately evoking the image of another crazed fan.

"This is Cynthia Pryce. We had a deal. I gave you the information, and you were supposed to report it. Was that so difficult?"

Gideon was driving up Hollywood Boulevard when he received the call. Traffic was bumper to bumper. Tourists wearing the latest strip-mall fashions walked in droves along the star-embedded street. Gideon pulled his car into a bus zone and continued. "We did not have any such deal," he said firmly. "I told you I would check out your story, but I never promised to report it."

"She got to you, didn't she?" Cynthia said coldly. "What did she do? Threaten you? Fuck you? Oh, wait a minute. I forgot. That wouldn't work on you."

Gideon took the phone away from his ear and looked at it in surprise. "I'm not sure who you think you're talking about, Mrs. Pryce. But I assure you no one 'got to me'. I simply chose not to pursue the story."

"Then why? This is the biggest story of your career. Don't you journalists have to take some kind of oath that says you have to report on stories that affect the public?"

"There is no such oath. Journalists have complete discretion as to what they report. I exercised my discretion," he said, attempting to manage his indignation.

"No, what you did was cover up a story. And the only reason I can think of is that somehow Samantha Cleaveland got to you. Did she pay you? God knows she's got plenty of my money and everyone else's to do it with."

"I resent you accusing me of accepting bribes," Gideon said, raising his voice. Cars continued to creep by as he spoke.

A tour bus filled with camera-toting tourists stopped next to his car. Someone on the bus yelled out, "Hey, look. It's Gideon Truman." Everyone on the bus immediately rushed to the windows and began shouting, "Oh my God. It is him," and "Hey, Gideon. Look over here," as they snapped pictures and waved in his direction.

Gideon ignored the gawking fans and continued, "If you must know, I considered the story to be in poor taste in light of the circumstances. The man was murdered, for Christ's sake. Why do you need to crucify him even further? You're a smart woman. I'm sure you can figure out a way to sleep your way to the top."

"I'm sure I can, too, Mr. Truman," Cynthia said sharply. "But as I've already told you, this is not about me. It's about doing what's right."

A Metro RTD bus wormed its way through the traffic and stopped inches from Gideon's bumper. The bus driver blasted his horn at Gideon, causing a chorus of more car horns from behind the bus.

"I don't have time for this bullshit," he finally said. "If you want to be the first lady of New Testament, you're going to have to find some other asshole to do your dirty work."

With that Gideon hung up the phone and dashed back into traffic, giving a wave of apology to the bus driver.

"Fucking bitch," Gideon said, slamming the steering wheel. "How dare she?"

Gideon honked his horn impatiently at cars he felt were moving too slowly as he wound up Hollywood Boulevard. Cynthia had touched a nerve. Was he now, in fact, participating in a cover-up? Had his attraction to Danny caused him to cross the line between reporter and story? Was he a part of the story? The prospect frightened him. Had he compromised everything he believed in for the remote possibility that Danny could ever feel the same way he did?

"Faggot," Cynthia cursed, tossing the phone on the bed. "Never send a gay boy to do a woman's job."

Cynthia grudgingly conceded one truth Gideon had spoken. She in fact was unashamedly willing to sleep her way to the top. She thought of the pounding she had endured from the balding *Chronicle* reporter, Lance Savage, in the front seat of her Mercedes. The sex had been in exchange for him running the story on Heze-kiah's affair.

It would have worked if the little bastard hadn't gotten himself killed, she thought. *His dick was so small, it wasn't really like fucking at all,* she recalled. *It was more like masturbation.*

Chapter 13

The sun slowly dipped behind the hills in the distance as streaks of clouds filtered the remains of the day in the orange Arizona sky. Cactus dotted the horizon like pitchforks retired for the day by exhausted ranch hands. The desert was still except for lizards darting between rocks as the sun ended its scorching assault on the barren landscape. It was eight o'clock and time for the evening group at the Desert Springs Drug Rehabilitation Center in Phoenix.

Paintings of dusty landscapes, cactus, and indigenous women toiling in the sun hung from adobe-plastered walls that arched to form a peak over the center of the meeting room. The bleached skull of an animal that had succumbed to the ravages of the sun hung over an adobe kiva fireplace protruding from a far corner in the room. A motley crew of eight adolescents made their way to a circle of chairs in the middle of the room. The glossy terra-cotta-tiled floor was cool against their feet, and the air conditioner emitted a nearly inaudible hum.

Desert Springs was the rehab facility the rich, the famous, and the notorious chose when they needed to send their alcohol-guzzling, pill-popping, and needle-poking children for treatment away from the prying eyes of paparazzi, police, and custody attorneys.

The group facilitator, Dr. Ron, appeared to be an adolescent himself, but he was not. His doctorate in addiction psychology, his seven published books on the treatment of every addiction know to modern man, and his numerous appearances on *Oprah, Dr. Phil,* and *The Dr. Oz Show* gave the parents of his wealthy young patients solace when they handed him their forty-thousand-dollar check for twenty-eight days of treatment.

"Its eight o'clock, everyone," Dr. Ron said in a voice that echoed his pubescent face. "Let's get started."

The last of the youths slumped into their seats. Tattoos, pierced noses and lips, spiked hair, and lit cigarettes were the accessories of choice for most in the group. Several, however, wore diamond tennis bracelets, Manolo sandals, and Rolex watches. The one thing they all had in common was they each looked at least ten years older than their fifteen, sixteen, and seventeen years.

"We're now two weeks into your four-week stay at Desert Springs," Dr. Ron said. "I think tonight is a good time to talk about our families. I want each of you to share what it's like in your home. Your parents, siblings, staff, pets, or anything else you'd like to share with the group. Who wants to start?"

"Why the fuck do you want to know that?" came the first response from the boy wearing the Rolex watch and sporting a two-hundred-dollar haircut. "You plan on selling our stories to *People* magazine? Forty thousand dollars for a month times twenty isn't enough for you?"

The comment elicited a smattering of uneasy snickers from the group and also from Dr. Ron.

"Forty thousand dollars a month is plenty for me," he said dismissively. "You all know that anything you say in this room will never leave this room. We've all signed confidentiality agreements. This is a safe place.

Probably one of the safest places some of you have ever been in your lives. Now, again, who wants to go first?"

"I'll go," was the earnest response from a girl with a loop ring in her nose and a burning cigarette on her fingertips. "I'll do anything to get this over with. Okay," she said, folding her legs beneath her. "I have a little brother and sister. A dog named Sammy Davis Jr., three nannies—two of um are fucking dear old dad— and God knows who all those other people are who are in our house twenty-four hours a day. My mother has her first vodka and tonic at ten in the morning, and I'm usually too fucked up at night to know when she's had her last one. The only time I see my father is when I pay ten bucks like every other asshole to see one of his crappy movies. Is that enough? Can I go home now? I think you cured me. Dr. Ron, you're a genius."

Some in the group laughed, while others stared blankly out the window, writhed in their seats, or struggled to keep their hands from shaking.

Dr. Ron smiled and said, "No, I'm not a genius. No, I don't think you're cured, and no, you can't go home yet."

"Oh, please, Dr. Ron. I'll give you another forty K," the girl said with smoke billowing from her mouth.

"That won't be necessary," he said patiently.

"How about a blow job? Everyone says I'm pretty good at it."

"I'll let you go home if you give me a blow job," said one of the twitching boys.

"I'm sure you're great at it, Rory," Dr. Ron interrupted, "but what I'd rather have from you is a little less sarcasm and a lot more honesty. Why don't you take a minute to think about what you'd like to get out of this session, and we'll come back to you? Ian, let's hear from you. Tell us about your family."

Ian was slightly overweight. His face was covered with freckles, and his flip-flop sandals clapped the terra-cotta tiles nervously when he spoke. "Me, uh," he stammered. "There's not much to tell. Uh, we live in D.C. My mom and dad are pretty cool. I'm home a lot by myself when my parents travel or when Congress is in session."

"Is that when you drink?" Dr. Ron asked.

"Yeah," the chubby adolescent said. "I, um, get bored alone in the house and, well, the place is full of liquor and, um . . ."

"How long have you been drinking?" asked Dr. Ron.

"Since I was about ten, I guess. I don't drink that much, though."

"Looked like you had a lot to drink when the paramedics rolled you out of your penthouse last month," said one of the other youths. "You looked like shit in that oxygen mask on the news, by the way."

"I saw that too," blurted another member. "Your father must have shit bricks when he saw the news. Guess he won't be running for president anytime soon."

There was more laughter from the group.

"How did your father react, Ian?" Dr. Ron asked.

"He, well, he was cool about it. . . . I mean, he was upset and everything. My mom freaked out, though. She said if I didn't come here, she was going to send me to military school."

Seven of the eight in the group told similar stories. Privilege, unlimited access to credit cards, minimal adult supervision, heroin overdoses, multiple sex partners, and numerous encounters with the law, all of which were neatly brushed under the rug by brooms made of money and power.

Dr. Ron looked in the direction of the one person in the room who had not spoken, and said, "I guess you're the last one, Jasmine. Why don't you tell us about your family?"

All the members looked sympathetically in her direction. Jasmine did not speak.

"I know it's difficult for you, Jasmine, but the only way you're going to make any progress is if you talk about it," Dr. Ron said gently. "Remember, you're among friends here. Everyone has a similar story to yours."

Jasmine looked in his direction. Her eyes were still puffy from weeks of crying. "Is that right?" she said coldly. "Who else in this group had their father killed in front of millions of people? Who else tried to commit suicide, only to have some son-of-a-bitch doctor pump their stomach and bring them back to this place?"

The room was silent. The hands stopped shaking, sandals stopped clapping the tile, and bodies stopped squirming in the seats.

"We all realize that part of your story is unique, Jasmine," Dr. Ron said softly. "But the process of healing is the same for all of us, regardless of what we've been through."

"He's right, Jasmine," said the ringed-nosed Rory. "I know I sound like a bitch sometimes, but I have to admit it does help to talk about it. It's nice to get the shit out in the open so other people can smell it, too, and sometimes they can tell you it doesn't smell as bad as you thought it did."

All eyes were still on Jasmine. She looked to the floor at the checkerboard tile, then to the skull hanging over the fireplace. After silent moments she said in a whisper, "My mother hasn't called me since I've been here. She's too busy saving the fucking world. She didn't love my father. As a matter of fact, I think she hated him. The only time they weren't arguing was when the cameras were on."

"How was your relationship with her?" Dr. Ron asked.

Jasmine released a pained chuckle and replied, "I don't have a relationship with my mother. The only time she paid any attention to me was when she trotted me out in front of the church or the cameras. I'm a stage prop. Most of the time shc doesn't even know or care if I'm in the house. I was raised by nannies, housekeepers, and security guards."

"How about your dad? What was that relationship like?" Dr. Ron asked, pressing on.

"I loved my father, and I know he loved me. But he was always so busy too. I remember when I was a kid, he used to take me with him everywhere. But . . ." Jasmine paused to clear her throat and stifle a tear and then continued. "But the church kept getting bigger and bigger. Then the television thing took off. After a while I just got left behind. There would be weeks when I would only see him on Sunday morning in church."

"Jasmine," said the boy with the Rolex watch. "Your mom must care about you. She sent you here, didn't she?"

Again Jasmine chuckled. "She sent me here because she didn't want anyone to find out I tried to commit suicide. She didn't want it getting out that the daughter of the perfect Samantha Cleaveland swallowed a bottle of sleeping pills and had to have her stomach pumped. When she shoved me in the car with her driver, she told me to tell anyone who asked that I was staying with family friends in Malibu. She didn't even bother to ride to the airport with me."

It was 8:20 on Thursday evening. The board of trustees sat nervously around the table in the recently christened Pastor Hezekiah T. Cleaveland Memorial Conference Room. The special closed meeting had been convened at the request of Reverend Kenneth Davis. The only item on the agenda was the selection of the permanent pastor of New Testament Cathedral.

Two armed security guards in full uniform were posted outside the door, with strict orders not to allow anyone to enter the room. A silver pitcher of water, five glasses, and a stack of neatly folded cloth napkins sat untouched on a side console. The shades on the two glass walls that looked onto the grounds of the cathedral were drawn. The room, which could easily accommodate fifty people, felt claustrophobic, even though there were only four people sitting in the thirty leather chairs around the table.

Kenneth sat at the head of the table as the convener of the meeting. Hattie Williams's wooden cane rested on the conference table. Her purse, filled with Kleenex, peppermints, and a pocket Bible, rested on her lap. Reverend Percy Pryce sat to her left, three chairs down. Despite his best attempts at appearing calm and detached, the moisture on his upper lip betrayed the churning in his stomach.

Kenneth nervously checked his watch. Scarlett Shackelford sat stiffly three chairs to his right. The pills she had taken before leaving her home that evening had effectively erased the remains of her shattered emotions.

"I don't think she's coming," Kenneth said, checking his watch again. "It's already twenty past eight. We were supposed to start at eight o'clock."

"Maybe we should start without her," Percy said softly.

"She'll be here."

All heads turned to Hattie Williams.

"How do you know that?" Scarlett asked coldly.

"Because she's already in the building," Hattie said. "I can feel her."

Scarlett rolled her eyes and said impatiently, "I say we call the meeting to order right now and get this over with."

As she spoke, the security guard swung one half of the double doors open and Samantha appeared in the threshold. Kenneth and Percy leapt to their feet, while Hattie and Scarlett remained seated. Before entering, Samantha made eye contact with everyone at the table.

"Good evening, brothers and sisters," she said confidently. "I apologize for my lateness, but I was attending to church business. Please sit down, brothers."

Kenneth walked to the console and poured a glass of water. "Would anyone else like a glass before we get started?"

A chorus of "No" and "No thank you, Reverend," followed, and he made his way back to the head of the table.

Samantha sat four chairs to the right of Scarlett, which placed her farthest from the head of the table. She crossed her legs and leaned back in the high-backed leather chair.

Kenneth placed the glass of water beside a single sheet of paper, five pens, a stack of index cards, and a small tape recorder. After pressing the RECORD button, he said, "I now call this special meeting of the Board of Trustees of New Testament Cathedral to order at 8:25 P.M. on this day of our Lord and Savior Jesus Christ. Thank you all for coming at such short notice. As you know, we are convened to decide an issue of the utmost importance. The sole agenda item is who will serve as the permanent pastor of New Testament Cathedral."

Samantha raised her hand and was immediately acknowledged by Kenneth.

"I would like to know what prompted this sudden need to appoint a permanent pastor," Samantha said calmly. "It was my understanding that I would be given ample time to demonstrate to this body and the congregation at large that I am fully capable of serving in that position on a permanent basis. Is one month the trustees' idea of 'ample time'?"

No one spoke as Samantha waited patiently to see who would lead the charge. Finally, Percy leaned forward and clasped his hands together on the table. "Pastor Cleaveland," he said, clearing his throat. "This is in no way a reflection on how we feel about your leadership during this trying time. I think I speak for us all when I say under the circumstances we feel you have done an amazing job in holding the congregation together and keeping the vision of Pastor Cleaveland alive and on track."

"Then what is this all about?" Samantha asked. This was punctuated by a flick of her French-tipped nail on the table.

Kenneth stepped in. "It's just some of us feel we may have not fully factored in your feelings when we placed you in the position. We . . . I mean I feel we may have acted too hastily, and selfishly, I might add. You just lost your husband, the center of your life. Reverend Pryce is willing to step in and give you the time you and Jasmine need to—"

"Reverend Davis, I am very aware that I just lost my husband," Samantha interrupted, "but contrary to popular belief, he was not the center of my life. God is the center of my life, as I hope He is yours. I loved my husband, but I also love New Testament Cathedral. I helped found this church when it was in a storefront on Imperial Highway. Before any of you ever heard of the Cleavelands or the Cleavelands had ever heard of any of you." Samantha leaned into the table. Her tone became firmer, and the words came more rapidly as she spoke. "Hezekiah and I built this ministry from the ground up, and now you think just because he's gone, you can snatch it from under my feet."

"Now hold on, Reverend Cleaveland," Percy said, jumping in and gesturing with both hands. "No one is trying to snatch New Testament away from you. We all recognize the significant contributions you have made to this church, and we all appreciate everything you've done to make New Testament what it is today. We're only thinking about what's best for you. That's all. This is not an indictment against you."

"You *appreciate* my contributions," Samantha said snidely. "I don't need your appreciation, Percy. It means nothing to me. Let me ask you something. How many millions of dollars have you brought into the ministry this year? How many new members have you brought into the church?"

Percy stiffened his back and said, "This isn't about money. It's about doing what's right by you. Hezekiah would have wanted us to look out for you, and by placing you in this position prematurely, we have failed him. You can wait a few years, can't you? Give it time, Samantha. You need time to heal."

"Let's be honest, Percy. This isn't about me at all. It's about you, isn't it? Did your wife put you up to this?" Samantha said, looking him directly in the eye. "Because let's face it, you don't have the guts to come up with a ridiculous plan like this on your own. Hezekiah always said you were a small-minded, weak little man, and I see now that he was right."

"That's uncalled for, Samantha," Kenneth interjected. "Please, I know this is a difficult conversation for us to have, but let's at least try to be civil with each other."

"Civil? You expect me to be civil when you jackals have plotted behind my back to steal my church. Well, let me say to you all, if you think you're going to pat me on the head and brush me aside, you are sadly mistaken."

Kenneth cleared his throat and said gently, "I'm afraid we do have the authority, Samantha. According to church bylaws section IIA, it is the responsibility of this body to select the pastor."

Kenneth reached for the single piece of paper in front of him and read it aloud. "A pastor shall be chosen and called whenever a vacancy occurs. A Pastor's Selection Committee shall be appointed by the church—that's us—to seek out a suitable pastor. The pastor's election shall take place at a meeting called for that purpose. That's this meeting. The pastor—for the time being, that's you, Samantha—shall be an ex officio member of all church standing committees, except the Pastor's Selection Committee."

Kenneth returned the paper to the table and said, "Because you are the interim pastor of New Testament Cathedral at the time this agenda item will be called to a vote, you will, unfortunately, not be allowed to vote on this matter."

"May I speak?" Scarlett said loudly.

Kenneth leaned back, relieved that someone else had entered the fray. "Please, Sister Shackelford, go ahead. You have the floor."

Scarlett spun her chair to face Samantha and said, "I'm not basing my vote on you or your feelings. I actually don't think you need time to heal. Do you know why? Because I think you're relieved that he's gone."

"Sister Shackelford!" Kenneth shouted.

"Let me finish," Scarlett said deliberately. "My decision is based on the fact that I don't think you are fit to be pastor. You are an evil woman who has demonstrated over the years that you are more than willing to destroy anyone and anything that stands between you and whatever it is you want at the time. New Testament Cathedral deserves better than that. God deserves better, and I know I deserve better. I'm ready to call this to a vote."

With her final words Scarlett spun her chair back to its original position. Samantha sat stunned and speechless.

Kenneth held his breath, waiting for Samantha to respond, but she remained silent. Kenneth then leaned forward and said, "We haven't heard from everyone. Mother Williams, do you have anything to add before we call for a vote?"

Hattie remembered the vision she saw in her garden of Samantha standing in the pulpit with thousands of lost souls standing at her feet, crying and raising their hands to the heavens. She clutched the handle of her cane and simply said, "I have nothing to add. I'm ready for the vote."

"Very well then," Kenneth said, reaching for the index cards and pens. "Please write your choice for pastor of New Testament Cathedral on these cards. Fold your card in half and pass it back to me when you're ready."

"May I ask a question before we vote?" Samantha said calmly.

"The discussion is over," Scarlett said. "Let's vote please."

"Hold on, Scarlett. Let her speak. Go ahead, Samantha. You have the floor," Kenneth said, leaning back in his chair.

Samantha looked to Percy and said, "Reverend Pryce?"

"Yes?" he said suspiciously.

"Do you know someone named Lance Savage?"

Kenneth jerked forward in his chair and lunged toward the tape recorder. He quickly pressed the STOP button and, in doing so, knocked over his glass of water.

"Oh God, I'm sorry," he blurted out. Water splattered down the center of the table, soaking the single white paper and forming a puddle around the tape recorder. Kenneth jumped from his seat and ran to the console for the cloth napkins. When he returned, the water had begun to drip onto his chair. Kenneth dabbed and blotted the table, the chair, and around the base of the tape recorder until much of the spill had been absorbed.

Samantha watched him curiously and noted the unexpected reaction to the name Lance Savage.

I'm so sorry, everyone," Kenneth said with a shaky voice. "I'm so sorry. I didn't mean to do it. It was an accident. I'm . . . I'm sorry."

Percy retrieved more napkins from the console and wiped the remaining drops of water while coolly saying, "It's all right, Reverend Davis. Calm down. It was just a little accident. Calm down."

Kenneth sank back into the damp leather chair and said through labored breaths, "Samantha, I don't see what that has to do with the matter on the table."

Samantha returned her gaze to Percy. "Answer my question, Reverend Pryce. Do you know Lance Savage?"

Percy looked helplessly to Kenneth and then back to Samantha and said, "No . . . I don't believe I know anyone by that name."

"From Kenneth's reaction I think you do."

"You're stalling, Samantha. What does this have to do with anything?" Scarlett said impatiently.

"To be perfectly honest, Scarlett, I'm not sure. But I'm curious. You see, my assistant gives me a monthly report on the church telephone records. I like to know if anyone is making any unauthorized calls. We had a problem with that a few years ago. You remember that, don't you, Mother Williams? Anyway, in doing so," Samantha continued methodically, "she noticed two calls were made to a Lance Savage."

Samantha looked around the room and said, "Did I forget to mention Mr. Savage was the *Los Angeles Chronicle* reporter who was found murdered in his home on the canals in Venice."

She then looked back to Percy and said, "The calls were made from your extension to his cell phone and home. And, ironically, they were made on the very same day that he was murdered. Quite a coincidence, don't you think? I've been meaning to ask you why you called him, but I've been so busy burying my husband and running the church."

There was silence in the room. All eyes were now on Percy. Kenneth sat stiff in his seat. The remnants of the spilled water soaked the seat of his pants. Beads of sweat formed on his brow, and his heart pounded in his chest.

"Looks like you might not remember right now. That's okay, though, because you see, if I'm not going to be pastor any longer, I'll have plenty of time on my hands to solve little mysteries like this." Samantha leaned back in her chair and said with a smile, "All righty then, Reverend Davis, I think I have my answer. Now, let's get on with that vote."

Kenneth's hand shook as he passed the cards and pens to Hattie, Scarlett, and Percy. He kept one for himself. He used a dry napkin to wipe the sweat from his brow, only to have it be replaced by even more.

Scarlett was the first to hand back her folded card. Hattie was next. Percy's hand rested on the table, with the tip of the pen suspended only centimeters above the card. Scarlett, Hattie, and Samantha watched him as the pen finally began to glide along the surface of the card. He stopped and started several times before he finished. He then opened his fingers slightly, and the pen dropped to the table with a thud that echoed off the walls of the conference room.

Percy stared at the card without moving. All he could think of was his wife's final words as he left their condo for the meeting. "Call me as soon as it's over," she'd said, brushing imaginary lint from his lapel at the door. "And, Percy," she'd added, "don't screw this up."

Samantha leaned toward the table and said, "Fold your car, Reverend Pryce, and hand it back to Reverend Davis."

Kenneth's card was soggy from the droplets of water that remained on the table in front of him. He was the last to fold his card and add it to the stack of four.

"Thank you, everyone," Kenneth said nervously. "Here we go."

"Wait a minute, Reverend Davis," Samantha said calmly.

"Yes, Pastor Cleaveland?" Kenneth said humbly.

"I think it might be a good idea if you turned the recorder back on, for the record."

"Of course . . . yes, of course. I'm sorry. I forgot."

"No need to apologize, again," Samantha said.

Kenneth reached forward and pressed the RECORD button. "Okay, where was I?"

Kenneth opened the first card and read out the name written on it. "Samantha Cleaveland."

He opened the second card and said, "Samantha Cleaveland."

Scarlett looked bewildered and betrayed. The numbing effects of the medication began to wear off rapidly with the reading of each card.

Kenneth unfolded the third card and let out a gush of air. "Percy Pryce," he said with a hint of disappointment.

The last card seemed to levitate above the table in front of him. He reached for it, hesitated halfway, and then picked it up. He looked around the room at each person. Scarlett looked at him with a longing glare. Hattie's eyes were closed. She still clutched the head of her cane. Percy's eyes were closed, as well.

Samantha looked at him with the cold, clenched eyes of a woman who was about to lose everything.

Kenneth opened the final card and read it. "Samantha Cleaveland," he said, dropping the card to the table. He then closed his eyes and released a puff of air. "Let the record show that Samantha Cleaveland is as of this day the permanent pastor of New Testament Cathedral. Congratulations, Pastor Cleaveland." Kenneth slapped the table with his open palm and said, "This meeting is adjourned."

Samantha stood immediately and walked over to Kenneth. She reached over his shoulder and pressed the EJECT button on the tape recorder, and the little cassette popped up.

"I'll take this," she said. Without making eye contact with anyone there, Samantha spun on her heels and left the room.

The others sat in stunned silence, and then one by one they slowly exited the conference room. The last person to leave was Percy, who slowly turned the lights off.

Chapter 14

Cynthia paced the floor of the condominium as she waited nervously for the call from Percy. A bottle of champagne chilling in a bucket of ice stood next to two glasses and a tin of caviar. In the bedroom she had placed twenty candles around the room and had laid an ivory-white negligee suggestively on the center of the satin-covered bed. It was already a quarter past ten at night, and she still hadn't received the call.

As she walked the length of the room, she gripped her cell phone in one hand and checked periodically to ensure the volume was turned up and the battery was fully charged.

With every step she took, she muttered a prayer. "Please don't let him fuck this up for me," and, "If you give me this, I promise I'll never do anything wrong again for the rest of my life."

Midway through one such prayer, Cynthia heard keys turn in the front door. Percy entered and gently closed the door behind him. He placed his keys on a table in the foyer and walked softly across the black-veined marble floor. Cynthia appeared beneath the arch that led to the living room before he could reach the hall to the bedrooms.

He could smell the perfume, a hint of sulfur, and burning candles in the air. He saw the chilled champagne over her shoulder.

"Why didn't you call?" Cynthia said, rushing to him and wrapping her arms around his barrel chest. "I've been going crazy waiting to hear from you. So what happened? Tell me everything."

Percy did not return her embrace. He changed his course and walked past her to the living room. Cynthia knew it was not a good sign that he had not spoken.

"Percy," she called behind him. "What happened?" This time she spoke more forcefully. "Are you the pastor? How did Samantha take it? She must be devastated. I'll have to call her tomorrow and reassure her we won't abandon her in her time of need."

Percy stood with his back to her, looking out the window. The city lights below looked to him like disapproving eyes all peering in his direction.

"You're scaring me Percy," Cynthia said, walking behind him. "Please tell me you are the pastor." She gripped his shoulder and spun him around. "You are the new pastor, aren't you?"

His silence and inability to make eye contact provided her with the answer. Blood rushed to her head, and time seemed to stand still. For a brief moment she thought she would faint. She clutched the arm of the sofa and braced herself. Her breathing became shallow, and the room blurred.

"I don't fucking believe this," she said in a pant. "Oh my God, I don't believe this."

"It's for the best, honey," Percy said calmly, holding her by the shoulders. "I didn't really want to be pastor. I'd rather spend more time with you. Honey . . . Cynthia, are you all right? Take a deep breath, honey. You look like you're going to pass out."

Cynthia straightened her back and pushed his hands from her shoulders. "Take your fucking hands off me," she shouted. "You didn't have to do a fucking thing. I set it all up for you. All you had to do was vote for your-self. Did you at least vote for yourself?"

Percy turned back to the window and did not re-spond.

"Oh my God," she said slowly. "You mean to tell me, you didn't even have the goddamned sense to vote for yourself? You stupid piece of shit! You fucking moron. You can't do anything right."

With her last words Cynthia reached for the bucket of ice and champagne and shoved it at the back of Percy's head. The metal made a loud clank when it con-nected with his skull, sending the bottle crashing into the window and spewing ice cubes around the room. This was followed in rapid succession by the chair she threw with such force that it shattered the window and plummeted twenty stories to the ground below. The cold of the city and the sounds of the night rushed in through the gaping hole.

Percy dropped to his knees from the blow and said, "Cynthia, what are you doing? Get a hold of yourself. It's not the end of the world."

Cynthia dropped the full weight of her body onto his back and began pounding his head with her fists. "You worthless piece of shit!" she shouted as she delivered blow after blow to his head and face. "I'm going to throw your useless ass out the motherfucking window."

Percy shielded his head from the blows. "Cynthia, stop," he shouted through the blood now dripping from his face and mouth. "Move away from the window. You're going to kill us both."

"I want to fall out. I want us both to fall out," she said, lowering her bloodstained fists again and again to his face. Her hair was tossed back and forth from each blow leveled with the full weight of her body. "I want us both to fall out the fucking window!"

Cynthia pushed the cowering man on his back. She then grabbed one of his ankles and began dragging him toward the gaping hole in the glass. "I'm going to throw your useless ass out the fucking window," she yelled through labored breaths. "You are worthless to me!"

"Stop, Cynthia. You're going to kill us," Percy shouted. He twisted and turned on the carpet, leaving a trail of blood as the two moved closer and closer to the window. "Stop, Cynthia, That's enough. You're going to kill us both!"

Percy grabbed the leg of an end table next to the sofa, but she pulled him harder. The table soon was on the same course as his sliding body. The lamp, the telephone, and the vase filled with flowers on the table came crashing to the floor.

Percy began to kick Cynthia with his free foot as they neared the hole in the wall. The first blow landed on her chest. The heel of his leather shoe struck the center of her howling, contorted face with the second kick. She continued to drag him, undaunted by the now vicious counterattack. He kicked her again and again, each blow harder than the one before.

The last jolt of his foot was delivered with such power that it caused Cynthia to lose her grip on his ankle and tumble backward. She landed with a crashing thud on the floor, with her head and shoulders hanging out the window and into the cold, dark night. Shards of glass scraped against her back as she squirmed on the floor, still screaming obscenities.

Percy rolled to his knees and quickly grabbed her waist, which was now at the edge of the building.

"Let me go!" she screamed, clawing at his bloody face. "I want to die. Let me go!"

Percy pulled the flailing woman away from the window with his last ounce of strength. When he reached a safe distance, he sat on the floor next to her and quickly wrapped his arms around her chest like a vise. "Calm down, Cynthia," he whispered repeatedly into her ear. "It's all right, honey."

Cynthia continued to squirm and wiggle to break free from his powerful grip and return to the window.

"It's all right, honey," he continued to say calmly. "Take a deep breath and calm down."

As she grew weaker, her resistance waned. The screams and rants gradually turned into wrenching whimpers and moans. "I want to die," she continued to cry. "Let me go. I hate you. Let me die."

"No, you don't, honey," Percy repeated over and over. "I know you're disappointed, but you don't want to die. You have everything to live for."

"I just want to die," were the last words Cynthia whimper before her twitching body fell limp in his arms on the living room floor.

The sky was clear and blue above the translucent gray layer of smog that hung over the city. Danny lay by the infinity pool in the hot Los Angeles afternoon sun. Parker was curled in a furry ball near the water's edge. The yard was a page from *Architectural Digest*. Towering pine trees lined the sides, leaving the rear property line unobstructed to display the spectacular view of downtown. Los Angeles Jacuzzi at the end of the pool gurgled like a volcano threatening to erupt. From the vantage point of Gideon's home in the Hollywood Hills Danny could almost see the streets where he handed out condoms, socks, and clean needles to the homeless.

Wicker furniture and freestanding stone and artificially aged copper fireplaces were arranged throughout the wooded, grounds, creating numerous cozy nooks for intimate conversations, alfresco dining, or dancing the night away under the stars.

"Come and stay with me for a few days," Gideon had said the night they held hands on Danny's couch. "You shouldn't be alone right now. You can sleep in one of the guest rooms. I promise I won't try anything. Parker can come, too, to keep me in line."

Exhausted from grief and weak from loneliness, Danny had cautiously accepted the invitation. Although his visit from Kay Braisden had given him some respite from his isolation, she was able to stay with him for only three days before she had to return home to D.C. Danny had dreaded the thought of crying alone in his apartment another night.

Gideon had been the perfect host since Danny arrived two days earlier. The two men would pop popcorn and watch movies in his media room when Gideon wasn't working in his home office. They ordered takeout from Gideon's favorite little Chinese restaurant on Sunset Boulevard and sat in the middle of the living room floor, eating shrimp egg foo yong and moo goo gai pan with cheap wooden chopsticks while sharing secrets, some of which they hadn't even told themselves.

"I haven't had sex in almost two years," went one such conversation. "It's just too risky. I'm afraid if I'm . . ." Gideon paused and stirred chow mein in a white box with his chopsticks before he continued. "I'm afraid if I'm intimate with someone, he'll go straight to the *Enquirer* and tell them everything, from how big my dick is to how I stutter like Porky Pig when I cum." Gideon raised his hands and stammered, "Tha-tha-tha-that's all folks."

Danny laughed and said, "You must be very lonely."

"You get used to it. I have my work. I have my friends, and I have my right hand," Gideon said, laughing. "But, yeah, I do get lonely sometimes. How about you? What was your life like before you met Hezekiah?"

"Strangely enough, it was very much like yours, except without the house in the Hills, the Mercedes, or my own television show," Danny said with a smile. "Before I met Hezekiah, I was almost a recluse. I had a small circle of friends and my work. That was it. I've always had a hard time with men. They were either only after quick sex, or they wanted to parade me in front of their friends like a mannequin."

"I can understand that. You are quite beautiful, Danny."

"Thank you, but I don't see myself that way."

"How do you see yourself?"

"To be honest, I didn't really see myself until I met Hezekiah. When we were together, every time I looked in his eyes, I swear I could see into my own soul. I could see how empty my life was. I could see how afraid I was. But I also saw how loving I could be. I saw how kind and compassionate I could be. But regardless of what I saw, he made me feel like it was okay. There was nothing about me that shocked or repulsed him. He made me feel like there was absolutely nothing about me that could make him stop loving me. He was an amazing man."

"You were very lucky to have him in your life, even for such a short time."

Danny looked away. "I don't feel very lucky right now. Sometimes I think I would have been better off if I'd never met him. At least I wouldn't be going through this hell."

"Do you believe in fate, Danny?"

"I guess. What do you mean?"

"I believe everything in life happens for a reason," Gideon said, looking directly at Danny. He could see his reflection in his eyes. "There are no coincidences, and wherever we find ourselves in our life, that is exactly where we were supposed to be at that time. There are no mistakes in the universe. Everything is perfect and as it should be."

Danny stretched his bare legs on the chaise lounge by the pool as he remembered the words Gideon had said to him the night before. He wore a pair of dark blue Speedos and sunglasses. The heat had caused his skin to shimmer in the afternoon sun. Dishes could be heard clanking and water running in the kitchen behind him. Danny stood and stretched his long limbs again, then made his way to the open French doors that led directly into the kitchen.

There he found Gideon, barefoot and wearing a yellow T-shirt and short khakis, standing at a green granite island, slicing peaches, a mango, and a cantaloupe. The kitchen was a stainless-steel shrine to food. A ten-burner Wolf range was against the wall; opposite it was a Sub-Zero refrigerator with double glass doors. The room was a series of red oak cabinets from the floor to the ceiling. Silver and black appliances and gadgets occupied almost every counter, and a flat-screen television hung from the ceiling. Pristine copper pots swung from a rack above the island where Gideon stood. "I thought you might like a snack before dinner," Gideon said, slicing into a melon. "Are you thirsty? There's Pellegrino, lemonade, beer, and juice in the fridge. Help yourself."

"Gideon, why are you doing this? Shouldn't you be interviewing some serial killer instead of making me a fruit salad?"

Gideon laughed and said, "I'm going in at four o'clock. I have to interview Tyler Perry. I'd rather hang around here with you, but hey, somebody's got to do it. I see the Speedo fits you."

"Yeah, just barely," Danny said, adjusting the tight briefs. "I didn't know anybody still owned these things."

"They were the only swim trunks I had that I thought would fit you," Gideon said and quickly looked away.

Danny laughed and replied, "Are you sure? I think you just wanted to see how I looked in them."

Danny would have seen him blush were it not for Gideon's amber skin.

"Nothing could be further from the truth," Gideon said with a smile. "But I do have to admit you look amazing in them."

"Gideon, you've been so kind to me and Parker these last two days, but I probably should be thinking about going home. I've been in your way too long already."

Gideon froze mid-cut but didn't look at Danny. "Don't be ridiculous," he said, resuming the slice. "You haven't been in my way at all. I've loved having you guys here. Besides, I think Parker's made friends with one of the raccoons. You wouldn't want to break them up."

"I'll promise to bring him back soon to visit."

Gideon began to arrange the sliced fruit on a tray. "I wish you would reconsider. I . . ." Gideon stopped and turned to face Danny. "I've kind of gotten used to you being here. The place isn't so lonely with you around."

Danny walked next to him at the island and said, "I know what you mean. For the first time since the day Hezekiah . . . since the day Hezekiah died, I've been able to sleep through the night."

"Then don't go," Gideon said, reaching for Danny's moist shoulder. "Stay until you know for sure that you're ready."

Danny leaned in and rested his head on Gideon's chest, and Gideon embraced him tenderly. The two stood in silence and luxuriated in their comforting, long embrace. After moments, Danny raised his head and looked into Gideon's eyes. Gideon slowly moved forward and pressed his lips to Danny's.

"I'm in love with you, Danny St. John," Gideon said through the passionate kiss. "Don't leave me. I need you."

Danny could feel Gideon's erection pressing through his khaki shorts as his own erection stretched the Speedo to its limit. Gideon slowly slipped his hand under the tight waistband and massaged him gently. Danny lifted Gideon's T-shirt over his head and kissed circles on his bare chest. He could feel Gideon's heart pound with each kiss. He lifted Gideon's hand to his mouth and kissed his palm and fingers. He could taste the nectar of the sweet fruit. With a flick of his finger Danny unbuttoned Gideon's shorts and slowly pulled the zipper, which allowed them to drop silently to the granite floor, forming a pool of fabric around his ankles.

The two made love for the first time on the cool granite floor in the house in the Hollywood Hills.

It was Saturday night at 11:55. Samantha drove her white Bentley sports coupe on Western Avenue. Even at that hour the street was filled with people going to or leaving their favorite nightclub, late-night restaurant, or theater. The duffel bag containing the two million dollars sat on the passenger seat.

While waiting for the light at Sunset Boulevard and Western, she looked in the rearview mirror to ensure David Shackelford was following closely behind. He had the gun in his pocket and passion in his heart. Samantha prayed he would use them both just as she had planned.

As she continued driving, the gritty street gradually transitioned from run-down storefronts, hamburger joints, bars, and dollar discount stores to a tree-lined residential neighborhood of two-story houses with Spanish tiled roofs and circular driveways. Samantha turned left at the first entrance to the park. A canopy of trees covered the road and blocked the ambient light. Vintage streetlamps with glass globes provided the only illumination on the road.

When David veered onto the road, he turned off his headlights and slowed down to increase the distance between them. Samantha could see him only when he rolled under one of the few dim streetlamps lining the road. His car would disappear seconds after he passed each lamp.

There were no other cars on the dark road. Dense layers of trees lined each side as she drove deeper into the empty park. She could see traces of buildings in the dark as she ascended a hill, but couldn't tell if they were houses or public restrooms. Suddenly the entrance to the parking lot appeared on her left. She made a cautious turn, and the incline increased dramatically. When she reached the top, Samantha saw the parking lot sprawled out under the beams of her headlights. It was empty. Samantha immediately noted that there was only one way into the parking lot and only one way out of the large space. It was walled on one side by the sheer face of a wooded hill, and on another a steep cliff dropped down to the main road below. She parked the car so that it was facing the cliff and turned off the ignition and the lights. She could see only a few feet on either side, in the front and the rear.

David drove a safe distance past the parking lot entrance on the main road below and parked. His heart was pounding hard against the gun in his breast pocket. His hands were moist from perspiration. The darkness seemed to close in on him like the walls of a coffin. His breathing became shallow as he braced himself to exit the car.

David placed his hand on the door handle, then paused. "You can do this, David," he said out loud. "Samantha needs you. Don't let her down." The longer he waited, the shallower his breaths became and the more fiercely his heart pounded against the gun in his pocket. David reached over and frantically fumbled at the latch to the glove compartment. From it he pulled a half-empty bottle of distilled courage. He took one long gulp and then followed it with two more.

Samantha looked at her watch. It was now 12:08. "Come on," she said softly, tapping the steering wheel. "Where are you?"

Seconds later she heard a gentle tap on the car window. She looked to her left and saw the torso and hands of a man wearing a dark coat and standing at the window. The figure motioned for her to roll down the window.

"Hello, Samantha," the man said, bending down to the open window. "It's nice to finally meet you. I'm Danny St. John."

Samantha looked him in the eye and said, "I should have guessed. So you're the man that was sleeping with my husband."

"Yes. I'm also the man who loved your husband. Is that the money?" he asked, pointing past her to the bag on the passenger seat. "May I have it please?"

Samantha tried to look around Danny for David, but his shoulders were too broad. *Come on, David. Where are you?* she thought as she slowly reached for the bag.

"They don't come much lower than you, do they, Danny?" she said, stalling for more time. "Sleeping with a married man, then blackmailing his widow."

Danny laughed out loud. "This coming from a woman who killed her husband. You're in no position to judge me. Now, give me the money, and you'll never hear from me again."

Danny saw blackmail as his only way out. The only way he could move beyond her dangerous reach. *If she's evil enough to kill her husband, she's certainly evil enough to kill me,* he had reasoned in the grief-stricken days that followed Hezekiah's death. *Get the money and disappear. Leave the country. Move to a place where she will never find me.* He'd concluded that leaving Los Angeles was the only way he would be free from the paralyzing fear that every stranger he saw on the street was potentially a deadly messenger sent to him by Samantha Cleaveland. He also needed so desperately to be away from every inch of the city that reminded him of Hezekiah.

The two looked intently at each other and simultaneously understood why Hezekiah had fallen in love with the other. They saw pure, raw passion burning in each other's eyes. Two people who would stop at nothing to get what they wanted, whether it be love or money. In the dark of the night there was no need for pretense or defense. They spoke as if they were looking into a mirror.

"Was this your plan all along?" Samantha asked, looking in his eyes. "Was it always about the money?"

"This might be difficult for someone like you to understand, but it was never about money," Danny said. "I loved Hezekiah. Did you ever love him?"

"At one time I did," Samantha responded with a slight nod of concession.

"Then why did you kill him?"

Samantha paused but at that moment saw no need for caution. "It's the law of the universe, Danny. In order to get something you want, you have to give up something you love."

"Then I guess that law worked well for you."

When Danny said the last word, he felt a hand on his shoulder. He turned around quickly and found himself standing nose to nose with David.

Samantha shouted out loud, "He's got a gun, David. Shoot him! Shoot him!"

David immediately pushed Danny into the side of the car. The two men wrestled to the ground and rolled on the pavement, with arms and legs flailing in every direction. Samantha unlocked the car door, jumped out and screamed over the jumble of flesh and cloth, "Shoot him, David. He tried to kill me. Shoot him now!"

Suddenly a shot rang out, and the bodies went limp on the pavement. Samantha could see the gun in one of the hands lying flat on the ground. She rushed to the heap and snatched the gun away, took three steps backward, all while aiming the gun with both hands at the still pile of flesh. A chest was heaving, but she couldn't tell if it was David or Danny.

"David," she said, still pointing the warm gun at the heap. "David, are you okay?"

Suddenly the bodies moved, and David struggled from beneath Danny.

"Get up, David," Samantha said, directing the gun to the lone figure on the ground. "Is he dead?"

"I think so," David panted. "He's not breathing."

"Good."

David stopped breathing and looked at Samantha. "What are you talking about? I just killed a man."

"It was self-defense. If you hadn't been here, he would have killed me."

David reached into his pocket for his cell phone and began to dial nine-one-one.

Samantha grabbed his arm and said, "What are you doing?"

"I'm calling the police," he yelled. "We just killed a man. I'm calling the police."

"David, honey, wait a minute," she said. "Let me at least check to see if he's dead. He may still be alive."

Samantha walked cautiously to Danny's still body. She knelt down and first checked his coat pockets and then the pockets of his pants. She stood up and faced David and said, "He doesn't have a gun."

"What?" David screamed.

"You just killed an unarmed man."

"Oh shit!" David said. "Oh shit! Oh God, Samantha, you said he had a gun," he said, holding his hands against the sides of his head. "You said he was going to kill you."

"It looked like he had a gun in his pocket. I thought he had a gun," Samantha said curtly.

David began to pace back and forth in the parking lot, with his arms waving in front of Danny's lifeless body. "What have I done?" he said. "Look what you made me do!"

Samantha threw the gun into her open car window and grabbed David by his shoulders. "David, stop," she said, trying to calm the frantic man. "Listen to me, David. We have to leave. No one knows we were here. We need to just leave now and never speak of this to anyone. Do you understand me?" she asked firmly.

"Leave?" he muttered. "Just leave him there? Are you sure?"

"Yes, I'm sure. Everything will be fine. I want you to go home to Scarlett and not say a word about this to anyone. Ever! Do you understand me?" she said, shaking his shoulders. "Someone will find him in the morning. They'll never be able to link any of this to either you or me as long as we both agree that it never happened. Okay? Do you agree?"

"I . . . I agree," David sputtered. "Are you sure no one will find out?"

"I'm sure. Now, go to your car and wait for me at the bottom of the hill. I'll follow you as far as Wilshire Boulevard. Then I want you to drive straight home and put this out of you mind. Do you understand?"

"I understand," he said, shaking.

"And make sure you are at church tomorrow," Samantha continued. "I want to see you there with Scarlett on one side and Natalie on the other. We have to act like this never happened. Do you understand?"

"Yes," he said, shaking harder.

"Good. Everything is going to be fine, David. I'll call you in the morning to check on you."

David took one look at Danny lying face down on the pavement and ran sporadically to the edge of the parking lot, looking over his shoulder at Samantha and Danny. When he reached the edge, he took one step over the ledge and slipped in the loose dirt. His heavy body tumbled headfirst and rolled until he hit the road below with a thud. He scrambled across the dark road, covered in dirt and spitting dust. Once inside his car he reached into the glove compartment again and retrieved the almost empty bottle and guzzled the remainder of its contents.

Samantha did nothing as she watched the shadow of David's hulking body tumble down the hill. When she heard the thud of his body hitting the pavement below, she moved quickly to Danny and removed his watch. She recognized the dial of the Rolex immediately and said, "I assume Hezekiah gave this to you, so technically it belongs to me." She then removed his wallet and said, "Good-bye, Danny St. John. I'm glad we finally met."

In the car Samantha unzipped the leather duffel bag, revealing the jumble of cash. She placed the gun, the watch, and the wallet inside the bag and shoved it to the floor of the car.

Once on the road, Samantha followed David down the hill until they each vanished into the night as silently as they had come.

Samantha opened the door to her closet. It was three o'clock on Sunday morning. Etta was asleep in the maids' quarters. The house resembled a mausoleum with its dark, cavernous halls and lifeless rooms. Little green lights blinked on security devices throughout the house, and red beams guarded the most valued treasures.

When she opened the door, lights around a floor-to-ceiling mirror that stretched the length of the wall in the closet turned on automatically and flooded the elaborate windowless room with what appeared to be natural sunlight. A crystal chandelier hanging over a Louis XV table that held an arrangement of tulips, roses, and white snapdragons marked the center of the room, which was almost as large as the master bedroom.

Clothes she had acquired over the years of her marriage were arranged by designer and occasion. Each of her favorite designers had their own individually lit nook. Sections were dedicated to couture gowns, black dresses, white dresses, business wear, formal, semi-formal, and every other conceivable occasion. Dozens of hats made especially for her face were displayed on pouting porcelain heads. A ladder on wheels leaned against shelves filled with cashmere sweaters and silk scarves stacked neatly according to color. A full set of Louis Vuitton luggage had been placed neatly in a section created especially for luggage. The mansion's central control room assured that the closet remained at a constant sixty degrees, the perfect temperature for storing her most valued collection.

The centerpiece was the hundreds of shoes displayed on shelves behind sliding glass doors. The shoes were arranged by color. Each pair had been chosen to complement a new ensemble added to the collection, or for its ability to carry Samantha as if she had wings on her feet.

Samantha stood in the threshold and admired the items that were so dear to her heart. Garments and shoes that had not been worn in years and would probably never be worn again were as admired as those she had just worn the day before. Some held sentimental value, while others were kept for their sheer beauty and exquisite craftsmanship.

Samantha normally took two hours early on Sunday morning to ready herself for church. But this was going to be another special Sunday. She needed more time to assemble the perfect image for her first Sunday as the permanent pastor of New Testament Cathedral. Samantha wanted to look her most radiant, while conveying an air of humility, with a backdrop of power. Her heels had to be just the right height. Her jewelry had to sparkle but not shine.

She had to select a look that would titillate the husbands but would not incense the wives.

Samantha grudgingly decided that because Hezekiah had been dead only a few weeks, she had to, for at least one more Sunday, wear black. After a lengthy search of the black dress section, Samantha selected three outfits from the racks and displayed them on hooks as if they were warriors preparing for battle. One was a simple two-piece suit with a loose-fitting skirt and a jacket with mid-length sleeves. The second was also a suit, but with a skirt that hugged the lines of her well-shaped lower half. As she studied the lineup, the third was clearly emerging as her favorite. She had purchased it the week earlier, on a shopping spree on Rodeo Drive. It was a Givenchy that caressed the contours of her body and offered a seductive peek at the V in her ample cleavage.

She tried on each of the outfits multiple times over the next hour, putting each one through a series of tests, posing and strutting, sitting and waving in front of the mirrored wall. Samantha kneeled in front of the large mirror, walked at a quick pace across the length of the dressing-room floor, and executed a series of abrupt twists and turns, mimicking the theatrics and gestures of her debut sermon.

She decided on the Givenchy suit at the conclusion of the high fashion aerobic session. Its color, shape, and easy movement suited her purposes well. The shoes she selected were not the pair purchased for the suit. Instead, she chose a pair with a slightly higher heel. The accessories were the easy part; the dress would tolerate only diamonds, a single-strand bracelet, and six-carat studs for her ears.

Samantha stood in front of the mirror to examine her final choice and was pleased. For a brief second the image of Danny's lifeless body flashed before her. "Give Hezekiah a kiss for me," she said out loud while surveying her figure from every angle.

***

It was now 7:45 on Sunday morning at New Testament Cathedral. The death of Hezekiah could still be
felt in the air and seen on the faces of members as
they filed down the aisles and into the pews. The entire length of the three steps that led up to the pulpit
was covered from top to bottom with flowers left by
thousands each Sunday. At the end of each Sunday the
maintenance crew would remove the flowers, and the
next Sunday there would be even more.

The pipe organ churned an upbeat hymn in an effort
to elevate the mood as members took their seat. An
eight-foot portrait of a smiling Hezekiah T. Cleaveland,
draped with black cloth, hanging above the choir stand
immediately reminded worshippers that a murder had
taken place only a few Sundays earlier.

Cameras captured, for the two jumbo screens, the
parade of colorful hats, mothers settling small children
into the pews, and men escorting their wives down the
aisles. The continuing saga of grief was felt not only
in the sanctuary. People across America watched and
cried along with them from the comfort and safety of
their homes.

"Where are you, David?" Samantha asked, clutching
her cell phone to her ear in the window of her office.

"I'm here, parking the car."

"Are Scarlett and Natalie with you?"

"Yeah, I dropped them at the entrance. She's getting
our seats before it gets too crowded."

"Perfect. Did you say anything to her last night?"

"What was I going to say? Honey, guess what Samantha and I did last night?"

"Good, and make sure you keep it that way. Did she
ask why you were out so late?"

"No. She was just surprised and relieved I came home. Stop asking me all these fucking questions," he snapped. "I told you I wasn't going to say anything, and I didn't. When am I going to see you? I want to hold you in my arms. I need to make love to you again. I love you, Samantha."

"Soon. Just be patient," Samantha said calmly. "David?" she continued.

"What?"

"You and I are in this together. Do not cross me, because as you now know, I can be a very dangerous woman."

When the clock struck eight, the side doors to the left and right of the pulpit swung open and the choir entered from both sides into the stand.

"We are on our way. We're on our journey home," the choir sang as they marched. "We are on our way. We're on our journey home."

The stage backdrop was an electric blue wall of light that periodically changed hues to match the desired mood of each moment during the service. The walls of the sanctuary pulsated from the brass instruments, drums, violins, guitars, organs, and pianos playing the rhythmic tune. Scenes on the two twenty-foot-high JumboTron screens alternated rapidly between panoramic shots of the congregation standing, clapping, and singing and the two-hundred-member choir and orchestra.

Another door at the foot of the pulpit opened. All heads in the room turned to the door. After a dramatic pause, Samantha Cleaveland appeared in the threshold. The cameras rushed to catch every second of her entrance. As befitting a widow still in mourning, she wore the two-piece black Givenchy suit, which traced with precision each curve, bend, and twist of her hour-glass figure. A sleek skirt sloped around her full hips down to the lips of a tulip shaped hemline just above her knees. The jacket was a cascade of satiny fabric, cinched at the waist and blossoming around her hips. The heels on her one-of-a-kind black Chanel sling-back pumps were the exact height necessary to mold her legs into the perfect female form.

Samantha entered the sanctuary with the gait of a woman straddling the line between courage and grief. Applause exploded throughout the sanctuary when the people saw her, and drowned out the singing of the choir. Samantha flashed her smile and waved triumphantly to the crowd. The diamond bracelet she wore twinkled like a cluster of stars in the midnight sky.

The image of Samantha Cleaveland standing at the front row, smiling and still waving to the crowd, filled the JumboTron screens. The caption below read, "Rev. Dr. Samantha Cleaveland—Pastor and Founder, New Testament Cathedral." She repositioned her body with each wave to ensure everyone in the room got a complete view.

David Shackelford walked swiftly down the aisle and slid sideways into a pew two rows from the front. He stepped over shoes and purses until he reached Scarlett and Natalie. David scooped up the little girl and sat her in his lap and kissed Scarlett on her cold cheek.

Scarlett looked up at the screen filled with a twenty-foot Samantha Cleaveland. God, what have we done? she thought. *As usual, Samantha got everything she wanted, but at least she didn't get my husband.* Scarlett reached over and covered David's hand with hers. She found it hard to believe he was sitting next to her. *Thank God he didn't leave me for that bitch.*

When the applause subsided and the audience returned to their seats, the music gradually transitioned to a melodic and reverent tone. A soprano began to sing an operatic tune, and the audience followed her word for word. The melody from the crowd rolled from the front of the church to the top row of the sanctuary and filled the room as congregants softly sang in unison and looked upward to heaven.

The cameras followed Samantha as she walked along a path in the sea of flowers and up the steps to the center of the stage. Again, the audience leapt to their feet, and thunderous applause erupted. Samantha stood at the mike center stage, raised her hands in victory, and blew a series of kisses to the crowd.

"I love you, too, New Testament Cathedral family," she declared, her amplified voice rising above the cheers and applause. "I love you too." She beamed.

The outpouring of love and adoration went on for five minutes, until Samantha finally raised her hands and tamed the crowd into submission.

Cynthia Pryce sat on the front row with her husband, Percy. Dark oval sunglasses and a thick mask of Dermablend covered the black eye and the scars inflicted by the heel of Percy's shoe. A wide-brimmed hat and a collar that reached her chin provided ample cover for the bruises on her neck and back. Under the glasses her left eye twitched as she watched Samantha on the stage.

Percy reached for her shaking hand, but she pushed him away. "Don't touch me," she said under her breath. "That should be you up there, not that bitch."

"Good morning, New Testament Cathedral!" Samantha said to the rapt crowd. "Does anybody here know that God is still a good God?"

Thousands of voices responded with, "Yes, Lord," or "Yes, He is," and "I know it, Pastor. I know He is."

"We don't have anything to cry about this morning, New Testament. We have every reason to rejoice. God has seen fit to allow us to see another day, and I don't know about you, but I'm going to praise Him."

With that there was no keeping the masses in their seats. Hands flew up in the air, and shouts of praise swept through the room.

"There's a verse in the Bible that says, 'Touch not mine anointed, and do my prophets no harm.' Do you believe that, saints?"

"We believe it, Pastor," was the unified response.

"Well, I'm a living witness that it's true."

For the next thirty minutes the room hung on every word that fell from Samantha's glossed lips. Hattie Williams sat stiff on the front row at the end of the pew. Her arthritic knee throbbed with each pound of the drums. The head of her cane rested against her thigh, and the purse filled with Kleenex, mints and a pocket bible sat on the cushion next to her.

Hattie looked up at Samantha in the pulpit and prayed silently. "Lord have mercy on New Testament Cathedral this Sunday morning."

The End